Priela

A NOVEL

by Jocelyn Bly Karney

Wolcott Publishing

Library of Congress Control Number: 2017907695

ISBN 978-0-9990119-0-4

First edition print copy, June 2017

Chapter One
MONDAY

Priela caught sight of the tree and whipped around, her corkscrew curls pausing a moment before following the motion. There was something wrong with the tree. Its branches stretched high above the classroom building in an oddly symmetric, almost mathematical pattern, and they hadn't been there at all the day before. She was sure of it. Priela leaned in to touch the leathery bark. It was too smooth somehow, cold to the touch like metal. Her hand recoiled from the texture and her heart skipped a beat.

"What are you doing?" said Kalista, pushing her thick glasses across the bridge of her nose. "You look like you're massaging that tree."

"Don't you remember? This tree wasn't here yesterday. It was just a black stump, charred from a fire or something."

"Um, I don't really go around memorizing the plants on campus, but sure. I'll take your word for it."

"No. Just look at it," said Priela, circling the base of the trunk. "It's too perfect. Like the tree's a fake. Like someone built it last night to hide cell phone receptors or cable wires."

"Uh huh." Kalista glanced over one shoulder and lowered her voice. "Priela you can't talk like this anymore. People already think that you're, you know, becoming like your mother."

Priela shuddered. It was one thing to know that she was different, to know she didn't fit in. But having her closest friend point out the obvious sent a shiver down her spine. Priela's mother was what some might call eccentric if they were being nice, and what others might call mentally unstable if they were being perfectly honest. These days, there were rumors that Priela was losing her mind too.

She didn't want to believe the gossip, but it was growing harder to ignore. Priela had always had this heightened insight. She knew things about people she simply shouldn't know, like their plans to ditch school, or to buy an essay online, or to cheat on a boyfriend. It was an ability that went beyond empathy, beyond well-honed intuition, as if Priela could genuinely hear people's thoughts and sense their emotions. It was definitely growing stronger. Not a good thing.

Priela couldn't help from letting her knowledge slip on occasion. One time, she complemented a girl's tattoo that had been inked the night before in a discrete location. Another time, she warned a girl to change her phone's password, knowing the girl's boyfriend was planning to read her texts and that there were messages she wouldn't want him to see. But the advice came across as creepy and the girl never spoke to her again.

Priela's clairvoyance made people defensive, relegating her to a sort of social purgatory. She mostly sat alone at lunch now. Hiding in the corner. Scarfing down her food. Pretending to be busy with her phone. She had never had a sip of beer, never smoked pot, never so much as kissed a boy, but not because she was unwilling. It was just that no one had asked her to join them. Priela wasn't cool enough to hang out in the parking lot afterschool or to attend those clandestine parties that the popular girls whispered about between classes. People simply

4

didn't want her around, dreading the information she might casually reveal.

It made Priela feel out of place and horribly alone. But at least people still acknowledged her existence, unlike Jacob, or Sterling, or Laura who were deemed legitimately insane. No one dared to bully or harass them. Instead, they were completely ignored.

Priela pulled on a long curl and sighed deeply. Kalista was right. She couldn't talk about some ominous tree rising out of nowhere. She couldn't let anyone know what was really going on inside her head.

"Don't worry," said Kalista, repositioning her backpack and taking Priela by one arm. "Your secret is safe. Come on, we're going to be late to algebra."

Priela allowed Kalista to guide her toward the classroom, lowering her eyes and partially shielding her face with a cupped hand as she walked through the door. She hated Mrs. Wilson's class. Not because there was anything wrong with the subject matter. She enjoyed the numbers, the puzzles, the simple perfection of algebra. Her feelings toward Mrs. Wilson were another matter.

"Take a seat to the right, Priela," said the woman in that horribly shrill tone. The right was the *'good'* side of the room, the side where students were getting passing grades. The students on the left were not so lucky.

"Move to the left, Violet," said Mrs. Wilson, tapping a long fingernail across the desk. "No, not your usual seat. Remember that 'F' last week? Further to the left by the slow kids. The very last chair. Yes, right there."

Violet's face paled and her shoulders stiffened as she pushed her way through the cluttered row of chairs. It was the only room in the school facing south and it lacked the standard florescent bulbs and the simple rectangular layout. Instead, the space was virtually triangular, with a single cracked window no larger than a laptop. It was obvious the space was an add-on, originally a storage closet or some kind of shed that was hastily converted when the school began overcrowding. But Mrs. Wilson seemed to relish in the dimness of the lighting and the awkwardness of the space.

Violet pulled out a textbook and attempted to angle into a seat, but Mrs. Wilson wasn't done with her yet. "I didn't say sit down, Violet. Remain standing. We can't allow our worst performers to fall through the cracks, now can we?"

Mrs. Wilson watched the girl tremble for a moment, clearly enjoying the ease with which she could intimidate a student. Then she swiveled around and pointed to an equation on the wipe board. "Now tell us, what is the value of X? If the textbook is any indication, you should be able to factor a quadratic equation by now. Of course the textbook assumes you have some modicum of intelligence."

Violet's body began cowering visibly and her eyes flickered downward, seeming to fixate on her skirt's simple geometric pattern. The girl had likely designed the outfit herself, doing more than just selecting the pieces, but actually sewing the fabric together and tailoring it to fit. The skirt layered over fitted leggings and its pattern contrasted sharply with a checkered purple vest. The assortment was odd, yet somehow it worked. Clearly, Violet had a natural sense of style, a gift, and she would have probably been popular if she had even slightly more confidence. Instead she was meek, her twig-like arms dangling inward and making her appear fragile.

"Ah yes, a student who won't even look at the board," sneered Mrs. Wilson, a glint in her eye. "Moments like these make me grateful to have someone of your caliber in my class. I would say that you're being disrespectful, but that would be giving you too much credit. Now walk us through this example, Violet."

Violet finally looked up but her expression was blank, her face drained of any color. Priela's face began to pale too and her knees grew stiff. It was happening. She was feeling Violet's emotions connecting with her own. Priela could never quite predict when it would occur or precisely what brought it on. Although, she guessed it had something to do with the strength of a person's feelings. The more intense the emotions, the more clear the thoughts, the more likely Priela could sense them.

"Three," thought Violet, and Priela could hear the number echo through her head like a far-away scream. It was the right answer, but instead of verbalizing it, Violet started muttering under her breath. "I think that uh… That X is… It's equal to…"

"My goodness. It spoke," said Mrs. Wilson, rounding her desk and slowly taking a seat on its edge, her eyes gloating. "Louder now, Violet. I'm trying to imagine you as something more than a failure but you're making it so very difficult. Perhaps I should recommend they move you to one of those programs for special kids? Somewhere you'd be considered normal. You do want to be normal, don't you Violet?"

Violet clenched her jaw and grasped her rigid chair, ramming it between the wall and the long desk, and Priela could feel her shame sweltering. The emotions were palpable, rising up like a volcano and tearing at her insides. Why did Mrs. Wilson always target the weak kids? Her ridicule had grown so frequent, her viciousness so extreme that it bordered on emotional abuse, yet no one said a word. The worst part was that Mrs. Wilson wasn't acting out of ignorance or frustration. Priela could tell she enjoyed it.

"Three," said Priela loudly, rising from her chair. She wasn't going to win any friends by defending Violet, but she didn't care. She couldn't bear to embody the girl's humiliation any longer. It was agonizing. She had to make it stop.

Mrs. Wilson's head turned sharply in her direction. "The question was not directed at you, Priela. Now sit down and remain quiet. We all know how smart you think you are. How much you like to shoot your mouth off in class. But it's Violet's turn to prove she's capable of basic math."

"No. The answer is three. Now let's move on."

Mrs. Wilson snickered. "Alright. If you really want to play this game, I'll go along. You think you're so clever, Priela? Some mathematical genius? Well, you'd better get every question correct or I'll send you to the principal's office for disrupting this class. It's such a lovely day. I would hate for you to waste it in detention. Do you understand me?"

Priela nodded and Mrs. Wilson rose to her feet and began hastily scrawling equations. But despite her explicit desire to embarrass Priela, the math problems weren't particularly difficult. They were examples taken directly from the homework. Even the sequence of the equations was identical. Priela knew the answers before Mrs. Wilson had finished writing.

"Twenty-two. Five. Twelve. Eighteen."

"Ah yes, so smug. You think a few correct answers proves anything? It only demonstrates that you're appallingly conceited. Aren't you ashamed of being such a show off, Priela? You should be. I'm certainly ashamed of you."

She scribbled down more equations. These ones were from the following chapter in the textbook, written in precisely the same order. It would be this week's homework for sure.

Mrs. Wilson's assignments were predictable, and in theory, she structured them so that the problems became more complex over time, requiring a teacher's instruction. But Priela's math skills went way beyond second year algebra. Numbers came naturally to her. Intuitively. She didn't need an explanation, not that Mrs. Wilson provided much of one anyway. Priela had completed the remainder of the year's homework in a single evening, turning in the pages one at a time as assigned.

"Sixty-five. Nine. Fourteen." She rattled off the answers with ease.

"Don't you know why everyone avoids you, Priela?" said Mrs. Wilson. She was skipping far ahead now and selecting an equation from the textbook's last chapter. "Being a know-it-all is such an unattractive quality. I'm shocked that anyone even acknowledges your existence."

Priela gritted her teeth and snapped her pencil between her fingers. "Thirty-four."

"Wrong," said Mrs. Wilson cackling. "The answer is twenty-six. Did you honestly believe that you could fool me by memorizing the answers in this textbook? A parrot can spit back answers. The goal here is to *solve* problems."

"I did solve it and the answer is thirty-four. Your teacher's edition has an error." Priela pulled out her phone and began typing rapidly, but her heart was pounding in her ears.

"Such arrogance. I highly doubt that it's the textbook that's wrong. Now put that phone away or you'll leave me with no alternative. I'm warning you."

"See?" Priela held up the device. "It's a list of typos in the textbook. Eighth edition, right? Look it up yourself, if you don't believe me. Maybe I'm not the one who only knows how to memorize answers?"

Mrs. Wilson's eyebrows narrowed and a vein on her forehead began throbbing. "Why you impertinent little…" She lunged forward, grabbed Priela's phone, and hurled it against a wall, but just then an alarm bell rang. Three quick rings, then a pause, then three more. It was a fire drill. Students rose from their chairs and started racing out the door. "This discussion isn't over, Priela. Mark my words, you will never forget fifth period."

Priela groaned. Fifth period referred to chemistry, a course the woman had been substitute teaching lately, and seeing Mrs. Wilson twice in one day had been excruciating.

"I really did know the answer," whispered Violet as she zoomed by.

"You see, Priela?" laughed Mrs. Wilson. "That girl needs a spine, not a savior."

"Whatever."

Priela scooped up her cell and managed to make it to the allocated fire drill spot on the lawn, but her muscles remained rigid, her heart exploding. At least her phone had survived the crash.

"That was awesome," said Noah, running his fingers through his hair and flashing her a smile. "I've always wanted to tell Mrs. Wilson off. Is the textbook really wrong or were you just making all that stuff up?"

"Nope. The book's wrong and the website only lists about half the errors."

"Brave and brainy. Not a bad combo, Priela. So are we still on for later?"

"Um…" She twisted one leg behind the other and her cheeks turned red. "Yes."

Chapter Two
UNDER THE BLEACHERS

Priela slipped past the cafeteria and headed down the long row of lockers. It was lunch period now, but she had an appointment to keep and she was running late. Besides, she didn't have much of an appetite. She turned in the direction of the gym. It was the place where she was supposed to meet Noah. Under the bleachers. The spot where kids went to hook up, to make out, to be alone together. Priela had never gone under the bleachers before, so to speak. She had never been kissed.

Although there was nothing about this get together that was the slightest bit romantic. It had been scheduled through a series of text messages, like some kind of business meeting. Everyone was supposed to have a first kiss by now. Well, everyone relatively normal. Since Noah hadn't had one yet either, the meeting was arranged on their behalf.

She stopped at her locker, shoved her backpack inside, and thought about their conversation on the lawn that morning, spoken between bursts from the fire alarm. Noah had been her classmate for years, but it was the most they had ever talked. She remembered the way he tossed his hair and how it fell in shaggy strands around his temples. She wasn't sure if she liked him, but he was kind of cute with a gentle smile that lit up his face and a frame that was short in stature, but on the verge of growing. Priela wouldn't be so lucky.

She was already a late birthday based on the school's calendar year and then she'd been bumped forward an additional grade level because of her math prowess. These days, she wished her parents hadn't allowed it. Priela was naturally short, or petite if one was being politically correct, with a flat chest, wide dark eyes, and soft facial features. She still looked like a little girl while her classmates all looked like women.

She glanced in a mirror stuck inside the locker's door and sighed at her reflection. Just the other day, a security guard had stopped her in a shopping mall while she was waiting for her friend Kalista to return from the restroom. *"Did she leave you all alone?"* he had asked. *"Is there someone I should call to come get you?"* It didn't make any sense until Priela realized the man thought Kalista was her babysitter. Ugh!

She yanked on a stray curl and attempted to smooth the frizz, wanting to gain some control over her own appearance. Depending on one's perspective, Priela's hair was either spectacular or a mess, but either way the curls distinguished her, reaching halfway down her back in wild disarray like a mane of dark fusilli noodles. Then her fingers touched the bandages and she winced. Great. She had forgotten about those.

Priela had an accident the night before. She was reading a book, walking down stairs, and there was a fall. Only eight steps or so. Although she had banged up her back pretty badly and the wounds weren't healing yet. She turned one shoulder away from the mirror and bit her lip. If anything, the injuries were worse now, protruding through her shirt in swollen lumps. Hopefully, Noah wouldn't notice. She slammed her locker shut and started jogging down the hall, checking her watch while she rounded a corner. Nine minutes late. Would he wait for her?

She rushed inside the auditorium, but instead of finding an empty space there was some kind of exhibition going on for seniors and the room was crawling with people. Little booths had been set up everywhere to sell things, and promote things, and give stuff away. An army recruiting station was at the center of the floor with a line of students snaked before it. There was a booth with plumbing equipment promoting some kind of apprenticeship program. There were student internships, and summer jobs, and a for-profit college giving away bumper stickers that read, *"CSL College – Where Learning is a Breeze."*

Directly on top of the bleachers was a Gateway Credit Card booth. The thing looked like it might collapse at any minute. Books propped up two of the station's legs, but even so the structure sloped unsteadily to one side. Priela slipped quietly under the stack of seats at the far end and saw Noah, just sitting there. Alone.

"I wasn't sure if you were gonna show," he said, gulping audibly. "I've been listening to those people up there at that credit card booth. You can see them through the slats if you lean back. And you can hear every word they're saying. That Garrett guy is such a douche."

Priela crouched down as she moved closer, taking a seat by his side and leaning backward. Just above her and to the right stood Robin. She was the newly elected student body president, the first African American to hold the office in the school's complicated history, and people respected her. Admired her. Now Robin was gesturing excitedly and extolling the virtues of Gateway Credit Cards. Apparently, she was working at the sales booth.

Garrett and Anton were there too, listening attentively to her pitch. Garrett was a senior with chiseled features, dark perfect hair, and a brash arrogance that gave him a certain allure, while Anton, his younger brother, had an awkward nature and pimples everywhere. Still, both brothers vied for Robin's attention with Garrett spewing lame pickup lines and Anton filling out an application just to edge his way in to the conversation. Garrett quickly reached for a credit card form too. The sibling rivalry was tangible.

"Listen, I got you something," said Noah, pulling a tangled bracelet from his pocket and dropping it limply in her lap.

"Uh, thanks." She held up the gift and straightened her posture, straining to divine some deeper meaning from the cheap bracelet, as if it could reveal what he was truly thinking. But her abilities were weirdly selective, rarely seeming to work when she really wanted them to.

Instead of connecting with Noah, Priela started to sense Anton of all people. She could feel his jaw tense and his joints lock, and she could hear the guy's mind obsessing, his thoughts radiating through the metal slats like radio waves pulsating through the air. *"Robin should be with me. Not Garrett. But I'm sure she thinks I'm a dork."* It was a mixture of desire and jealousy, and the sensation made Priela a bit nauseated.

The contrast with Noah couldn't have been more stark. There was no excitement in Noah's voice. No flirtation in his gestures. He seemed distracted, his eyes focusing on everything other than her, his movements mechanical and rushed. "So you ready?" he asked, puckering his lips.

Priela nodded meekly, but her throat turned dry and she couldn't bring herself to move any closer. Deep down, she knew this kiss was a very big deal. Her first intimate experience. She was terrified of her own body and the sensations it might feel, but she was even more afraid of being rejected. Had Noah chosen her for this kiss or was she just the only girl left? Could this whole thing be some sort of set up, a joke to make her look stupid?

14

He reached behind her now and began to draw her toward him. She could feel his breath on her face and the warmth of his hand through her shirt, and she tightened her fingers around the bracelet, squeezing so strongly that little spokes from the clasp dug into her skin.

Then his hand brushed across the bandages and he flinched. His eyebrows furrowed together. His nose squinted at the tip and his lips flattened in a puzzled expression. Why was he squinting like that? Did he think she was disgusting? Priela interpreted his demeanor as proof that his motives were shaky. Proof he didn't really want her. She couldn't do this.

"Get away from me Noah," she said, pushing his hand away.

"But I thought…"

"What did you think? That you'd give me a piece of crappy jewelry and I'd just make out with you?" She threw the bracelet back in his face.

"No. It's just… we had a deal."

"Really? A deal? Did you honestly believe that I had anything to do with those text messages? That I wanted you even the slightest bit? Let me guess, this whole thing was supposed to make me look bad. You're going to tell your friends that we met here and then you'll all laugh at me."

"That's not it at all," he said, shaking his head and seeming genuinely perplexed. "I like you, Priela."

At that moment, the conversation from above came to an abrupt conclusion and Garrett kicked the leg of the sales booth, angry that Robin had rejected him. It pushed one of the books sideways and the station teetered. Then a loud crashing noise. Books started falling through the slats, landing squarely on Priela's head one at a time. Thump, thump, thump. The blows were hard, the pain immediate.

Tears welled up in her eyes, although Priela's emotions had nothing to do with the sudden whacks. She felt embarrassed. Confused.

"Are you okay?" said Noah.

Priela didn't answer. She merely shielded her head and ran away.

Chapter Three
MRS. WILSON'S REVENGE

Priela didn't know why it upset her so greatly that things hadn't gone well with Noah. Her tears certainly had nothing to do with the guy himself. Still, she couldn't stop them from streaming down her cheeks, one after the other. She ducked into a restroom but the popular girls were there.

Lacey noticed Priela, rolled her eyes, and nudged Julie with an elbow. "Why are you crying, lice-bait? Did someone know more than you in math?"

Andrea snickered, "Yes, please tell us what's so tragic. Just ignore the yawn."

Priela's hands balled into fists, but she backed up and headed down the hall, her eyes scanning open doors through a lock of hair. She was searching for a room that was empty, a place to hide, but the computer lab was packed and the classrooms all had teachers. Even the library was busy. She reached Mrs. Wilson's triangular room at the end of the hall. The space made her bristle but at least no one was there.

She crept inside and glimpsed the familiar textbook, still resting on the desk, opened to the same page as before. The page with the error. She took a deep breath, wiped a tear from her cheek, and scrawled the number *"thirty four"* in the margin.

Mrs. Wilson would be furious at this act of vandalism but wrong answers bothered Priela, particularly when it came to

17

math. Fixing them was a compulsion. She couldn't stop herself any more than some kids could refrain from washing their hands multiple times or from counting every calorie. In a chaotic world, it was something she could control. Something that made sense.

She flipped to the beginning of the textbook and began scanning pages, correcting another error and then another, marking up the sheets in wide messy strokes. A few pages were stuck together. She pried them apart with a nail and hesitated, not recognizing the new page. It was as if the textbook printer had accidentally glued in an extra sheet from a different volume. A more advanced volume. She leaned in and studied the Greek characters for a moment, unaccustomed to math problems that required effort.

Sigma. That usually stood for the sum. Delta. That symbol represented change. The answer came to her in pieces so that she had to jot down her logic and think through each step. Something about the exercise was strangely cathartic, as if she was decoding an ancient treasure map. With each finding, her muscles relaxed and her tears stopped falling.

"Dude, do you think Priela's gonna ditch?" said a voice from beyond the door.

"I dunno. But if she does show up, Mrs. Wilson's gonna do something epic for sure… She's so pissed."

Priela's stomach churned. It was fifth period already, chemistry class with Mrs. Wilson, and an increasingly large throng of students were chatting just outside the door. There was no escaping now. She moved to the edge of the classroom and took a seat, rearranging her curls as she walked to conceal her swollen eyes, like a sheep dog.

Then a bell rang and students started filing in around her, including Noah. He ignored her as he shuffled past her desk.

Was he upset about what had happened too? Or had he already told people that she was disgusting or a prude?

Someone stepped on Priela's foot. Someone else bumped into her chair, compressing her chest into the desk. It didn't hurt, but still they didn't apologize. What exactly had Noah told everyone? People were treating her like she wasn't even there.

"Let's begin with a pop quiz," said Mrs. Wilson waltzing in and passing out papers. Typical. The woman loved impromptu examinations and they factored heavily toward one's final grade in the class.

"I'm not expecting much from you," she said, dropping a quiz in front of Alice. Then she turned to Zachary. "Grading your papers is such a bore since we both know what you're going to get. Why not just mark an 'X' through the entire page and save us both some time?"

With each passing remark, the invectives grew crueler and more personal. So when Mrs. Wilson finally snaked toward her desk, Priela was expecting the worst. Instead, the woman didn't say a word and she didn't give Priela a quiz. She just kept walking.

"Um, you missed me," said Priela. Her voice was certainly loud enough for Mrs. Wilson to hear it, but the teacher returned to the front of the room and dropped her remaining paperwork directly on top of the algebra textbook with a thud.

"Now, you'll have twenty minutes for the quiz. If you don't finish… you don't finish. I'll grade them immediately. Whomever gets the lowest score will stand before the class and fill in a blank periodic table of elements from memory. The chart must be perfect before anyone is dismissed, no matter how long it takes. Understood?"

So this would be Mrs. Wilson's revenge? She'd give Priela a zero by default, making her stand in front of everyone and embarrass herself. Priela didn't know the periodic table by heart. She'd get stuff wrong and make everyone late. They'd all hate her. She peeked over one shoulder at Noah. Would he laugh at her while she was up there?

"The clock begins now."

There was a flurry of movement as students took out their pencils and began scribbling away.

Priela raised her hand. "I'm sorry about this morning, Mrs. Wilson. Can I please get a quiz?"

No response.

A minute ticked by on the large round clock. Then another. Although it felt like time was moving in a prolonged motion, as if it was genuinely slowing down. The fierce scribbling became more deliberate and drawn out.

"Fine," said Priela, shaking her head. "I'll volunteer to do the periodic table, if you'll just give me a quiz. There's no reason to make me totally flunk this."

Again her pleas were ignored. Mrs. Wilson didn't even make eye contact. Instead, she leaned back in her chair, crossed one leg over the other, and curled her lips in a vicious sneer. Her movements were maddeningly slow and exaggerated.

Maybe Priela could have handled the disdain if her nerves weren't so frayed. Maybe she could have dealt with the periodic table charade if her self-esteem wasn't already shaken from her encounter with Noah. But now, the hair on her arms stood on end and her pulse quickened. Conflict was one thing. Conflict Priela could manage. If anything, she thrived under pressure, seeking out the occasional dispute. Being ignored was something else. It was Priela's greatest fear. A punishment reserved for those unworthy of attention, like those who were dumb or crazy.

"Okay well… if that's how it's going to be Mrs. Wilson," she said, rising to her feet. "Then let me tell you something. You're a horrible teacher. Just terrible."

As she spoke, a weird light started to glow. Was someone directing a laser pointer at the back of her head? Could it be Noah, mocking her? She ignored the brightness and continued with her rant, but her body was trembling.

"You certainly shouldn't be teaching math or science, Mrs. Wilson. You think you're helping people by embarrassing them? You're not. Try saying 'good job' once in a while. How about that? People aren't failing your classes because of the subject matter. It's your teaching that sucks."

Priela gritted her teeth and glanced away, trying to force her emotions back under control. What was she doing? Did she honestly believe that arguing with Mrs. Wilson was going to help anything or endear her to her peers? The woman could get knocked in the head by a boulder and it wouldn't make a difference.

Priela held her breath and returned her gaze to the front of the room, but now the light was gone and Mrs. Wilson was staring directly at her. Although the woman's eyes were strangely unfocused and her expression was hard to read.

"I know…" said Priela, edging around a desk. "Go to the principal's office, right? I'm going."

She zoomed through the open door and down the hall. Although Priela wasn't heading to the administration building. She was going home and nobody tried to stop her.

Chapter Four
THE CHOICE

"Why are you home already?" said Calliope, putting down her purse and flipping off the television set. "Is everything okay?"

"I'm fine, Mom," said Priela, but the guilt was already mounting. She sank into the sofa and glanced at her fingernails. "I yelled at one of my teachers, but honestly Mrs. Wilson deserved it. If you saw the way she tortures people in her class, you'd totally agree with me."

"Tell me exactly what Mrs. Wilson said… word for word."

"What she said?" Priela rolled the question over in her mind. "She didn't say anything. She was ignoring me. That's why I got so angry. She gave everyone else a quiz and then she just walked right past me, like I wasn't even there."

Calliope lowered her eyes and let out a deep sigh. Then she shut the drapes and began pacing around the den, gesturing with her hands as she moved. "Something must have triggered the change," she muttered to herself. "I mean, it couldn't have happened without prompting. Priela certainly wasn't born this way." She removed a painting from the wall, grasped it tightly with both hands, and closed her eyes as if she could divine something supernatural from its essence. "No, definitely not born this way."

Priela's mother was a brilliant painter and her pieces covered every inch of available wall space. Dad had them appraised once. The works were valuable, even for an unknown artist, but she refused to sell them.

"If the change was going to happen…" she mumbled, removing yet another abstract image from its hook, turning the piece upside down, and holding it to her ear as if the painting might whisper something. "It should have started years ago. I've never known it to develop this late."

Priela groaned. Sometimes her mother was like this. Nuts. Her head filled with fantastic notions about things. Her words illogical and erratic. Priela usually tried to rationalize her mom's thought patterns, to put them in a context that made them seem less crazy. Now was not one of those times. "What are you talking about, Mom? You're not making any sense."

Calliope lowered her hood. She was wearing a dark cloak, the kind one might wear to a renaissance festival. It was far from her most bizarre attire. "Your teacher wasn't ignoring you, honey. You're invisible now."

"Uh huh, sure."

"By any chance did you paint a portrait today, Priela? Or maybe you sang a song?"

"No."

"Did you recite a poem in class? Or write an essay?"

Priela shook her head.

"I need to make certain." Calliope kneeled down and placed a hand on Priela's shoulder. "Those bandages on your back. You've had them since last night, right? Would you mind taking them off, so I can see?"

"What? No. I'm fine, Mom. Don't touch me."

"Please, Priela. I have to be sure." Calliope's eyes turned inward at the edges and her forehead creased, revealing fine lines. It was a look of determination, a look that said she wouldn't let this issue go until she'd had her way.

Priela sighed. "Fine." She rose from the sofa, raised her shoulders, and removed her shirt to reveal a pink bra that was pathetically unneeded. Then she began slowly peeling off the bandages.

"Oh, they're coming in beautifully, honey. Still small and no color yet, but don't worry. They should reach their full size fairly quickly. I'd imagine within a few weeks."

"What will?"

"Your wings, of course."

"My what?"

There was a framed mirror adjacent to the hallway closet. Priela walked over to it now and looked at her reflection. She gasped, not believing. The lumps on her back were gone, replaced by two small wings. She reached one hand over her shoulder to touch them. They were translucent, paper thin, and frail. She tensed a muscle. They fluttered. She tensed it again. They fluttered faster. How was this possible?

"Is this some kind of trick? Are you recording me or something?"

Calliope just stood there, watching her.

"Get these things off. Get them off, Mom." Priela grabbed one wing between her fingers and started pulling, yanking until she could feel her skin stretch uncomfortably. Then she started scratching with her nails. Despite being light, skeletal even, the wing didn't rip or tear. Instead, it started bleeding. The color vanished from Priela's face and the room suddenly felt like its walls were closing in, like it was being drained of oxygen, leaving her gasping for air.

"I'm so sorry, honey. But you can't take off your wings any more than you can take off your right arm. They're a part of you now, but don't worry. Humans won't be able to see them."

"Humans? What are you talking about?" she shrieked. "I don't want these things. I don't want them at all. Please Mom… Help me." She continued to tug and scrape until she could feel the pain, until her hands were shaking and the blood was trickling down her fingers.

"Stop," said Calliope, grabbing a hold of her wrists and twisting them before her, so that Priela's movements were restrained in a tight embrace. "Stop."

Priela collapsed to her knees, instantly sobbing. Her day had been horrific. All of it. She couldn't grasp what was happening to her. But she felt an immediate and absolute sense of loss. She had lost control over her own physical being, her own sense of self. There was confusion and shock. Her tears fell in giant droplets. Her body shuddered.

Calliope just sighed and held her as if she was still a young child. She wiped away her tears, and petted her hair, and dabbed gently at the blood with a dry cloth.

When the sobs finally slowed, Calliope rose to her feet and grabbed a loose pink gown from the closet. "Here honey, put this on. You can't really wear a t-shirt with wings."

Priela nodded and slipped the thing over her head. It had no buttons, no snaps, no zippers. Instead it was fluid, cascading around her as it fell over her shoulders, with a narrow opening that slid gently around her wings. "Mom, please tell me what's really going on. I don't understand."

"I can't imagine how you must feel Priela, learning all of this at your age. You see, I was born with mine." Calliope removed her cloak and Priela could see them. Her mother's wings. They

25

were large, and silver, and they shimmered in the light. "You're a muse, Priela. A magical creature gifted in the arts."

Priela swallowed hard. "And I take it that you're a muse too?"

"Yes. I know this is a lot to absorb."

"Is Dad a muse?"

"No, your father is human." Calliope took a seat on the edge of the sofa now and her wings started to flutter.

"What about Moriela?"

"Well, we don't know with your sister yet. Like you, she was born without wings. So I suppose she could go either way."

"Okay, so muses are invisible," said Priela. She staggered upward and began to pace in front of the coffee table, dragging her feet along the carpet as she moved, but her mind was reeling. "Can people hear me?"

"No, Priela. People cannot hear you speak. They cannot feel your touch. They do not know you are here."

"So if no one knows muses are here, then how can people see you? How can Dad see you?"

"Honey, I was your father's muse for many years. From the time he was a boy really. And he could always sense me, feel me on some level. Then one day he fell in love with his inspiration. With me. And just like that, I became real in his world. In the human world. I still disappear at times, although it doesn't happen much anymore."

"So will Dad be able to see me too?"

"Of course. He loves you Priela. Anyone who loves you can see you. You exist as a human in their presence."

Priela gritted her teeth. "Stop saying the word 'human' like it doesn't apply to me anymore. You're creeping me out, Mom."

Anger was replacing her confusion, making her muscles tense and her skin hot. She imagined it was the same sensation people felt after learning they were adopted. A feeling of being lied to by those one trusted most. But this was even worse because apparently her biological mother was a different species. "Why didn't you ever tell me any of this?"

"There was simply no reason to tell you before."

"Really? You thought there was no reason to say anything? My whole life I've felt different, like some kind of freak. I don't fit in with the kids at East. I hate it there."

Calliope rose to her feet and straightened a painting that was now askew. "Teenagers aren't supposed to enjoy high school. Everyone feels like she's different somehow. It's all perfectly normal. You'll get through this phase."

"It's not a phase, Mom. I can hear people's thoughts. I bet you didn't know that about me, did you? I've tried to hide it. You know why? Because I was afraid of turning in to you, Mom. Because I thought you were crazy."

Calliope's calm expression suddenly hardened and her shoulders tensed. Priela had clearly struck a nerve. "You thought I was crazy? But I've been trying so hard to act normal, just like you and your sister."

"But I'm not normal, Mom. I've never been normal. I'm not even sure why this whole muse thing comes as a surprise. I've already got a sixth sense. Why not one more, right? Why not become an invisible creature who flies through the sky and inspires art?" Priela's lip quivered. "Oh yeah, I know why. Because I'm not insane. That stuff isn't real."

Her voice trailed off and the word 'real' began to echo through her mind. She could feel something shifting inside her and suddenly it all made sense. The weird clairvoyance. The intuition. The not fitting-in. It was as if she had been putting together pieces of a jigsaw puzzle all of her life, making connections here or there, and now she was seeing the puzzle in its entirety for the very first time, its picture snapping sharply into view. "I'm a muse," she whispered.

At that moment, Priela heard the garage door opening. She heard the trunk slam, the lumbering footsteps. It was her father, Daniel. He only came home this early when he was heading in from the airport. The rear kitchen door swung open and he stepped inside, dressed in his standard suit and hauling a large laptop case, beads of sweat dotting his forehead. "Hello," he said, rubbing his left shoulder and wincing in discomfort. Priela didn't need magic powers to sense his stress and exhaustion. Still, she stiffened and turned away.

"What's going on?" he said, moving closer and glancing from Priela to Calliope. "Is everything okay?"

"Remember what I told you last night, Daniel? About those bandages? I was right. It's happened."

He shook his head and sighed. Then he crouched down and opened his laptop case, pulling out a gift. "I had a feeling. I got you something, Priela."

She took the present and ripped in to the wrapping paper, but when she saw what it was, a doll in a purple box, the hair on the back of her neck stood up. Priela's father was always getting her gifts designed for children. It made her feel like he didn't really know her, like he didn't understand her at all. "Is this supposed to be for Moriela?"

"It has wings, so no. I got the doll for you, sweetheart."

"Seriously? You think this thing is going to make me feel better? Just because some doll has wings too?" She let out a grunt and pushed the box aside.

"You know Priela, you really need to show some appreciation when I get you things. Most of the time, I don't even get a 'thank you.'" He stomped over to a side table and began aggressively sorting through mail, ripping up the advertisements and tossing them in the trash.

"Thanks for the doll, Dad," she said, but her tone was dry and she crossed her arms over her chest.

"Priela, I realize you've had a tough day but you have zero gratitude, zero understanding of the meaning of work. I kill myself every day to support this family and you act as if money grows on trees."

"So we're going to make this about you now, Dad? My whole life has been a lie and you're worried about what? My lack of appreciation for some token souvenir you picked up at the airport?"

"I understand that you're angry, but that's no excuse for disrespect." He tossed the remaining mail and turned around. "Look Priela, I don't want to argue. How about we just focus on tomorrow? You're going to need to go back to school."

"What? No. I'm not going back to that place and you and Mom can't make me. I don't belong there. I never did. Besides, I'm invisible now and you're the only person who can see me. So I don't know how school is supposed to happen."

Calliope stepped closer. "Priela that isn't the way invisibility works. Think of it like Wi-Fi. When your father is nearby, the signal strength is strong and everyone can see you, not just him. When he leaves, it weakens and you disappear."

"I don't get how that fixes my problem, Mom."

"Well, there's nothing particularly special about your father. It's his love that triggers the switch. So you'll just need to stay around someone who loves you while you're at school, like your best friend Kalista."

"Kalista's not in all of my classes."

"Well, Mrs. Vasquez adores you and she's in that big house all alone these days. Maybe she could go with you for a little while?"

"Honestly? You want me to attend school with a chaperone?" Priela looked down at her frilly dress now and clutched a handful of fabric, holding it up for her parents to see. "And what exactly do you think will happen if I show up to school in this thing? You think no one will notice? I already look younger than everyone. Now I'm supposed to walk around in a princess dress?"

Priela could almost feel the steam coming out of her ears, but being a muse wasn't the only reason she didn't want to go back to East High School. She thought about Noah and his disgusted expression. Seeing him again would be mortifying, particularly if he'd told people about their encounter and he must have by now. She had no idea what he'd say but it wouldn't be good, and it was the kind of gossip that had a way of spreading. And then there was Mrs. Wilson, and the popular girls who hated her, and the lunchroom where she sat all alone.

"No," screamed Priela. "There's no way I'm going back to that place."

"You know, you can't just run away from your problems, sweetheart."

"Dad, I've just learned that I'm not human. It's not exactly a small problem."

"Look, if you don't want to go back to East, I'll understand. I get it. Your mother went to a muse academy. I'm sure we can enroll you over there instead. But you need to make a choice, Priela. You need to make a choice, pick yourself up, and move on."

"It's called The Muse Institute of Learning, Daniel," said Calliope, edging between them. "And it isn't as simple as just enrolling her. I really think East is a better fit."

"So you're saying that it's not my choice, Mom? You're saying that you'll force me to stay at East no matter what I want?"

"No. That's not what she's saying," said Priela's father, turning to his wife now. "Calliope we've always known this day might come. You can't protect her forever."

"Daniel, I know you mean well but you have no idea what you're talking about. You've never visited Gaia. You don't realize how unprepared Priela is for the muse world. It would eat her alive. She hasn't studied the arts. Not really. And art is all they care about there. Maybe in time with some additional training she could make it work, but she simply isn't ready. She hasn't even found her talent." Calliope clasped her hands together now and glanced back at Priela. "Trust me, I left that place for a reason. Besides, you're half-human. It will be easier for you than it was for me. I think it's best if…"

"Enough, Calliope. You've won this battle for years. Priela's old enough to make her own choices. If she wants to go to the muse academy then we need to support her."

"The Muse Institute."

"Academy, institute… whatever."

Both of Priela's parents were furious, their eyes scowling, their posture stiff, a vein bulging from her father's neck. But the apparent concern they both expressed for her well-being only made Priela angrier. Neither of them truly understood.

"You're both making it sound like it's no big deal. Like I'm just picking one school or the other. But I'm choosing between two worlds, two lives, and I'm just not sure I can do that right now. What if I just stayed home for a while?"

Daniel's head snapped sharply in her direction. "Staying home isn't an option, Priela. This won't be your only life changing event. We all have moments, choices that change our worlds forever. Giving up isn't the answer."

"But I have no idea what to do, Dad. It's terrifying."

"I know," he said, loosening his collar. "But tell me, where do you think you'll be more successful?"

"Daniel, how can you expect Priela to make an informed decision here? She has no frame of reference."

"You're the one with no frame of reference, Mom. I've always listened to you and I'm miserable. How do you know that the muse institute isn't a good fit? Just because you left that world doesn't mean that I should avoid it too. Just because you wanted to be human doesn't mean that it's what I want. I'm not you, Mom. I'm not you."

Priela pivoted around and raced up the stairs, but her entire body was shaking. She wasn't sure what to think or how to feel. She wasn't sure of anything anymore.

Chapter Five
A PARALLEL UNIVERSE

Morning came much too quickly for Priela to make a decision. It wasn't fair. She'd only had one night to ponder her future. One night to decide if she should return to East High School, a place she found insufferable, or attend The Muse Institute of Learning, a place she hadn't even known existed until now. People usually agonized over these kinds of choices, taking months to select the best-fit college, but Priela was supposed to pick a school in a few hours? She took more time choosing what to eat for dinner.

Priela pulled herself out of bed and glanced at her reflection in a mirror. Her eyes were bloodshot. Her hair was a mess. She had spent most of the night researching muses online until her eyelids drooped shut from exhaustion and the tablet slid from her hands and fell to the floor, leaving her fitful and restless.

The internet was great, except for when it wasn't. It had reams of information on Greek mythology, although the material was clearly out of date with most muse lineage data stopping around the last millennium. There were quotes from famous writers about muses. Homer. Virgil. Dante. Shakespeare. But Priela couldn't really relate to those dead guys. There were plenty of depictions of muses as well, mostly sculptures and paintings, although the artists had portrayed the wings wrong, looking much too bird-like. That was, if they had bothered to include wings at all.

Still in all her research, Priela couldn't find what she really wanted to know, like what it felt like to be a muse or how to inspire people. She limped into the hallway and her eyes scanned her mother's art. Calliope's paintings were bold and abstract. They came from deep within so that the act of painting took her mother from somewhere bizarre and very far away, to a place of deep contemplation. Would this be Priela's future too? She touched one of the pieces, her fingers tracing the terse lines and angles, but she didn't feel any visceral connection. She just felt foolish.

"What are you doing, La la?" said Moriela, entering the hallway. She still called her sister La la after all these years, not having been able to pronounce Priela's name as a toddler. "You're acting weird."

Priela looked over, feeling a sudden wave of jealousy at Moriela's simple existence, her unknowing bliss. "I've just had a horrible week, that's all."

"It's Tuesday morning."

"Um, yeah…" Priela bit her lip. "Dad said that I could switch schools. So I've been up all night trying to decide what to do."

"Oh, are you thinking of transferring to Chesterfield High? Because I've heard they have a really good math and science program."

Priela shook her head. At some point she'd need to tell her sister the truth, but she wasn't ready to discuss it yet. "It's more like an arts academy."

"Really? No offense, but you kinda suck at art."

Moriela walked into the bathroom, stretched her neck, and began brushing her teeth. She was the real prodigy, the sister with all of the talent in art, and music, and dance. And she was the one who resembled their mother with the same green eyes and soft, manageable curls, while Priela resembled their dad with olive skin and dark hair.

But Priela's similarities with her father went beyond physical appearance. He was a pragmatic man. He couldn't sing or dance. He didn't even have a sense of rhythm. His art was amateurish at best and Priela was certain he'd never written a poem in his lifetime. In fact, he had no artistic talent to speak of at all. So if Mom was his muse, for years presumably, then what exactly had she inspired?

"You're right, Morgie," said Priela with a sigh. "I do suck at art. So do you think I should stay at East?"

"No, that's not what I meant." Moriela spit out a mouthful of toothpaste and spun around. "I think you should get as far away from that place as possible, even if it's to go to an arts school. This isn't the first time you've had a bad week, La la. You're always moping around. You're always saying that you don't have any friends. That you hate your classes. Either they're too easy or the teachers are awful."

"Yeah, but I was thinking…"

"What's there to think about? You're miserable. I don't see what you have to lose by trying something new." Then Moriela smiled and headed down the stairs.

Priela watched her go. Her sister made the choice sound so simple, so obvious. She pivoted toward the bathroom and her wings fluttered. The movement was an involuntary reflex, like yawning in response to a yawn, and the sensation felt peculiar. But flying did seem kind of cool. And really, how much worse could the institute be than her current situation? Sure, she wouldn't know anyone. But at least there wouldn't be any haters either. Maybe she'd even fit in. And yes she wasn't much of an artist, but excelling academically hadn't exactly made her happy at East.

"I really wish you understood what you were signing up for, honey," said Calliope, suddenly beside her.

"Mom, could you stop sneaking around all the time? You're like a cat, just appearing out of nowhere."

Priela nudged her mother aside and slammed the bathroom door in her face. She was still upset about the lifetime of lies and she needed her space, but Calliope wouldn't give her any. Priela could hear the floorboards creak as her mother started pacing outside the threshold, waiting to make her case, waiting to explain the numerous reasons she shouldn't switch schools.

It made Priela's pulse race. This decision wasn't anyone else's to make. She leaned against the bathroom tile and put a hand up to her forehead, breathing in quick mouthfuls of air. The anger helped clarify her thought process and strengthen her resolve. It was time for her to make a change and nothing her mother said could persuade her otherwise.

"Mom, I've made up my mind," she said, banging open the door. "I'm going to the institute and you can't stop me."

"I know," said Calliope. Then she headed toward Priela's bedroom and gestured for her to follow. "I just thought you might need some help getting ready. Things are going to be different now." She opened the closet to reveal dozens of glittery gowns. "See?"

"Did you put all of those dresses in there?"

"I didn't need to, honey. They arrived on their own. Creativity is what defines muses. It's a part of you now and the creativity extends to your clothing."

"Uh huh. Sure."

Priela thumbed through the pastel dresses, removing one from its hanger and examining the thing. Its bodice had shiny beads sown into the seams with sheer white sleeves that cinched at the wrists and swayed outward. Tufts of fabric flowed from the waistline in various shades of pink, making the outfit nauseatingly girly, but at least it would fit around her wings. Priela slipped it on. The texture was elastic, yet strong. "What is this fabric?"

"Oh, that's silk from a spiders' web."

"Of course it is." Priela rolled her eyes, ran her fingers through her messy curls, and glanced in the mirror. She looked ridiculous. She slipped on a pair of sneakers.

"You won't need shoes anymore."

"Right, because muses just walk around barefoot since they're all so delightful and perfect."

"What's with the sarcasm, Priela? Enough. If you'd rather grab your backpack and head over to East, I'm sure that we can…"

"No." Priela kicked off the shoes and stiffened her posture. "The outfit is fine. I'll get used to it." Then she marched through the hall and down the stairs, hesitating when she reached the back door. "So how am I supposed to get to the institute anyway, Mom?"

"It's precisely where your old school was, so you shouldn't have any difficulty finding it. Although, you'll have to walk there until those wings come in."

"No, I mean… How am I supposed to switch worlds?"

Calliope's expression softened and she placed a hand on her daughter's shoulder. "Priela, you're a muse now. The moment you walk out that door and leave your father's realm, you'll already exist in Gaia. You see, the muse world is layered on top of the human one. It exists in the same place, at the same time, but in a wholly separate dimension."

"Seriously? A separate dimension? I don't know what that means."

"Well…" Her eyes flickered upward, like she was searching for the right words. "Time is its own dimension too. Imagine traveling backwards in time by fifty years. You'd still be in the same location. The streets would seem familiar, the city's blueprint remaining very much the same. And yet, the world would be irrevocably altered. Gaia is like that. It has the same basic framework but its details, its sensibilities, are painted by a different brush. An artist's brush."

"So it's an alternate reality, like in a video game. Got it. But I still don't understand how these two worlds can overlap without anybody knowing?"

"Honey, someone standing on a street corner fifty years ago wouldn't be able to see another person standing there today. They wouldn't be able to interact. They wouldn't even know the other person was there."

"Uh huh. And how long will I exist in the muse world?"

"For as long as you have wings."

"So basically forever?" Priela grunted. "Fantastic. I guess I'll see you when I get back from this parallel universe." Then she swung the door open and stepped outside.

Chapter Six
AUDITION WEEK

Priela shut the back door to her house and squinted. It was as if the sun suddenly shone brighter, as if her eyes weren't adjusting to the light so that they stung from the glare. She shielded her vision with one hand until the world faded in to view, but its colors were more vibrant than normal, the reds redder, the blues bluer. It was a dawn like she had never seen, vivid, dazzling, with a sky streaked in a full spectrum of hues and punctuated in turquoise and gold. So this was Gaia?

She started walking. She could feel the pavement beneath her feet. It was warm and strangely smooth, and her feet made a faint tapping noise as they stepped. She whispered the word, "Hello." The sound reverberated through the air, echoing over and again, until her ears were quietly ringing. Even the smells were more intense, the air having an aroma of fir leaves and freshly cut grass, so that her awareness of everything was intensified. It was fantastic, and weird, and a bit frightening all at once.

Priela headed to school in the same direction as always, with the same stops, the same turns, but the streets were now changed. She could see why her mother compared the muse world to time travel. The place had an old fashioned feel. But it wasn't the dirty, chaotic world of the actual past. It was a sanitized version that lacked the blaring traffic, and the cracked sidewalks, and the dumpsters overflowing with trash, and yet there was an eeriness to it all.

She approached the corner hardware store that she passed every day and glanced at its usual display of tools in the window. Something was definitely off. She pressed her nose to the glass and noticed that the tips of the screwdrivers were blunt, the edges of the saws weren't serrated, and the pliers lacked rivets to open and close. The tools were nothing more than props. She tried to open the store's front door, but it didn't budge. The door didn't even have hinges. What was this place?

She pivoted around and her eyes scanned the quiet storefronts and the deserted streets. Every window display was illuminated. Every surface was sparkling clean. But odd things were missing like road signs, and parking meters, and storm drains. Was everything fake? It was as if someone had built an entire city without needing it to function.

When Priela finally arrived at The Muse Institute of Learning, she breathed a sigh of relief. At least the school showed signs of life, with voices floating through open windows and music in the distance. Even the tree was flourishing, the strange one that had caught Priela's attention the day before. She walked closer and examined the square green leaves which now sprouted from its branches. Her arms prickled with goose bumps. They weren't leaves at all. They were dollar bills. Was this curious tree a money tree now? The whole concept seemed wrong.

"Aren't you Calliope's daughter?"

Priela glanced upward and saw a muse flying through the sky right above her. It was one thing to have wings, to touch them. It was another to see them in motion, carrying a muse effortlessly in broad sweeping waves. "Uh, huh," she muttered, her mouth dropping open.

"I'm Edessa," she said, gliding closer. Then she landed softly on the grass and brought her wings to a halt. "Please tell your mother I'm so very sorry."

"How do you know my mom?"

"Well, I don't know her personally. I just know that she lives in that monochrome, dreary place. I can't even imagine it. To be an art muse like me and to be stuck there. You aren't an art muse too, by any chance?"

"Uh, no," said Priela shifting her weight. "I don't think so."

"See I told you," said another muse, who floated down too. "I'm Dion, by the way. I'm a literature muse."

"Um, okay. I'm Priela," she said, attempting to smile. But it was immediately clear that despite her pink gown and her small fluttering wings, Priela still looked very human compared to these creatures.

Both Edessa and Dion had fully grown wings in rich, iridescent hues that radiated a subtle glow. Both had luminous dresses that shimmered when they moved. And they were tall. Strictly speaking, height was nothing new. In the human world Priela was always the shortest. Still, it made her feel different.

"Do you know if there's a schedule posted somewhere?" said Priela, clearing her throat. "I'm not really sure where to go."

"Oh, everyone starts with singing trials today. Come on."

The muses led Priela into a theater that hadn't existed at all at East High and her eyes widened. She felt like Dorothy entering the Emerald City. The space was packed with muses and all of them were fantastic and magical.

One muse cast a fleeting glance in Priela's direction and whispered something, but it wasn't the low murmur of human gossip. Her voice was melodic, traveling through the air in a harmonious lilt, her laughter sounding like song. Another muse sashayed by and eyed Priela, but her stride was graceful with each leg outstretched, each toe pointed. Would Priela ever fit in here? She was so ordinary and awkward compared to everyone else.

"Class, it's time," said a teacher, clapping her hands.

There was a flurry of movement as the muses took their seats. Then one muse leapt onto the stage and started to sing. Just like that, she belted out a song with no preparation and it was spectacular. The timbre of her voice was stunning, the pitch perfectly on key, and as she sang her wings changed from a deep purple to gold.

"Is everyone this good?" whispered Priela.

"Oh, that's Clio," said Edessa. "She's a direct descendant of the original Clio. You know, one of the nine ancient muses from Greece? Her mother was a really good singer too. But in my family, I'm the first artist."

"So then, every muse has a talent?"

Edessa flashed her a confused look, "You're joking, right?"

Priela bit her lip. At East High the arts were never really emphasized in the curriculum, and even if they had been, she wasn't particularly gifted in that arena.

The song ended and the room erupted in applause. "Beautiful," said the teacher and the name *"Clio"* appeared in the air, floating in a swirling amber font.

"Why did her name appear?"

"Oh, Clio's been chosen for this class," said Dion.

"So these songs are a test?"

"Uh, they're more like auditions."

"Do we have to audition for every class? What happens if we don't get in to anything?"

Dion raised an eyebrow and her mouth fell open but she didn't say a word, as if she was unsure how to answer the question.

42

Another muse hopped onto the stage. Her voice was exquisite as well. To Priela's ear, they all sounded good. But as the auditions wore on, she noticed the teacher frown a couple of times and not everyone's names appeared. Neither Edessa nor Dion were chosen, despite having pleasant voices.

Then it was Priela's turn. She was the only muse who hadn't yet performed and she crept onto the stage slowly, her head bowed, her stomach twisting in knots.

"You're Calliope's daughter," said the teacher, watching her. "We've all been wondering about you. A muse raised in the human world. Do you mind if a few others watch your performance as well?"

"Okay, but I'm a horrible singer."

"Nonsense."

The teacher waved her arm in a circular motion and additional audience members showed up out of nowhere, filling the theater to capacity. Most of them were muses, but there were a few green elf-like creatures, and two or three horned animals that stood on two feet, and even a lone giantess. How many mythical creatures existed here?

"Welcome Headmistress," said the teacher, gesturing toward an older muse with silvery white hair. "Welcome all. I'd like to introduce Calliope's daughter."

"What lovely curls," someone said.

"Such a petite little thing."

"And those wings. So wonderfully immature."

Priela's jaw stiffened. She knew the words were intended as praise but she hated these kinds of microaggressive compliments. She hated being reduced to a description of her physical appearance, specifically those traits that made her stand apart from everyone else. Of course, any comments about her singing

43

voice would be far worse. She had never performed before an audience in her life. She had no talent at all.

"Go on," said the teacher.

Priela gulped down a lump in her throat and stepped forward. Then she started to sing a peculiar melody based on an ancient Greek poem. It was the only muse-like song she knew.

> *"I too wish to sing of heroic deeds but the lyre's strings can only produce sounds of love"*

There was a collective groan throughout the room. Had Priela selected the wrong song or was she just horribly off key? Her cheeks flushed and her wings started changing from white to a crimson hue. So that's how wings changed color? They reflected her mood. Great. Now the entire room knew she was embarrassed.

> *"Recently I changed the strings and then the lyre itself and tried to sing the feats of Hercules, but still the lyre kept singing songs of love"*

Her pitch was getting worse with each stanza. Someone coughed loudly in the back of the room. Someone else murmured to a neighbor. The headmistress looked down at her hands and a few of the elves simply disappeared. Priela started trembling.

> *"So farewell you heroes because my lyre sings only songs of love"*

She couldn't remember if the song had another verse. It didn't matter. She was done. But there was no applause, no name appearing in the air, only awkward silence.

"Wow, that was painful," said Clio, the gifted singer. "She should just go back to where she came from. After a performance like that, I'd certainly never want to show my face here again."

Several muses laughed and Priela rushed off the stage, her heart pounding, her eyes fighting back tears. What was she thinking, coming to this place?

***

Unfortunately, Priela's embarrassments at the institute didn't end on that first day. The horrible singing performance merely launched a string of disappointments. During the dance auditions the instructor asked Priela to perform a solo, only to move her to the back of the chorus line, and then off the stage entirely. The art teacher wouldn't leave her alone, hovering over Priela's shoulder, watching each muddled brushstroke, wincing at every new color selection. And when her painting was done, the teacher threw it away.

The orchestra conductor was no better. She gave Priela the coveted first violin, ostensibly shoving it into her arms when she walked in the concert hall.

"But I've never played the violin before."

"Ludicrous. You're a gifted muse. I can sense it."

It didn't take long for the conductor's enthusiasm to wane. After Priela improperly positioned the wooden instrument under her chin and squeaked the bow across its strings, the conductor grabbed the violin away.

"Here," she said, thrusting a triangle into Priela's hands. "Just clink this when I point to you. Can you handle that?"

Apparently she couldn't.

With each failure Priela felt increasingly lost, increasingly alone. But of all the auditions, the literature trials were the worst. Writing was an area where she had at least a little training, where she wasn't totally pathetic, or so she had thought. But then, each muse was assigned a type of literature to compose.

Dion received her style first, written on a glittering slip of parchment paper. "Oh, an original poem," she said, unfolding the sheet and smiling. Then she wrote a poem in a single stroke without any hesitation or editing at all, and read it aloud.

> *"Oh human, how our world would seem to you*
> *So vibrant, so melodic, so beautiful*
> *The blues a shade of azure, the reds a hue of fire*
> *The whites too glaring for your eyes*
>
> *And yet this world, layered atop your world*
> *Invisible, fleeting, exists because of you*
> *We muses provide guidance*
> *But you are the inspiration"*

Priela unfolded her slip of paper. *"Please compose an original novel,"* it read. A novel, really? Without saying a word, Priela rose to her feet and bolted out the door. But she couldn't escape the sniggering, the finger pointing, the whispers that followed her, growing louder and more sinister with each failure. Everything had changed and yet nothing had changed at all. She was still an outcast.

There was no mistaking the fact that Priela was less talented than her peers. Although it wasn't the only reason her auditions were so horrible, her efforts so emotionally draining. She was also being held to a very different bar, so that even her modest successes seemed pathetic when compared to the elevated standard.

The references to her mother were unrelenting. Calliope was simultaneously lauded for her great artistic talent and despised for her rejection of the muse world. And there was a fascination with Priela and expectations that were wholly unrealistic. What was her talent? What secret gifts did she possess? Was she really a muse or only human?

On more than one occasion, it was suggested that Priela discover an entirely new field of art. Apparently it had been done many times before, as immortalized by dozens of statues and monuments that dotted the campus, each marked with a prominent engraving. *"The Study of Ceramics, founded by Melete,"* read a colossal vase that was situated outside the pottery studio. *"The School of Singing, founded by Euterpe,"* read another monument shaped like a musical note. But how did one create a new field of art anyway? They expected her to know things they didn't know, to excel in ways the rest of them couldn't. To be a teacher. A leader. A star. It was overwhelming.

At least tomorrow would be the last day of auditions. Priela had very mixed feelings on the topic. On the one hand, she couldn't wait for this week to be over. On the other hand, Priela had yet to be chosen for a single course and the thought of not being selected was terrifying. Did she just go back to the human world? She dreaded the thought. Or was there some kind of remedial path for muses who failed at everything?

The whole paradox made Priela doubt if she really was a muse after all. Sure, she had wings and they were growing larger every day, their default color changing from white to a pale pink hue. But she had no discernible talent and a muse wasn't a muse without one, right? Clearly, she didn't belong in Gaia. She didn't belong anywhere.

Priela approached the trails board where a gathering of muses was reviewing the schedule for the final day. There were still plenty of classes available but Priela's name was only written beside a single subject, *"Muse Essentials."*

Edessa traced her finger down the glittery panel. "Architecture, sculpture, lithography," she read, her wings fluttering. "Jewelry making. I suppose that makes sense for an art muse. Oh, and Muse Essentials. Ugh."

"What is Muse Essentials?" asked Priela.

"Um, it's kind of like a magic class. It's where you learn how to guide humans, that sort of thing. Everyone says it's really hard, but they won't let you graduate without it."

Priela swallowed audibly. Muse Essentials. Magic class. Was that where muses learned to fly? She couldn't imagine what the auditions would be like, but if singing was out of her comfort zone then magic was in a whole other league. She'd fail this last audition for certain. Her face fell and her body shivered from an intense wave of self-doubt.

Edessa watched her. "Don't worry about tomorrow," she said gently. "Everyone gets in to Muse Essentials. Everyone."

Chapter Seven

MUSE ESSENTIALS

Priela couldn't imagine a scenario in which the magic class tryouts would go well. If they asked her to mix a potion she'd probably turn herself into a frog. If they asked her to use a wand she'd likely zap herself with electric shocks. And if she needed to fly in a race she'd certainly finish in last place, without ever lifting off the ground. The stress weighed on her heavily, making her stomach nauseated and her body ache.

Why couldn't she fit in anywhere? Why did she have to be so different? Priela wished she could just drop out of school entirely, but her parents wouldn't allow it, making it unnervingly clear that if she wanted to stay under their roof school was mandatory.

She grabbed a duffle bag and shoved some clothing inside. Running away would give her power over her own destiny, a measure of control she desperately craved, and it seemed like a more sensible course of action than humiliating herself again. Besides, not trying at all was better than failing and choosing to be alone was better than feeling ostracized, even if it amounted to more or less the same thing.

Priela envisioned herself alone on a mountaintop or lost in the forest somewhere. But who was she kidding? It wasn't like she had wilderness survival skills. She couldn't even make mac and cheese unless it came from a package. Plus, she was invisible in the human world these days which seemed like it might be a problem.

Really she had no choice. She'd have to suffer through this last audition and allow the consequences to play out. Although her heart wasn't in it. She abandoned the duffle bag and slipped out the back door without bothering to eat, or shower, or even brush her teeth. What difference did it make? It wasn't as though she was going to impress anyone. Then she passed through Gaia like a walking zombie, her thoughts stuck in a hypnotic daze, her eyes barely focusing on the oddities around her.

When she reached the Muse Essentials room, she had to squeeze inside. The space was set up like an old-fashioned classroom with tiny desktops attached to each chair and a sizable black chalkboard. Although the room was too small for the dozens of muses who were already there with scarcely enough standing room, let alone enough desk space. Priela spotted Edessa and Dion and inched closer. They weren't exactly friends, but at least they smiled when they saw her.

"I'm Lady Raymere," said an instructor, who appeared out of nowhere.

Priela turned her head and gawked. Most muses were proportioned like humans. Tall humans. But this teacher was giant, her waist the height of Priela's shoulders, her wings spanning virtually the width of the classroom, her sparkling gown trailing several feet behind her.

"For your Muse Essentials trials, you will take a written examination."

Most of the muses groaned but Priela relaxed her shoulders, feeling relieved. In the human world she had hated test taking, but now she longed for its anonymity, missing the certainty of right and wrong answers.

"Based on your examination results, four students will be chosen."

There was a noisy murmur. At every other audition, dozens of students were selected. Wasn't this supposed to be a required course? Wasn't everyone supposed to get in? Priela scanned the room and did a quick mental headcount. There were thirty-nine muses and four slots. The odds weren't in her favor.

"You can't just accept four," said Clio, the talented singer. "Last year, you enrolled twenty three students."

"Yes, that was last year," said Lady Raymere, her deep voice reverberating through the space. "Now shall I allow your classmates to begin the examination while we discuss this matter further?"

"But I'm on track for an early graduation. To be the youngest ever. Younger even than Calliope."

"Then I'd suggest you score highly on the exam."

Clio crossed her arms over her chest and looked away.

"Class, this chalkboard will track your progress," said Lady Raymere, shifting her gaze and gesturing with a golden sleeve, and the muses' names appeared along the bottom of the board. Then she tossed a handful of papers and colored chalk into the air, and the things swirled through the room and landed in the muses' hands. "Please begin."

Many of the muses without desks took seats on the floor, but Priela remained standing and glanced at the page. On it were three ovals along with a single question. *"Which oval is the most important?"*

She glanced around. Dion was already covering her paper in multiple long paragraphs. Edessa was also scribbling feverishly. Did all of the muses have the same question? Probably not. Priela's question certainly didn't warrant an essay.

She looked back at her exam. It didn't make a whole lot of sense. The ovals were nearly identical, although one was almost imperceptibly larger, but it's bigger size didn't necessarily make it more important. Priela pressed her paper against a wall and wrote, *"It depends."* Then she glanced at the chalkboard. Some of the muses' names had started to inch upward. Hers was not among them.

She looked back at the page. The ovals and her messy handwriting were gone, and a second question appeared. *"What time is it?"*

It was a strange question. Why did the time matter? How was it relevant to anything? Priela checked her watch. She still wore the thing even though she knew it was an anomaly in the muse world. *"8:46 a.m.,"* she scribbled.

"WRONG." The word appeared in a capitalized red font. *"How disappointing…"* the test continued, its letters skipping across the page. *"Aren't you Calliope's daughter? Your mother was such a gifted muse. We expected so much more from you."*

Priela's face flushed but she didn't know what to make of the test's insults.

A few muses began rising from the floor. One muse tore her exam to shreds before storming out of the room. Another muse snapped her chalk in half, threw her paper down, and then hurried off. At least Priela wasn't the only one being affronted by her exam. She took a deep breath and glanced at the chalkboard. It had fewer names now, but hers was still at the bottom.

"You know, Priela," wrote the exam, erasing the words that had come before. *"You chose to come to Gaia for all the wrong reasons. You were so desperate for someone to like you and then you ran away from the one boy who did… NOAH."*

A chill went down Priela's spine. How did this bizarre examination paper know about Noah? She hadn't told anyone. Her mind flashed through the events under the bleachers. It was only a week ago, yet it seemed like a different lifetime. *"Noah didn't like me. I would have sensed it,"* she wrote.

"Are you certain, Priela?" The words appeared all at once. *"Do you really have a sixth sense or are you simply losing your mind? Everyone thinks your mother is crazy. And you're so much like her. Is everyone wrong?"*

Priela's muscles stiffened and her wings turned red. She'd had enough. It was one thing to endure insults from other students but she wasn't going to take them from a stupid piece of paper. She crumpled the page and stomped through the room toward Lady Raymere. She was done trying to save herself from embarrassment. Priela was angry.

"This test makes no sense. All it does is insult me."

"Well, you must admit," said Clio with a sneer. "There's a lot worth insulting."

A few muses laughed but Priela ignored them. "I don't understand why my name is at the bottom of the board?"

"What makes you believe that the bottom of the board is a bad thing?" said Lady Raymere, straightening to her full lofty height. "You didn't think the largest oval was more important than the rest."

Priela glanced again at the chalkboard and all of the names switched positions with her name jumping off the board entirely and landing on the wall.

"Uh well, this exam doesn't have anything to do with anything. What skills is it testing anyway?"

"For one thing, it's testing your composure. It's testing your self-control. The human world can be a very dark place. I need students equipped to handle it."

"I think I know how dark the human world is."

"I don't believe you do, Priela. I'm familiar with your background. Your home. Your family. You've lived a charmed life. Not all humans are so fortunate." Then she glided closer until she was towering over Priela. Her gaze was piercing. "Tell me, what does a muse do precisely? What's her job?"

"You know, muses conduct humans' music. They guide their hands when they're painting. They hold them steady when they're dancing. That sort of thing."

"No. We do not give charges their talents. Their talents are their own. They belong to humans themselves, not to muses."

"Okay, so then what do muses do?" Priela placed her hands on her hips and tapped one foot against the floor, but she wasn't trying to be confrontational. Not really. It was just such a simple question and she was suddenly aware that she didn't know its answer. She felt ignorant.

"Muses foster creativity," said Lady Raymere, snaking between the desks now, her long robe sweeping the floor behind her. "We harness our charges' natural talents and set them free."

The other muses were no longer looking at their exams. Instead, their eyes were trained on Lady Raymere and Priela realized the instructor was teaching a lesson for the benefit of the entire class.

"So for a muse to be successful," said Priela, pulling on a curl. "She makes it possible for…what did you call them? Charges? She makes it possible for her charges to thrive, to reach their full potential."

"Indeed. A muse helps her charges thrive, but our influence is limited to the arts. We are not permitted to interfere in the human realm in any other way. Is that understood?"

Priela nodded and suddenly her name bounced from the wall back to the chalkboard, erasing all the others. Then its letters transformed from a chalky white to a shimmering gold. She stared at her name, her eyes wide, her wings fluttering.

"Priela, you have been chosen."

"What? You chose her? Her?" said Clio, throwing down her examination paper and rising from her chair. "She's not even a real muse. She doesn't deserve to be at this school at all. I watched her auditions. That wretched orchestra recital with the triangle. That laughable dance performance. She has no artistic talent. None. She's pathetic. I'm the one who deserves a spot in this class."

Edessa jumped up, "We all want to be chosen, Clio."

Dion rose too. "Yeah, and Priela deserves it as much as anyone. More probably. She knows the human world. Taking this class just makes sense."

"You two are defending her? Really? I bet that neophyte doesn't even know how to fly. Do you, Priela? The rest of us have had wings since birth. I could fly before I could walk. And your little wings are still growing in. You're the physical equivalent of a toddler." Her eyes quickly scanned Priela's short stature, her flat chest, her prepubescent frame, and she snickered. "In quite a few more ways than one."

Priela's mouth dropped open but she didn't know how to respond. She just stood there gaping.

"Nothing to say, huh? You see? She's useless."

"Clio, enough" said Lady Raymere glaring.

Then the name 'Clio' appeared on the chalkboard beneath Priela's name. The names 'Edessa' and 'Dion' appeared too, in sparkling golden letters.

"This subject has been filled," said Lady Raymere, her tone unequivocal. "To my new students, I will see you first thing next week. Please assemble in the auditorium. To everyone else, thank you. You're welcome to reapply next year."

A hush fell over the room as muses began rising from their seats and filing out the door, and Priela could sense a weightiness, a feeling of disappointment among them.

"Thank you," she said to Lady Raymere, but the instructor merely nodded in Priela's direction and vanished.

Chapter Eight
TAKING FLIGHT

Clio's words kept rolling over in Priela's mind, taunting her. *"I bet that neophyte doesn't even know how to fly. Do you, Priela?"* All of the other muses had flown their whole lives, starting around birth apparently.

Priela examined her wings in the long mirror in her bedroom. They had mushroomed in size, developing in less time than it took for a tadpole to transform into a frog. Still, they weren't as large as everyone else's wings. But then, Priela wasn't as large either and they certainly seemed proportionate.

She touched them with her fingertips. Each wing stretched perhaps a foot and a half in width and about twice that from end to end. Their shape was full and rounded, growing narrower as they approached her back, much like the wings of a honeybee, but frayed at the edges in loose wisps and spirals. Veins arched in an elaborate winding pattern, giving them a texture that was strong, yet malleable.

Priela arched her back, wanting to fly. She considered asking her mother to teach her, but Mom would probably say something like, *"I told you, honey. You aren't ready for the muse world. East is a better fit."* If Priela was going to learn, she'd have to teach herself.

She grabbed a notepad and started scribbling equations, calculating the biomechanics she'd need to lift into the air. It was simple physics, not that she had really studied physics in depth. East High School merely scratched the surface and she wasn't sure that science fiction novels counted. Still, she determined the necessary wing force, the lift, the trajectory. Then she waited until her parents were sleeping, snuck downstairs, and slipped out the back door.

But when the door shut, the world looked different. Its shadows were particularly heavy, its filth pervasive. It was the human world. How had that happened? What had caused her to transition all of a sudden?

She took a few steps, her bare feet touching down on the pavement, but there was no sensation at all. It was like her feet had grown thick with callouses and they were weirdly heavy. An airplane flew by overhead and she jumped, letting out a faint shriek. The noise had caught her off guard. In the human world, sounds were relatively flat but there were so many of them. She could even hear traffic coming from the main highway several blocks to the north. It was disconcerting, as if her ears were losing their ability to filter out the background noise.

She looked at the weathered homes, the cluttered street signs, the weeds poking through the sidewalk. Everything was visible from the streetlamps, yet she felt like she had gone colorblind. Gaia had a broader spectrum of hues, even at night, as if there was a fourth primary color in the muse world that blended with the blues, and the yellows, and the reds to make sunsets that were unbelievable.

Priela's depth perception was different now too. The human world was less three dimensional, so that as she moved stationary objects no longer shifted in relation to each other in the same way. It made the experience of walking feel odd, causing her footsteps to amble in an uneven pattern, as if she were drunk.

She had changed so much in such a short time, and Priela suddenly understood that the longer she stayed in Gaia the harder it would become to transition back to the human world, if she ever wanted to return. She'd be like a foreigner who moved away and lost her accent, forever sounding strange when she visited home. But this adjustment was even more dramatic than an altered speech pattern. She'd had a total change in sensory perception. It would be more like choosing to live with dark sunglasses, and poorly attuned hearing aids, and permanent weights attached to each ankle. The human world was simply so ugly, its sounds so irritating, its physical sensations so dull.

Priela's mother must have had a difficult time adjusting. It explained so much. Calliope was still easily startled, reacting disproportionately to loud noises, and flickering lights, and crowds. She had never driven a car, never taken public transportation, never traveled alone. She was reclusive, and erratic, and intensely afraid of change. But she wasn't crazy. And given the circumstances, she'd actually done a fairly good job of acting human. Priela's stomach tinged with guilt. Why had she always given her mom such a hard time?

It made Priela realize that she'd chosen the institute for the wrong reasons, to escape from a school and a life that she'd hated. But it wasn't enough to leave one place. She needed to figure out if Gaia was where she wanted to stay. Going back and forth no longer seemed like a viable option. She breathed in deeply. Maybe flying would help clarify things?

Priela headed toward the vacant lot as intended. The place was perfect for flying purposes with wide open space and soft grass. Then she slipped under the chain link fence, walked to the center of the lot, and spread her wings. She tensed her muscles and her wings fluttered behind her. She tensed them again and again. The motion created a gentle wind and some scattered leaves spun upward, but nothing else happened. She flapped harder. Still nothing.

Toddlers had to crawl before they could walk. Did muses have some kind of intermediate stage too or were they more like baby birds, pushed from the nest and forced to fly?

Plan B was to gain momentum. Priela walked to the edge of the lot and then sprinted to the other side while fluttering rapidly and jumping as high as she could manage. But it didn't work. She felt like an ostrich, possessing the needed wings and speed, but lumbering, and awkward, and unable to lift off the ground.

She needed to add height. But height would only help if she used a dangerous amount. She swallowed hard and glanced around. At the rear of the lot was a thick pine tree that stretched to a rooftop. She could make it up there. She headed to the tree and started scaling branches but needles scraped her wings, feeling like a dozen paper cuts. Ugh! At least none of the scratches broke the surface. Then she climbed from the roof's low sloping edge to its highest point at the center and peered over the side.

How far was she from the ground? Thirty feet? More? Scrapes and bruises were one thing, but if the flying didn't work now there would be no bed of feathers, no powdered snow, no swimming pool to soften her landing. She'd be in trouble.

Clio's words repeated again in her head. *"You see? She's useless."*

Priela balled her hands into fists and straightened her spine. "Here goes nothing," she whispered. Then she extended her wings, ran along the roof's flat upper plane, and jumped. Fortunately, a gust of wind whizzed through the air right at that moment, lifting her into the sky. She began flapping. Her body tilted strongly to one side and then turned sharply to the other. She pulled one leg in, narrowly avoiding a telephone pole, and then quickly pushed it out again. There was nothing elegant about her movements. Still, they were working.

She flew over the empty lot and above the house by its side. It was exhilarating and terrifying all at once, like a ski slope or a rollercoaster, but better. Her heart pounded, her breathing intensified, and her wings changed colors with each flap, turning bronze, orange, rose.

How high could she go? How long could she fly before growing tired? She willed herself to flap harder and harder, until she reached a point where the air started to thin. Then she stretched her wings and began gliding down in large sweeping circles. All around her the moon shone brightly, bathing her in its soft light. She peered at the tree-lined streets, the glowing street lamps, the scattered rooftops. It was a birds' eye view. A magical view. And there was something cathartic about it, something that filled her with wonder and awe and made her feel free.

That's when she made up her mind. Yes, she wanted to stay in Gaia. To live in a world of color and light. To fly. To inspire humans. To be a muse. Priela would carve out a place for herself. She'd work hard and discover her talents. Maybe she'd even fit in. And for the first time, Priela could imagine her future unfolding in magnificent and wonderful ways.

Then the wind stopped suddenly, causing her to stall mid-air and plummet toward the ground. She wasn't that high up anymore, only about a dozen feet or so, but she didn't know how to prevent the fall. She put out her hands instinctively and tensed her muscles. Smash. The ground was rigid. The asphalt rough. A pain shot through her hands and knees which absorbed the brunt of the impact. She remained still for a moment. Her body shaking. Afraid to move. She would have to work on that landing.

She held up one hand. A chunk of skin was hanging loosely, dotted with beads of asphalt and a stream of blood. To avoid scarring, she'd probably need a stitch or two, but that would necessitate her mother's involvement. It wasn't worth the hassle. Ointment and an adhesive bandage would have to do. In the meantime, she ripped off the loose skin and brushed the asphalt away. Then she yanked a tuft of fabric from her gown and wrapped it around her palm. It soaked with blood. At least, she didn't seem to have any broken bones.

Take off 'C minus' she thought, mentally grading her flying efforts. Other muses didn't need to jump from buildings, they could just lift off the ground. Cruising ability, 'B plus.' Other muses didn't need wind and they were so graceful. Landing, 'F'. Too bad it was the only part of flying that wasn't optional.

Priela heard footsteps and turned her head. A figure emerged from the shadows and darted across the street. It was Noah. He stopped for a moment, brushed his hair from his face, and glanced right through her invisible frame, not seeing her at all. She stared into his eyes and felt a rush.

Chapter Nine
KALISTA'S HOUSE

It struck Priela as odd that Noah was roaming the streets alone at night. She was pretty sure he didn't live in this neighborhood. Plus, he was acting strangely. He kept glancing around, fretfully looking over one shoulder, as if he was worried about being seen. Noah was up to something and Priela sensed that it was something he shouldn't be doing, something dangerous.

She rose to her feet, wincing from the pain in her swollen knees, and glanced at her watch. It was late and it would take a while to get home from here, but instead of turning back she started hobbling behind him. Curiosity was part of it. His blue eyes probably played a role too. But mostly, she was driven by a strange, almost instinctual need to watch over him.

Noah turned left in the direction of the mansions, passing a series of imposing facades with tall stone pillars, dramatic arched doorways, and balconies that stretched from one window to the next, before stopping in front of a quiet brick house. He pulled a slip of paper from his pocket and checked a number on the sheet against the number on the house. They matched.

Priela gulped. She knew the house well. It belonged to her best friend Kalista. Why was Noah visiting her? It couldn't be for romantic reasons. Kalista had a crush on someone else.

Then he unfolded the slip further to reveal a date that was etched into Priela's psyche the way all horrific events were remembered and she felt an immediate sense of foreboding. Seven years earlier, on this very same night, Kalista's mother had been killed. Police referred to the tragedy as a home invasion gone bad, but her friend never learned what really happened. All she knew was that her mom was there one day, baking cookies with giant chunks of toffee, and that she was gone the next.

On these distressing anniversaries, neither Kalista nor her father could handle being home. So they always took trips to go hiking, or camping, or to amusement parks, although the excursions did little to distract from the memory. Did Noah know the house was probably empty? Was that why he had marked down this date?

He shoved the paper back in his pocket and headed up the driveway, jumping the fence into Kalista's backyard. Priela followed, hoisting herself over the fence too and dropping to the ground. A sharp pain shot through her injured knees. Ugh!

Then Noah pulled a Swiss army knife from his pocket and clicked through the various tools. He located the screwdriver, approached Kalista's back door, and jammed the tool into the lock with his fist. What was he doing? Trying to break in? Priela cringed at the thought. Noah wasn't a hardened criminal. He was a good guy. Why would he do this?

She recalled yelling at Noah that afternoon under the bleachers and her stomach churned. Was Noah one of her charges, one of the humans she was linked to? He must be. Priela must have caused this, messed him up somehow, screwed with his head. She shuffled closer and placed a hand on his shoulder. She could feel the shape of his muscles and the warmth of his body emanating through his shirt.

64

"Come on, sixth sense" she whispered, trying to tap into his thoughts. "Work."

But she couldn't hear anything. Instead her hands started shaking, just like his. Her breathing became heavier, like his. And her stance adjusted to mirror the way he was standing even though it put strain on her knees. Along with the physical sensations came a certainty, a powerful sense that this was just something that had to be done. But the conviction now stirring inside Priela was not her own. It was Noah's. It had happened before, this embodiment of someone else, although never with such intensity.

Priela bit her lip and leaned in, and suddenly a vision swirled through her thoughts. The image was blurred as if she was seeing it through a waterfall, like an old memory. It was exactly the kind of psychic apparition that typically filled her with fear, causing her to run away or mutter a series of prime number tables to force the images from her head. But now, she narrowed her eyes and concentrated harder.

A man's face with a crooked smile slowly sharpened in to view. The man looked like Noah but with darker eyes and wiry hair on his chin. It must be his father. Then the image panned outward and details started to emerge in the open spaces of her mind. Noah's father was in handcuffs and he was being pushed into the back of a police car by two shadowy figures.

"You're the man of the house now, Noah," his father called out. The words were broken, yet unmistakable. *"Take care of your mother. Take care of Benjamin."*

A light flickered and Priela looked upward. A faint glow was coming from Kalista's bathroom, one story up and just to the left of the back door. Was that light on before or was someone home? Priela wasn't sure. She needed to look through that window, but she couldn't just fly up there. She couldn't lift off the ground without the added height of a rooftop and the added force of wind. At least, she couldn't do it yet.

Directly in front of the window was a gnarled maple tree. Priela eyed its branches and groaned. She wasn't particularly eager to climb yet another tree with her scratched up wings, and her injured hand, and her throbbing knees, but at least this one didn't have pine needles. She made her way up cautiously, securing each foothold before reaching for the next branch. Then she peered through the glass.

Kalista was there, crouched over the toilet, vomiting violently. Her father was there too, pacing back and forth down the hallway, his expression concerned. Clearly, they had cancelled their annual trip because Kalista was ill. It made Priela feel awful. She hadn't known her friend was sick and she probably would have figured it out if she'd bothered to respond to a single text.

"Why aren't you at school today?" Kalista had asked repeatedly. *"Where are you? Is everything okay?"*

Priela avoided the texts because she simply hadn't known what to say. She still didn't know. She yanked on a curl aggressively, tugging at it in a symbolic act of repentance, but the motion caused her to lose her balance and fall from the tree. Smash. Again, really?

She looked over at Noah. He was grating his screwdriver against the lock now as if he was trying to copy a weird technique from an online instructional video or something, but the door remained impervious causing his scraping to grow louder and more frenzied with each twist of the hand. Any minute now, Kalista's father would hear him and head downstairs.

Priela moved closer and another vision flashed through her thoughts. This time, she saw a boy of nine or ten. His cheeks were rounded and his hair was short, but otherwise he resembled Noah. His brother? The boy started moving, walking across her field of vision, but there was something wrong with him. Priela could tell by the way he favored the right side of his body, not placing weight on one leg, and his left hand was frozen in a claw-like manner as if his tendons were being pulled taut. And again the words echoed, *"Take care of Benjamin."*

Noah wiped the sweat from his forehead, clicked through the tools, and located the knife. Then he shoved the knife into the space between the door and its frame, and attempted to wedge the thing open.

"I'll only steal enough to pay for the medicine and not a cent more," he rationalized in his head, and Priela could hear the words unravel like a spool of yarn, coming to her in one continuous stream of consciousness. *"So that Benjamin can walk again. It shouldn't take long if I can get through this door. Nobody's home."*

Priela's throat filled with bile. She empathized with Noah's situation, she really did, but he was making a horrible mistake. He would frighten Kalista if she saw him in the shadows with a knife. She'd think of her mother and that awful night. Kalista's father would think of it too and he'd do anything to protect his daughter from the same fate. This wouldn't end well.

She had to stop this robbery. To make it right. But being invisible had its disadvantages. She couldn't just talk to Noah and she had yet to learn how muses influenced humans. She waved her arms in a circle, mimicking instructors who made similar movements to spark magical things. Nothing happened. She waved them again. Still nothing. She flapped her wings so that air blew in his direction. Noah shivered from a sudden gust of wind, but otherwise it had no impact. He kept jabbing at the door.

She put her hands over his, feeling the sweat on his palms, and tried to yank the knife away. But the edge of the blade pressed against the cut on her hand, reopening the wound, and she recoiled in pain. She needed another approach. She kicked him. Nothing. She pulled his hair. Nothing. She pushed him. Nothing. Then slowly, he lowered the tool, reached out one hand, and turned the knob. The door was unlocked and it swung right open.

No. No. No. Priela couldn't let this happen. She couldn't let anyone get hurt. But what could she do? She spotted Kalista's cat. The animal was curled up on the counter and he was staring directly at her. Could he see her? She took a step sideways and the cat's eyes followed. Then she bent down and patted the floor.

"Come here, Toffee. Come here."

The cat jumped off the counter and moved closer. Noah was watching. Priela arched her back, curled her fingers like claws, and hissed.

Toffee turned his ears outward and bristled his fur. "Hissssss," he said.

Something about the cat spooked Noah and in one continuous motion he clicked the blade closed, bolted back over the fence, and raced down the driveway so quickly that Priela completely lost sight of him. Not a moment later, Kalista's father appeared at the base of the stairs. He saw the open door, marched through the kitchen, and slammed it shut, not seeing Priela at all.

She stood there for a moment in shock, allowing her breathing to return to normal. Then she glanced across the sky. In the distance, the sun was beginning to rise. She had to return home before her parents discovered she was missing. She took one final look at Kalista's bathroom window. The light was still glowing. Then she limped away.

Chapter Ten
THE POOL OF POLLY

Priela awoke early in a sweat. She told herself that it was excitement over her first Muse Essentials class, but in truth her hands were hot, her breathing fast. She had dreamed about Noah and she saw little point in going back to sleep.

She arrived at the institute long before the morning bell, her thoughts still picturing the way his lips creased at the edges and how his eyes narrowed when he was concentrating. The last time she had been in the auditorium it was buzzing with sales booths, but even so he had waited for her under the bleachers. It was the place where she had felt his breath on her face and where he had said, "I like you, Priela."

But now she opened the door to find the room dark and quiet, with only a faint lantern in the corner. She felt along the wall for a light switch. There was none. Instead, her knee brushed against something smooth and cool. It must be the metal slats, the bleachers. She ducked beneath them and crept forward, to visit that place where she had been alone with Noah.

Splash.

She was now immersed in water. What just happened? Had she fallen into some kind of pool? If so, the water was so murky she couldn't tell which way was up.

Priela circled her arms in a breaststroke fashion and kicked her legs. She had always been a decent swimmer, but that was before she had wings. Now they were holding her back, tugging in the opposite direction. She tried to flap them in a smooth, continuous stroke, but pushing wings against fluid was like pushing one's hands against a brick wall, it didn't accomplish much. How was she supposed to swim? She stopped moving entirely and stretched her body in a flat plane in an attempt to float to the surface, but still she felt herself sinking.

Don't panic. Whatever you do, don't panic. She sealed her lips tightly, willed her nostrils not to inhale, and rubbed her eyes. When she opened them, she saw a face in the water. It was Noah's face but it was ethereal, ghost-like. She reached for him but his image faded as soon as her fingers touched it. She looked around. More faces. Hundreds of them. She reached out again, hoping to grasp one of the people and stop herself from descending further, but they were only illusions.

Her lungs started yearning for air. Was this really happening? Was she really drowning? Priela couldn't die now. She hadn't even made her bed that morning. It was such a simple thing, such a mundane thought, but her mother would see the messy covers and shake her head in disappointment. That unmade bed would be Priela's last impression, her only epitaph, as if she were saying goodbye by letting her mother down.

Then her body reached a breaking point. She had run out of oxygen and her instincts began taking over, causing her to breath in a mouthful of water, dragging it past her windpipe in a frightening gulp. She tried to cough it out but it only made the situation worse. She could feel her throat start to spasm and her heart exploding. Her mind was losing consciousness. Darkness was closing in. Help me, she thought, but there was no way to voice the words. No way to scream.

Then suddenly, a yank. The motion was swift and forceful. Clio was pulling her out of the water. Priela emerged gasping, her dress damp and heavy against her skin, her wings a dusky black.

"It's astonishing that anyone could be so idiotic," said Clio, dropping Priela onto a hard surface. "Of course if I had to live with your singing voice, I'd probably drown myself too. I'm shocked you have the capacity to visit Gaia at all."

"You saved me?"

"Oh, don't be too grateful, Priela. Do you have any idea what happens in Gaia when a muse dies tragically? Every literature muse writes a poem. Every lyrical muse sings a song. Every art muse paints a portrait in her honor. Do you honestly believe I would let them immortalize you like that? You don't deserve to be honored. You haven't earned it."

"I'm not trying to be honored, Clio."

"Good. Because it isn't going to happen. Just look at you, dripping like a wet rag. Everyone thinks you possess some buried talent deep inside. Unlock it, they say, and she'll amaze us all. But you're worthless. I truly don't know how you've managed to fool everyone."

Priela's eye twitched. "Don't worry, Clio. I know I'll never be as talented as you are. I'm not trying to be anything special. All I want is to be a normal muse."

"But you're not normal, Priela. Do you think fitting in is a modest goal? This place will grind you up and spit you out. If I was you, I'd just leave now and save myself the embarrassment of flunking. That way, we can all pretend like you had a different reason for leaving here… like you're not some talentless freak." She slanted one eyebrow and pursed her lips in a malicious grin. "Fortunately, I'm not you."

Priela shuddered. The popular girls at East High had always been mean, but this attack felt more personal somehow. Was Clio just a typical queen bee, asserting her dominance over the new girl, or was there validity to her bullying? Was Priela truly a talentless freak? She shook her head and pushed the thought away. No. Clio had to be wrong. Gaia was where Priela belonged and she'd discover her talents soon enough. She was certain of it.

"Are you okay? You're soaking," said Edessa, entering the auditorium.

"What happened?" said Dion, who entered by her side. Then she unraveled her scarf and wrapped it around Priela's shoulders.

"It was awful," said Clio. "Priela almost drown. But I couldn't let that happen. So I yanked her out of that water even though I knew it could suck us both under. That pool is like quicksand."

"You saved Priela? Oh, Clio. You're a hero! Can I paint your portrait?"

"And I'll compose a poem in your honor."

Clio glanced at Priela and smirked.

Whatever. At least Priela's eyes were finally adjusting to the light. She could now see an altered version of that very same East High gymnasium, as it existed at the institute. Here the room contained a massive pool that was mirrored, yet murky as if its water had been polluted by a leaking oil rig.

"What is that water?" asked Priela, tightening the scarf more firmly around her shoulders and shivering.

"It is the pool of Polyhymnia," said Lady Raymere, who suddenly appeared out of nowhere.

"The Pool of Polly," said Dion.

"Indeed. It is older than the institute, having been here for millennia. The campus was designed around it." Lady Raymere looked at Priela and sighed, as if to say *poor thing*, although she didn't actually voice the words. Instead, she began pacing by the water's edge. As she moved, the tiny lantern acted as her personal spotlight and shadows darted out of her way. "You see, in the human world Polyhymnia is known as the muse of sacred poetry, but in our world she is known for solving the pairing dilemma."

"The pairing dilemma?" asked Priela.

"Yes, before Polyhymnia there was no real system. Muses would wander the earth hoping fate would bring them together with their charges."

"So this pool assigns us to our humans?"

"No, Priela. Your charges are a part of you. They are linked to you irrevocably. But it is the Pool of Polly that will reveal their images. And once you have seen your humans, sensed their unique nature, they can be found."

"So those faces I saw in the water... Those were my charges? There were so many of them."

"A muse is paired with many charges in her lifetime. Some muses are paired with thousands." Lady Raymere cleared her throat and her eyes lingered on Priela. "But for now, you will each guide a single human. Only one. Is that understood?"

Priela nodded.

"Good. Shall we begin?"

Lady Raymere started passing out tiny marbles, one to each muse. Priela looked at the stone. It was icy cold and disproportionately heavy for its small size.

Then Dion, Edessa, and Clio knelt beside the pool and tossed their marbles inside. Priela knelt down too, looking for a moment at her own reflection. Her dress was still damp and clinging to her bones, but her wings had started to regain some color and her hair was already a frizzy mess.

She pressed the marble against her chest and tossed it. For a few minutes, nothing happened, or nothing Priela could discern. The stone didn't even cause a ripple. Then gradually, a mist started to rise. At first the fog was dark, but as it rose it faded to a deep grey and then to white. In the haze, glowed several images. Human faces.

Violet, the girl who had once been intimidated in algebra class, appeared before Clio, her face blinking and shifting in the mist. Robin appeared before Dion. Robin was the senior girl who had been working at that credit card sales booth above the bleachers while Priela listened below. The brothers who were also standing above the bleachers appeared too. Anton's face swirled directly before Edessa, while Priela was paired with… Garrett. Ugh.

She sighed deeply and looked him over. Garrett's image, only inches away, winked in her direction. Even in the fog he was handsome, his cheekbones pronounced and marked with dimples, and those piercing eyes. Still, Priela felt nothing. No emotional connection. Just a sinking sensation. She had assumed her charge would be Noah, not someone else. Then the images faded, the mist dissolved, and the room returned to darkness.

"You seem disappointed in the pool's revelation, Priela?" said Lady Raymere, her golden robes sparkling in the dim light. "Everyone else's wings are glowing."

Priela shrugged. "Yeah, Garrett's kind of full of himself."

"You mean, you know him?" asked Dion.

"Well, uh, sort of. Garrett went to my old school. They all did."

"Really? What's my charge's talent?" asked Edessa. "Is he an artist like me?"

Was Anton an artist? Priela didn't think so. She guessed that he was a decent student based on his circle of nerdy friends. But Anton was younger than Priela and aside from passing him in the hallways, the guy hadn't made much of an impression. Not like the creative kids, who dressed eclectically and made their presence known.

"Probably not."

"Enough," said Lady Raymere. "Of course your charge is an artist, Edessa. Why else would you two be linked?" She spoke with a definitive air, but there was something about the sharpness of her tone that seemed disingenuous, as if Lady Raymere was knowingly glossing something over. Then she turned to Priela and lowered her voice. "You thought it was going to be that boy, didn't you? The one you followed the other night."

Priela shivered. How did Lady Raymere know about Noah? It was creepy. Was this how people felt when Priela knew stuff about them, irritated and a bit alarmed? She pulled on a frizzy curl. Then she did what everyone else did when their secrets came to light. She lied.

"Um, I don't know who you're talking about."

"Yes you do," said Clio, waving a finger. "You were reaching for his face when you fell in the water. I saw you. You like him."

Lady Raymere's expression hardened and she straightened her back so that her figure loomed particularly high. "Tell me, Priela. Do you want to remain at the institute? Do you want to inspire charges? To become a real muse?"

"Yes. I really do."

"Then you must understand. Your actions toward that boy served no artistic purpose. I know you were only trying to help him, but it is simply not our role. We must guide our charges for the sake of art alone. Fortunately, you failed to harness your true powers as a muse, to inspire him. Instead, you merely solicited a cat."

Dion giggled and Lady Raymere glanced at the small glowing lantern, her eyes seeming to lose their focus.

"I'm not suggesting that you cannot watch over him at all. He is your charge. It is your duty. But soon enough you will refine your glimmers. You will understand how muses awaken the human imagination and set their talents free. And I'm warning you, Priela. If you ever use your powers for reasons beyond art, I will expel you from my class immediately. I simply cannot be held responsible for such behavior. Is that clear?"

Priela gulped down a lump in her throat and nodded.

"Isn't that what happened to Priela's mother?" whispered Edessa. "Didn't she inspire a human in ways of love instead of art… and that's why she left Gaia?"

"Oh, I can't even imagine it," said Clio, sashaying closer and picking a piece of lint off Priela's shoulder. "To have a whole family line tarnished in disgrace. But don't worry Priela, I'll keep an eye on you and that boy."

"I'm sure you will, Clio," said Lady Raymere, her eyes snapping back into focus. "Muses, for tomorrow, please assemble again in the classroom and bring your artistic tools." Then she waved a glittering sleeve and was gone.

Priela gritted her teeth. It wasn't fair. All she wanted was to be a part of this world, to belong. And now, Lady Raymere had handed Clio a roadmap to sabotage her. She grounded her feet, puffed out her chest, and waited for Dion and Edessa to shuffle out the door. Then Priela spun around.

"I know what you're thinking, Clio," she said. "But it won't work. I'm not going to guide Noah in any way that's not artistic. I won't do anything to get myself kicked out of this class and you can't make me."

Clio laughed. "Calm down, Priela. I have no intention of forcing you to do anything. There's no need. You're more than capable of messing this up all by yourself."

"I'm serious, Clio."

"Uh, huh. You're so serious about my behavior, when you should really focus on your own. I can't be your savior for every pathetic accident, Priela. So please… be careful walking home. We wouldn't want you to trip over a pebble and bash open that skull."

"Is that supposed to be a threat?"

"Absolutely not," she sneered. "I couldn't care less about your well-being. Not that anyone would even notice head injuries under that rat's nest of hair. But if you did harm yourself… well, what would your boyfriend think?"

"He's not my…"

"Great. Then there's no need to be so sensitive, is there? Now if you'll excuse me, some of us have other classes to attend." Then Clio pushed her aside and slammed the door, leaving Priela alone in the darkness, still shivering and cold.

Chapter Eleven
FLOATING PRACTICE

Priela carefully timed her arrival to class. She didn't want to be late, but after her near-death experience in the Pool of Polly, she didn't want to arrive too early either in case there was something dangerous waiting. She opened the door cautiously and peeked around its surface. But the room contained only its simple chalkboard, its old-fashioned desk chairs, and her classmates.

Dion glanced over and her wings fluttered. "I can't wait to visit my charge," she said. "I feel connected to her already, like she's been a part of me my whole life."

"Me too," said Edessa. "I can't stop thinking about mine. What about you, Priela?"

"Yes," said Clio, swiveling around and smirking. "What about Priela? Still feeling… disappointed?"

"No. It's fine that I'm guiding Garrett for now. Muses are paired with lots of humans. We can't have an instant connection with all of them."

"I'm afraid you'll need to feel some attachment," said Lady Raymere, who appeared in her usual instantaneous fashion. "Or your powers will not be effective."

Priela bit her lip and angled into a chair. Appearing out of nowhere was something her mother did too, although Priela's mom was less obvious about it, materializing first behind a door, or a wall, or a curtain before hopping out. Still, Priela had never grasped that she was genuinely emerging from thin air. Everything she thought she knew about her mother was wrong.

Lady Raymere took a seat on the edge of a desk and waved a golden-hued fingernail. "Today we will commence with floating practice. Floating is how muses transition to the human realm. It is how we shift dimensions and move through time."

Priela raised her hand. "What do you mean… move through time? Is that like time travel?"

"Yes. Time passes very differently here than in the human world. It is more flexible and less linear."

"Don't you see, Priela?" said Clio. "It's the reason why a true muse would never wear something as impractical as a watch. They don't work in our world. But then, creatures like you wouldn't know such things."

"Clio," said Lady Raymere.

"Oh, I meant that as a compliment. I'm sure Priela knows that, right? It must just be so magnificent for her. To be so different. To be blessed with such peculiarities, such blissful ignorance."

Priela tensed her jaw and checked her watch reflexively. The secondhand was ticking but it was agonizingly slow. Then it halted for a moment and then it started moving again only faster. Had the device been like this before and she just hadn't noticed, or was it broken now from being submerged in the Pool of Polly? And what did it mean that time could be flexible anyway?

Nothing was making sense. Priela had always excelled in physics, finding concepts like gravity, inertia, and matter to be straightforward enough. Even Einstein's theories which she had learned more from popular culture than anywhere else, like his theory that time was a relative concept or that mass could be converted into energy, all made intuitive sense. But genuine time travel?

In Gaia, the universal rules that governed matter didn't seem to apply, or more likely, they were stretched and thwarted so that Priela couldn't comprehend them fully. She shook her head and sighed. If she planned to live as a muse, she might have to accept that there were some things beyond her grasp.

"You must understand," said Lady Raymere, clearing her throat and leaning in. "We have the power to visit the past. We have the power to see the future. But we are only able to guide our charges, to influence them, in the present time."

"So if we can only guide humans in the present," said Dion. "Then why bother traveling through time? What's the point?"

"I'm not sure you've thought that inquiry all the way through. Consider it. Why would a muse wish to visit her charge in the past?"

"Well, maybe…" said Dion, tapping a feathered quill against the desk. "To learn about her? To understand what talents she possesses inside?"

"And the future?"

"Um, I guess if we visit the future we'll see if our guidance has worked? We'll see if the life of our charge has become… more inspired?"

"Indeed," said Lady Raymere. Then she rose from the desk and began pacing around the room, her golden robes twisting along the floor behind her. "Without knowledge of a human's past we are flying blind. We cannot know how best to guide him. And without knowledge of a human's future we cannot know if our guidance has succeeded. Sometimes our influence changes the world in magnificent and unforeseen ways, and sometimes it does nothing at all."

"What does floating feel like?" asked Edessa. "I've heard it's really intense?"

"Unfortunately, that is true. With practice, I expect you will all learn to control the experience. But for now, these sessions will be extremely disconcerting. The light is blinding, the wind tunnel sensation is dizzying, much like traveling through a tornado."

"Try not to vomit all over yourself, Priela," said Clio, under her breath. "I don't think I could handle the stench."

Priela rolled her eyes. But in truth, she didn't have the most iron-clad stomach and even long car rides made her queasy. Whatever. It was best not to overthink it, the way a person jumping into ice water or walking on hot coals avoided testing the temperature first when they genuinely wanted to go through with the experience.

"Now you will each need to create a piece of art. The art will be used like a map, directing the floating air and light to your charges. Please identify your human clearly and indicate the date in time when you wish to visit."

"I think I'll visit my charge on the day she was born," said Dion, lifting her quill into the air. "I might as well start from the beginning."

"I appreciate the enthusiasm, Dion. But for purposes of this assignment, let's limit our visits to moments in the future, shall we? I've found those to be the least disruptive."

"So if I want to visit my charge in the future," said Edessa, "should I paint a portrait of him as an older man? Is that how it works for an art muse?"

"Precisely. Now please begin. I will return when your art is complete." Then Lady Raymere raised her arm and vanished.

Edessa began unpacking an easel from her bag, unfolding the tripod frame, and stabilizing a canvas on its ledge. Then she laid out a palette of oil paints and started painting in smooth, graceful strokes. Dion opened a large knapsack, removed a scroll of parchment paper and several vials of ink, and began writing feverishly with her feathered quill. Even Clio's preparation was elaborate, stacking sheets of music paper into neat little piles.

For a few moments, Priela just sat there. She had brought paper too, one blank letter-sized page. She'd also grabbed a sharpened pencil and an eraser, which seemed like a safe bet skill-wise. Priela still didn't know her particular talent but it definitely wasn't going to be the violin. Maybe start with an essay?

She penciled, *"Why Garrett has Nice Hair."* Then she sat back and looked at her messy handwriting. The title was missing something. She added a few more words, *"Why Garrett has Nice Hair in the Future."*

Minutes ticked by, or more correctly, the sun's rays traveled some distance across the window since minutes were no longer an accurate unit of measure. Priela reread the header over and over, imagining a future with intelligent robots, and gleaming metallic clothing, and vehicles that drove through the sky. But when it came to Garrett, she couldn't think of anything else to write. She felt no inspiration. Nothing.

Dion's scroll of parchment paper, stretching several feet long, rolled under Priela's desk. The entire sheet was covered in calligraphy. "Sorry," she said, leaning over to pick it up.

"Did you just write all of that right now?" asked Priela.

"Well, sort of. This lyric poem is new. And so is this sonnet. It's pretty good. But uh, this short story is actually a rewrite of something I used for my literature class. I commit most of my works to memory, so all I had to do was change the names and update the verbs to the future tense."

"And what about those symbols?"

"Oh that's Sanskrit, and that's Arabic, and that's Mandarin Chinese. I translated my poem into different languages. It's sort of a nervous habit. I would have translated the sonnet too, but it's really hard to get the iambic pentameter right."

"Uh, huh."

Dion returned to her desk and Priela glanced at Edessa. "Your paintings are amazing."

"Thanks," she said, angling a life-sized portrait in Priela's direction. "I'm trying to use different styles, Impressionism, Cubism, Photo-Realism. But I have no idea what my charge will look like in the future. You know him. Do these seem right?"

"Uh, sure. That one definitely looks like an older version of Anton. It could be a photograph. When I draw people they barely look human."

"Yes," said Clio. "We know."

Priela frowned, glancing back at her own page. *"Why Garrett has Nice Hair in the Future."* She didn't know much about floating but she was pretty sure this essay wasn't going to work. Who was she kidding? Maybe she could just skip the whole floating assignment and find her charges the old-fashioned way? By wandering the earth until fate brought them together. It had worked with Noah. It could work again. She put her pencil between her teeth and bit down hard.

But Lady Raymere materialized and shook her head. "Muses, you appear to have stopped working. I presume it means that you've completed the assignment?"

Priela knew the question was directed at her but Clio jumped up. "Yes," she said, holding out her sheets of music paper which were now covered in notes and lyrics. "I'm done."

Lady Raymere glided over and paged through them. "Tell me, Clio. How did you select these moments in time? This 'stormy Tuesday' for instance?"

Clio shrugged.

"I see. Next time you'll want to select dates that are meaningful, dates that have significance. The more relevant our art, the smoother our floating becomes." Then Lady Raymere lifted the sheet to her ear as if she could hear its melody jump off the page. "But this melody is exquisite. Yes. It should be of sufficient quality to take us to your charge. We will visit her today."

Dion stood now and handed over her scroll of parchment paper, but Lady Raymere scanned the writings and grimaced.

"I'm sorry Dion, but this story won't do. It's as though you wrote it with someone other than your charge in mind. And this lyric poem isn't your best work. For our floating to succeed, the art must be of the highest quality." She sighed, her eyes continuing to dart down the page. "But this sonnet is adequate." She read it again. "Yes, it should be satisfactory. We will visit your charge tomorrow."

Then she turned her attention to Edessa's stack of paintings. "No, no," she said, setting a few canvases aside. "But this cubist portrait will do nicely and I'd like to try this one as well. Let's aim for Thursday."

Fortunately, Lady Raymere didn't go through the charade of examining Priela's single sheet of paper with its ridiculous title. Instead, she returned to the front of the room. "As for you Priela, we will visit your charge on Monday."

But Clio wouldn't let it slide. She leaned over, grabbed the sheet, and laughed. "Oh, Priela. I knew that you were terribly unprepared for the institute, but I had no idea that you couldn't even compose a topic sentence." Her eyes shifted to Lady Raymere. "There's no way she'll be able to complete this assignment by Monday. Honestly, I'm only thinking of her best interests. Priela's art is wretched. You should give her more time… like an eternity."

"Nonsense. Priela has the whole weekend. I've seen architecture muses design cathedrals with less notice."

Nonsense? Really? Priela yanked on a curl and a hollowness engulfed her. She imagined it was the same emotion a hiker might experience at the bottom of Mount Everest, a feeling where a challenge that she had signed up for on purpose and wanted desperately, now loomed high overhead. Still, she had expected to have weeks, even months, to find her talent. Not days. Priela wasn't accustomed to being the slow kid, the one who couldn't complete the assignments. How did anyone handle it day in and day out? It was mortifying.

"Good luck," Clio sneered.

Then Lady Raymere pushed aside a few desk chairs, clearing a space in the center of the room. "Please form a line and link your hands together," she instructed and the muses hurried over. "Clio, you may begin."

Clio lifted her chin, broadened her chest, and started to sing.

> *"Violet a color, a flower, a name*
> *found in a dank place on a stormy Tuesday*
> *Will that devil of a man make you feel shame,*
> *or will you be saved from self-loathing?*
>
> *And then to a place of glass and marble*
> *sparks a habit that overwhelms fully*
> *Will the song on that stage be a mess, a garble*
> *or will your true talent shine through?"*

A whirling air circled around them, slowly at first and then faster. It was happening. There was light too, slicing through the room in opaque rays that gradually sealed together, like vertical blinds tilting closed until the classroom disappeared from view.

Priela no longer had any means of orienting herself and her mind couldn't make sense of the messages it was receiving. There was a jolting, churning pressure, as if she was being yanked like a rope during tug-of-war. She locked her joints and tensed her abdominal muscles to minimize the motion sickness, but it didn't work. How long would this floating continue? How disorienting would it become?

The wind tunnel grew faster, the force more intense for a period that felt like forever but was probably only moments. Then it all came to a halt. There was a sudden weightlessness, as though she was now floating in an antigravity chamber. The sensation would have been fun, except that it unleashed Priela's nausea and she vomited in a single, disgusting heave.

"Go ahead, Clio," she said, buckling over. "Insult me."

"Why would I insult someone who's clearly incapacitated? Seriously Priela, you have a warped mind."

"Enough," said Lady Raymere.

Then the forces of gravity returned to normal and the rays started moving apart. Priela wiped her mouth and straightened her posture. She could feel her emotions shifting with the light, as if the human realm was pushing aside her queasiness, her humiliation, her anxiety, and replacing it with excitement. Was she really in the future now? Was she really about to see Violet through the lens of a muse?

Chapter Twelve
VIOLET

The fierce air and brilliant light had carried the muses into the future, landing them in a cramped, barren space with walls made from cinderblocks, exposed pipes that smelled of mold, and some old music equipment lying in the corner.

Priela blinked her eyes in rapid succession, but they struggled to adjust to the dimness. She knew why. The room's single low-wattage bulb was a factor, as was the overcast sky, but the gloominess also pointed to a more universal change. They were in the human world now. It was a place where colors were muted, where sounds were devoid of reverberation, and where even the muses moved with less grace.

"It's so ugly here," whispered Edessa.

Thunder sounded in the distance and a tattooed man waltzed through the door, shaking off his wet hair like a dog. Then he wiped his nose, slung a guitar over one shoulder, and nodded at a man carrying a keyboard who squeezed inside behind him. Next came a woman with a partially shaved head and a thin, bearded man, followed by Violet.

Violet didn't look much different from that day in algebra class. She was still carrying the same backpack, still dressed in those signature striped shoes, still walking with a teenager's self-conscious gait, as if she were crossing a rope bridge.

How much time had passed? They couldn't be that far in the future. Priela glanced around for a better indication, noting the date on the thin man's cellphone screen and sighing audibly. It was mid-May now, exactly seven months into the future. Was all muse time-travel this subtle? If so, she wasn't likely to see any sentient robots or flying cars.

"So I talked to Gloria," said the tattooed man.

"The talent scout?" asked Violet.

"Uh, huh. I told her we had a new singer. Someone special. So she's gonna watch the band on Thursday."

"Really?"

Violet clasped her hands together and the phrase, *"someone special,"* started repeating on a continuous loop through her thoughts, echoing with a sort of haunting resonance. Priela couldn't help from overhearing it. *"Someone special... someone special."* Clearly, the phrase was something Violet longed to hear.

"You know," he continued, strumming a dissonant chord. "If you really wanna make it as a singer, you're gonna need to commit to the band full time. You get what that means, don't you Violet?"

"I know, Damien," she said, letting out a nervous laugh. "I can forget about high school, right?" Then she dropped her backpack to the floor and pulled out a long, indigo blue gown. "But look, I have the perfect thing to wear on Thursday. I bought it at a thrift store but it's a Dior. Can you believe it? I got it for nothing."

Damien sneered. "You need to look hot, not like a whale. That thing's enormous."

"I know, but don't you see? I could hem it. Take it in right here and clean it up. It would be beautiful." Violet ran the couture cloth through her fingers, cradling the dress so that it didn't touch the floor, and a vision appeared in her thoughts.

Priela could see the image vividly. It was a vision of a dress remade. A spectacular dress with an angular neckline, an A-line skirt that flared below the knee, and a whimsical uneven hem. Priela glanced at Clio. Could she see Violet's thoughts too? Did she know that her charge had a gift for fashion?

Damien grabbed a loose thread and started unspooling the fabric until a sleeve dropped to the floor. Then he ground the scrap into the filth with his heel. His movements were slow and exaggerated, his expression chillingly calm. It was clearly a power move, used more for the purpose of establishing his dominance than to make any specific point.

"Don't…" said Violet, gasping. "Please." She collapsed to the ground and shoved the dress back in her backpack. "The dress was so beautiful."

"It was crap. Now get up. We need to rehearse."

But Violet remained crouched, her frame cowering, her emotions emanating like a beating drum and Priela could feel the unease pound through her chest. Violet was definitely frightened by this man and yet she had a powerful desire to please him. The need was both desperate and all-consuming. But was it enough to make her follow this jerk blindly and drop out of high school?

Priela knew that Violet was isolated, keeping to herself most of the time. She knew she was from modest means, having worn those striped shoes for years, relying on the computers in the school library for homework, and participating in a free lunch program. Had Damien promised to change all of that? Had he promised Violet the lifestyle of a star, where she'd be both adored and wealthy? Or was this improbable goal merely a fantasy that she had built up in her own head?

"Look," said Damien, his tone softening. "I just want you to wow Gloria, okay? She could really promote the band. I'll take you to buy something better. We'll go to that new Palomar Boutique place before the gig. Sound good?"

Violet nodded and rose to her feet, but before the muses could hear her sing, a bright light punctuated the air. It was happening again. They were floating to the next moment in time, to the *"place of glass and marble"* from Clio's song. The muses clasped their hands together and Priela's dizziness returned, hitting her with such brutal intensity that she almost lost consciousness, but at least she didn't vomit this time.

A moment later, they were in a clothing store. It was an upscale establishment with the words 'Palomar Boutique' etched in a delicate font on the windows. The floor was white marble, the aisles pristine, and the walls mostly mirrored.

"This place is spectacular," said Edessa, her eyes coming alive. She approached a stylized mannequin and touched a small tag that dangled from its hem. "Is this some kind of jewelry?"

"Uh, that's a price tag," said Priela.

"It's so distracting, don't you think? The tag really obscures the hemline and it isn't even a matching color. They should really make these things sparkle, at the very least."

"Um, sure."

A door pushed open and Damien and Violet walked inside. Damien looked as disheveled as before, his jeans filthy, his hair an oily mess. Priela assumed that he was trying to cultivate that perfect rock-star image, racy yet desirable, carefree yet indelibly cool, but the effect was more unkempt than anything else. He sauntered down an aisle, allowing his greasy hands to graze the fabric while a sales woman glared from a distance.

"Try this one," he said, yanking a coral dress from its hanger.

Violet took the dress and hurried to a dressing room, but when she emerged the muses let out a collective gasp. The outfit was all wrong. It made her look like a reality television star with geometrical cutouts that revealed far too much and a plunging neckline that went down to her navel.

"I don't know, Damien," she said, eying her reflection in a mirror.

"What's to know? You look amazing."

Violet nodded and disappeared again, returning in her original outfit. She looked both more comfortable and more distinctive in her own, likely self-designed clothing, which managed to flatter her without resorting to overt displays of naked skin. Her gift for fashion was like the talent of a great comedian who didn't need crass language to elicit laughter.

Damien approached the register and handed over the dress.

"By any chance, would you be interested in a store card?" asked the sales woman. "We offer a ten percent discount on your first purchase. Plus the card allows you to pay off the dress over time."

"Yeah, sure."

"Great. I'll need some identification."

Damien took Violet's purse and began rummaging through it. Then he removed her wallet, located her Driver's License, and slapped it on the counter. The sales woman began typing Violet's details into a screen.

"Can I talk to you a minute?" said Violet, grabbing his elbow and ushering him aside. "Why are you putting the card in my name?"

"Well, it's your dress. I'm certainly not gonna wear the thing."

"But I don't have that kind of money."

"You need to trust me. If this gig is gonna work out, we need our lead singer to look hot. Besides, you heard what she said… you can pay off the dress over time. So I don't see why this is such a big deal?"

"But…"

"But what? You're special, Violet. You know that's how I feel. But do you honestly believe the band won't replace you if you don't do your part?"

Violet's shoulders slumped forward but she nodded her tacit consent and Priela could feel her emotions shoot across the room like darts. It was a mix of mortification and yearning, as if she were knowingly breaking the rules.

"Occupation?" said the sales woman. "Employer? Gross Monthly Income?"

Violet rattled off exaggerated answers, providing numbers as if the band was already a success. It wasn't lying so much as it was wishful thinking, a deeply emotional response. But even so, Violet winced with each reply, her eyes unable to make direct contact, her knees quietly shaking. Did the sales woman know it was all pretense? Did she care? Did she have any obligation to protect Violet from herself?

The sales woman finally folded the dress in tissue paper, placed it in a gleaming Palomar Boutique bag, and handed it over. Violet traced her fingers across the logo and her adrenaline surged, as if everything she had ever purchased before now had arrived in a brown paper bag. Priela's breathing quickened too, feeling Violet's simple, yet electrifying rush in buying something so pricey. But the other muses just looked puzzled.

Priela studied their expressions. Their confusion made sense. Muses had no use for money. In Gaia, dollars grew on trees and belongings just appeared when needed, when desired. It was why Priela's closet was now filled with silky gowns even though she had never purchased any. It was why distinguishing between needs and wants made little sense to her peers. Muses could afford to focus on artistic beauty above all. They had that luxury.

Then the wind rose up again, floating the muses to the final moment in Clio's song, the moment with a *"song on that stage."* The sensation was smoother this time, landing them in a small nightclub with a dusty floor and a ceiling so low that Lady Raymere had to lean over.

Violet was standing on a raised platform, dressed in the expensive coral dress, although she had paired the outfit with clunky boots which toned down the look. Damien was strumming his guitar behind her and the rest of the band was playing along. Gloria, the talent scout, was seated on a barstool. Priela could tell who she was because Damien kept glancing in her direction.

Then Violet began to sing. She was hesitant at first but after the first stanza her vocals became more audible, not that they were particularly impressive. Her pitch sounded okay and Violet seemed to be more or less on key, but she had no natural gift for singing. The song lyrics didn't help. They were halting, disconnected from the background noise as though they were written for a different tune, and every time Violet took liberties with the melody something seemed off. Priela glanced at Clio. Her expression said it all. The singing wasn't very good.

After a few minutes, Gloria ducked her head and slipped out the rear exit. Violet's eyes shifted from the empty barstool to Damien, shooting him a gaze infused with longing, and her hand reached out in his direction. Priela could sense that Violet blamed herself for the woman's disappearance. But instead of realizing that her dreams might be misguided, it only seemed to endear her to Damien with more fervor the way a cult member clung desperately to her leader when the world's promised end never materialized.

"Don't worry, Violet," whispered Clio. "Your singing may be uneven now. Your tone… rough. But I can teach you those things. I can improve your technique and hone your ear. This doesn't have to be your future. I can fix it."

Really? Clio planned to make Violet a better singer? Was that truly what she needed? In Priela's view, she'd be better off with a shot of confidence, a decent friend, and perhaps a math tutor. Priela shuddered, realizing the irony of her thought process. As a human she could have been that friend. She could have been that math tutor. But now she was powerless to genuinely help Violet. Instead the girl would be swayed by a man who didn't share her best interests and a muse who didn't understand them.

Suddenly, a violent wind sucked the muses back in time. The gust came without warning, pulling the air from Priela's lungs like a vacuum cleaner and leaving her gasping. It returned the muses to the classroom with its tiny desk chairs and its dark chalkboard. But in Gaia no time had passed at all and the sun was still shining through the windows at precisely the same angle.

"Clio, your floating was awesome," said Dion, collapsing into a chair.

Priela shook her head, "Yes, the floating was good. But we have to get Violet away from that man."

"We are not here to discuss Violet's choice of companionship," said Lady Raymere. "Only her talents."

"I know and it's her talents that I'm worried about. That man wants to make her a rock star but I'm not sure if singing is…"

"Violet is not your charge, Priela," said Clio. "So before you launch into some idiotic speech about what you think she needs, why don't you learn a few basics about our world, or maybe try finding your talent, or I don't know… how about cleaning that vomit out of your hair."

Priela touched her curls and felt a damp spot.

"Clio is right, Priela. You need to focus on your own assignments." Then she raised her golden sleeve as though she was preparing to disappear.

"Wait, shouldn't we at least talk about what happened?"

"You may discuss whatever you wish on your own time, Priela. But this is a muse essentials course. I see no reason to question Violet's life choices any more than a dance instructor would need to recite multiplication tables."

"Oh, she wouldn't know anything about proper class etiquette," said Clio, tapping a finger against her chin. "Tell us Priela, do you disrupt every class you attend or only the ones that aren't already centered around you?"

Lady Raymere cleared her throat. "Now, if there's nothing more…" and then she was gone.

Chapter Thirteen
THE MEANING OF ART

Five days. That's it. Priela had five days to find her talent and create some sort of artistic masterpiece. It was doable, but she'd need to have the right mindset. A calm, focused one. Not like audition week where each choice was heavily scrutinized and each misstep resulted in public humiliation, a stress-infused nightmare that would make anyone fail.

She went for a brisk jog, showered, and ate her favorite comfort food, vegetable soup with saltine crackers. Then she put on some earbuds, found a soothing stream of music, and wandered around her house. If divine inspiration were to find her, it was here at home, in a familiar environment that could foster experimentation and creativity. She ambled toward a storage closet beneath the stairs and opened the door. Inside were discarded toys, and old tile samples, and random knick-knacks, a treasure trove of artistic paraphernalia.

"What are you doing, La la?" asked Priela's sister.

"Um, it's an assignment for my new school," said Priela, swiveling around and removing her earbuds. "I have to create a work of art. I thought I could find something in here to use."

"Can I help?"

"Thanks. But I have to do this myself."

"Okay. Can I keep you company?"

Priela shifted her weight. She didn't mind a companion but she still hadn't told Moriela that she was a muse and she wasn't sure how her sister would react if she got lucky enough to find her talent. Muses typically described that first moment of artistic discovery the same way someone might discuss getting hit by a car, or falling off a cliff, so that the experience sounded both dangerous and wholly unexpected.

"I don't know, Morgie. This isn't like a normal art project. I'll probably be inspired all of a sudden and it might be kind of intense to watch."

"Oh, like when someone is inspired by a muse?"

Priela did a double-take, glancing at her sister, then away, and then back again. "Uh, sort of. But even more extreme. Imagine the muse thing but on steroids." Then she placed one hand on her sister's shoulder and lowered her voice. "I just don't want to frighten you, that's all."

Moriela rolled her eyes. "You're so melodramatic, La la. Do you really think I'm going to be scared because you're suddenly good at art?"

"Okay, fine. You can keep me company. But don't say I didn't warn you."

Priela turned back around and her eyes scanned the objects in the closet, darting from one item to the next. She was hoping something would magically stand out. Nothing did. She grabbed an old container of Play-Doh. Muses seemed to love earthenware bowls, and ceramic vases, and statues fashioned from clay. She pried open the lid and removed a hardened pink glob.

"You might want to add some water," suggested Moriela. "That Play-Doh is like five years old."

"Thanks, but I don't need your help."

Priela walked to the bathroom faucet and added a few drops of water. Then she started kneading the dough, returning the substance to a moderate state of squishiness, and fashioning it into a teacup-sized bowl.

"You know that thing is lopsided, right?"

"Shhhh… I'm not done yet."

Priela continued to mold the clay, smoothing out the edges and perfecting the shape. Then she held up her creation with one hand. How could she evoke her charge through pottery? She grabbed a toothpick and carved out Garrett's name and a random date, etching the marks into the malleable substance so that the floating air and brilliant light would know whom to visit and when.

Moriela leaned in. "Is that supposed to be your signature? Because it looks like you wrote the word, 'Grunt.' And you realize that's not today's date, right?"

Priela's jaw stiffened. "I know, I did that on purpose." But her sister's running commentary had aggravated her and she dumped the bowl in the trash.

"What are you doing, La la? I'm sorry. It doesn't look that bad. I can help you fix it."

"No. You're right, Morgie. It's terrible. I don't know why I was thinking that Play-Doh was a good idea. At my school, they have kilns the size of wood-fire pizza ovens, and they have potter's wheels, and real clay that doesn't come in florescent shades of color."

"Okay, so we'll go to an art supply store."

"That's not the point. It isn't the Play-Doh. It's me. Everyone else knows how to make these super realistic statues."

"Well, don't worry, La la. You'll find something else."

Priela bit her lip and returned to the closet, banging open the door so that it slammed into the wall. There had to be something hidden in there that was worthy of her efforts. Her eyes caught sight of a recorder that she'd used in the second grade. It was buried beneath a pile of porcelain figurines and she yanked it out, like a magician pulling a tablecloth from beneath a pile of dishes. But her movements didn't have the desired effect and the figurines smashed to the floor.

Moriela grabbed a broom and a dustpan. "A recorder?" she said, sweeping up the broken pieces. "Are you sure, La la? Isn't the only song you know, 'Twinkle, Twinkle Little Star?'"

Priela breathed an exasperated sigh. In Gaia, prior experience wasn't a necessary requirement for artistic expertise. "I don't need a backseat driver, Morgie. If you're planning to comment on everything I do, then please leave me alone."

"Alright, alright," she said, dumping the porcelain shards in the trash.

Then Priela wiped off the instrument, held it to her lips, and exhaled. But air whooshed through the tool without making a sound. She straightened her posture, covered a few holes, and tried again. Still nothing. She blew harder. Finally, the recorder squealed in a high-pitched burst, as if she were strangling a pig.

"When did you say this assignment was due?"

"Monday."

"I guess that's enough time."

"No, it's not enough time at all." Priela threw the recorder down and stepped on it, snapping the cheap instrument in half. "I'm so far behind, Morgie. It's like I'm running a race a week after they fired off the starter pistol."

"Uh, huh. Well if time is so important then I don't see why you're wasting it with all of these toys. Why not just use Mom's studio?"

"For your information, I can't use it because…" But Priela's voice trailed off. She didn't have a valid reason for avoiding her mother's art studio. The truth was that it hadn't occurred to her.

Technically the place wasn't off limits, but the family treated the room like a kind of sanctuary, a spiritual space where shoes were removed, where voices were lowered, and where unfinished works were only viewed with explicit permission. But now it seemed like an obvious choice, especially since muses were always talking about their lineage, as if creative talent was an inherited characteristic.

"Okay, fine," said Priela, heading up the stairs with her sister at her heels.

She entered the studio, grabbed a smock, and placed a blank canvas onto an easel. Then she stared at its white surface. She knew that any realistic portraits of Garrett would end in an abysmal mess. But paintings didn't have to be realistic to be considered art. They could be stylized, or abstract, or conceptual.

She grabbed a palette with a swatch of red paint, dipped a brush, and painted a square. It was a little uneven but perfection wasn't the goal. She used the blue next, drawing a straight line from one corner of the canvas to the opposite edge, and allowing the paint to drip. Then she splashed the piece with random flicks of black and yellow.

Moriela observed her from across the room. "Is that supposed to be like a Mondrian?"

"More like a Kandinsky."

"Oh."

Over the years Priela's mother had taught them a veritable course in art history, casting aside her fear of leaving the house whenever a visiting exhibit came to town, and dragging them to museums, and art festivals, and even sidewalk displays. Why had

Priela always zoned out when her mother explained the different techniques? Sure, those detailed descriptions were excruciatingly dull, but even so Priela could have paid a little more attention.

She stepped back from her piece, tilted her head sideways, and gritted her teeth. What was she thinking? Her painting was horrible, its lines clumsy, its splatter chaotic.

"So are you feeling that rush of inspiration now, La la?"

"Are you making fun of me?"

"No. I think that your painting is pretty good, for a first try."

"This isn't supposed to require multiple tries, Morgie. It's supposed to be brilliant without effort. If I show up to class with this thing they'll laugh at me or worse. They'll send me away."

"No they won't, La la. They can't expect perfection from a beginner."

"That's exactly my point. I can't be a beginner."

Moriela sighed audibly and took a step closer. "Do you remember that time when Mom took us to see a urinal in a museum? She called it a masterpiece."

"So you think my painting looks like a toilet?"

"No, that's not what I'm saying. It's just that art is subjective. It's open to interpretation."

"Well then why am I bothering to paint anything at all? What's the meaning of art anyway? I should just show up to class with a used toothbrush or a dirty spoon and call it art. Or maybe I'll have convulsions and say it's an interpretive dance. Or I know... how about I just stare at the wall and clip my toenails. That's performance art, right?"

"Why are you getting so angry? I'm just trying to help you."

"I know, Morgie. But you have no idea what I need to accomplish here. You don't understand anything at all."

Priela threw down her smock, ran to her room, and slammed the door. Then she collapsed across her bed and a hollowness engulfed her, making her chest ache. She felt as if she were trapped in a cell with the keys lying just beyond the bars, out of reach. She knew precisely what she needed to do, she just couldn't accomplish it. It was crushing.

As she lay there, visions swirled through her thoughts, horrifying visions of people taunting her and calling her a failure. Hours passed and she could hear her sister knocking sporadically on her door. But she ignored her, remaining perfectly still until tears had soaked her pillow and exhaustion finally overcame her.

Chapter Fourteen
THE MONEY TREE

Priela dragged herself to school just as rain was beginning to fall, as if she had channeled it somehow to accentuate her mood. But rain in Gaia was different, its droplets like illusions, melting away when they touched her skin without making it wet. She rubbed her bloodshot eyes and stuck out her tongue. The rain tasted like sugar. She walked to campus with her head tilted backward, sipping in droplets until she could no longer stomach the sweetness.

When Priela reached the school's front courtyard, she glanced at the money tree. Watching it change had become something of a habit, so that she noticed its roots were now outstretched to soak up the precipitation, while it's paper leaves remained crisp and dry. She ran her fingers through her rapidly frizzing hair and studied the foliage, seeing fives, tens, twenties, with the denominations growing larger as they sprouted toward the top. There were even hundred dollar bills budding from the highest offshoots.

She thought of Noah. That night at Kalista's house he was trying to steal money for his brother's medication. She recalled the sweat on his forehead. His shaking hands. The palpable desperation. It wasn't fair. Noah shouldn't need to resort to such stupidity when a handful of those leaves could solve everything.

Maybe she could climb up there and grab a few hundreds just in case she ever bumped into him again?

She waited for clusters of muses to disappear into their respective classrooms, and theaters, and concert halls, signaling the start of class. She'd be late but this was the only time when the courtyard was empty and climbing the tree shouldn't take long. Then she grabbed onto the branches and hoisted herself upward, scaling the rubbery bark with her bare feet.

As she moved, Lady Raymere's warning flashed though her thoughts. *"If you ever use your powers for reasons beyond art, I will expel you from my class immediately."*

Was giving a human cash the same thing as using one's powers? Priela didn't think so. It definitely didn't involve performing magic or creating art. She was just being practical. She reached the upper branches and plucked a handful of hundred dollar bills, stuffing them into her bra.

"What are you doing up there, Priela? Stealing money? How absolutely pathetic. You realize it can't purchase anything in Gaia, right?"

Priela's head snapped around. It was Clio, standing beneath the branches. She was dressed in a slick magenta raincoat that covered her wings and made her look almost human. Why hadn't Priela noticed her approaching? Could Clio materialize out of nowhere like Lady Raymere or was she just bizarrely sneaky?

"I know, Clio. For your information, I just climbed up here to get a better view of the school."

"Uh, huh. I didn't realize that your extracurricular activities mirrored your juvenile figure in terms of maturity. Although I must say that I'm impressed you have so much leisure time, what with needing to find your talent and all."

"Not that it's any of your business, but I spent hours last night working on my talent and I'm making progress because… well, you see…"

As Priela spoke she waved her hands, unintentionally releasing her grip and her body started to slide. One wing bent painfully against a branch, a knee twisted sideways, and her hair became entangled with twigs until she finally yanked herself free and fell to the grass, bumping down on her rear in a seated position. Ouch. The collision would leave black and blue marks for certain but she kept her composure.

"I did that on purpose."

"I'm sure."

Then Clio sauntered closer, leaning inward until her face was only inches away and picking a crumb of Play-Doh from Priela's hair. "Florescent pink? Yes, I can see that your search for talent is making very impressive progress."

Priela winced.

"Oh, but don't worry. Someday you will find your talent, and then you'll be just as disappointed in your art as the rest of us."

"Just go away."

"With pleasure." Clio straightened back up, removed her glossy jacket, and dropped it in Priela's lap. "Here, this raincoat is for you."

"I don't want anything of yours. Besides, this rain isn't even wet."

"It isn't for the rain. I thought you'd appreciate the pockets for all of that money you stuffed in your bra. Granted, the bills do give you some semblance of a chest. A lumpy, lopsided, uniboob one. But they must also be horribly uncomfortable."

Priela kicked the raincoat away.

"Suit yourself. But remember that I'm watching you, Priela. If you ever do anything to cross the line, like helping out that tragic boyfriend of yours, I'll make sure that you're banished from this place once and for all." Then Clio tossed her hair over one shoulder and headed toward the Muse Essential's classroom.

Priela watched her walk away and her hands balled into fists. It was more than anger. It was rage. She wanted to punch Clio. But aside from the obvious futility of violence, Clio was over a head taller than Priela. Not to mention the fact that Clio was an excellent flier which seemed like an inherent advantage in hand to hand combat. Plus Priela's body was already sore from falling out of the money tree and any fistfight was certain to end in more pain.

She grabbed the slick jacket, draped it over her shoulders, and moved the bills from her bra into its pockets. Whatever. She had to hold the money somehow and the crisp dollars were already chafing against her skin. Then she stumbled to her feet and headed to class. Lady Raymere, Edessa, and Dion were already there, standing with their hands linked in a chain.

"Muses, please arrive to class on schedule," said Lady Raymere, as Clio and Priela rushed to join them. "The next time you are late we will commence without you. Now Dion, you may begin."

Dion wrapped one leg behind the other, held up her parchment paper with her free hand, and recited her sonnet. Her voice wavered as she spoke but her wings remained perfectly still, frozen in apt concentration.

> *"Robin my charge, 'tis thee I seek to find*
> *In time of youth, you work above the boards*
> *Until a stand, does twist, and bend, and wind*
> *She finds you there to bring you her accords*

106

A letter does indeed use words of joy
Destroyed by scorn, jealousy fierce, and hate
Then tears grow thick and comes with hope, a boy
Too late to save you from the vicious fate

And then, to see you on a day unknown
Where crazy tigers clad in stripes abound
A fearful choice you may someday bemoan
'Till poise and strength, your muse in you has found..."

Before Dion reached the poem's final couplet, rays of light sliced through the air in dense, slanted beams. Priela tensed her muscles and braced herself for the inevitable swirl. It was shorter this time, although no less jolting, and when the air suddenly screeched to a halt and the beams tilted sideways, Priela knew the location immediately. She was back at East High school. Seeing it again sent a chill down her spine.

Chapter Fifteen
ROBIN

The muses were now in Priela's old high school auditorium, standing directly on top of the bleachers and little sales booths were everywhere. There was an army recruiting station, a college giving out bumper stickers that read, *"CSL College – Where Learning is a Breeze,"* and a Gateway Credit Card booth just to the right of where the muses had landed.

"Dion," said Lady Raymere, shaking her head. "Your sonnet has taken us to a moment in the past, not the future."

"How can you tell?" whispered Dion.

"It's quite obvious. Just observe the slants of the shadows and the haziness of the air."

Priela glanced around, trying to ascertain what Lady Raymere was referring to. They were unmistakably in the human world now with its grit and its commotion, but aside from the fact that Priela had already been in this exact place at this exact moment, she wasn't sure what Lady Raymere was talking about.

"If you sign up today, you could win fifty thousand free airline miles."

Priela turned her head. It was Robin, the school's student body president. Once again she was working at the sales booth, signing up Garrett and his younger brother Anton with credit cards, and having the exact same conversation as before. Priela's former self was probably there too, hiding underneath her own

108

feet right at this moment with Noah. She leaned over and tilted her head sideways, trying to see. But there was no way to spy beneath the bleachers from this vantage point.

"What are you doing, Priela?" asked Clio.

"Nothing," she said, straightening back up. It was probably a good thing that she couldn't watch the events unfolding beneath her. It meant that the other muses couldn't see them either. But Priela remained fixated on the metal slats, her eyes staring downward, her ears straining to hear what was going on.

"So you ready?"

The muffled voice was Noah's and the words were the same ones he had used right before leaning in to kiss her. Priela's face grew warm, her stomach flooded with butterflies, and her limbs prickled. She wasn't sure if it was excitement or humiliation, but either way the sensation embarrassed her and she took a few steps away.

Then Garrett kicked the leg of the Gateway booth while leading Anton down the steps. The station teetered to one side, rebounded to its other edge, and then toppled over with a starling crash. Thump, thump, thump. Books were falling through the slats and pummeling the earlier Priela right now. She cringed, remembering the pain, and her eyes shifted to the side of the bleachers. Then she saw herself, ducking out from below.

"Is that you, Priela?" asked Dion, gesturing. The other muses swiveled around, catching a glimpse of curls disappearing through the auditorium's side door.

"Yeah, this was my old school."

"You looked so different," said Dion. "So human."

She was right. Priela didn't look the same back then, so that seeing herself was a bit like looking at a before-picture of a person who had undergone radical weight loss or plastic surgery.

But it wasn't her physical appearance that had changed. It was her aura. Her earlier incarnation lacked a certain inner artistry and grace. She hadn't noticed the transition happening, but somehow she had acquired these divine qualities, as if they had soaked through her skin and transformed her from the inside out.

"I'm so sorry that you ever had to stay here," said Edessa, her body noticeably recoiling. "It's horrid. Just look at those flags on the wall. What are they supposed to be? Art? The designs are terrible."

"No, those are championship banners for the sports teams," said Priela. "So they're kind of like all those statues at the institute. You know, the ones that honor muses for discovering new fields of art?"

"Those are hardly the same," said Edessa with a grimace, twisting her black ponytail. "I can certainly understand why you were hiding beneath these stairs, Priela. I couldn't bear to look at such ugliness either."

"Um, yeah. That's exactly why I was under there."

"Really?" Clio raised one eyebrow and pointed. "Isn't that your boyfriend?"

Priela pivoted around. Noah had now emerged from the far side of the bleachers and he was wiping his eyes. Had he been crying? Priela tried to get a better glimpse but he shielded his face and slipped out the main door.

"He looked upset," said Dion.

"Yes. He was in close proximity to Priela," said Clio. "It's enough to make anyone miserable."

"Clio, would you just shut up already? You have no idea what you're talking about. Noah liked me."

"Uh, huh. You may not have any artistic talent, Priela. But I'd never accuse you of lacking a creative imagination."

"Enough," said Lady Raymere glaring. "You are acting like humans. Now please keep your composure and remember why we are here… for Robin."

The muses collectively turned their eyes to Robin, who had been trying to fix the toppled sales booth.

"I have something for you," said a woman, ascending the metal stairs. It was Mrs. Tucker, the school's college counselor and she was dressed in her familiar turtleneck sweater with a heavily powdered face, bleached hair, and long false eyelashes. She shoved a large white envelope into Robin's hands. "Open it."

Robin adjusted her stance and ran her dark fingers across the envelope's seam. Then she opened the seal, lifted out the top sheet, and scanned the page.

"Well, what does it say?"

"It says, 'Yes!'"

"What? Let me see that." Mrs. Tucker yanked the page from Robin's hands, ripping it in the process. "You were accepted at Princeton University? I didn't even know you were applying to schools like that. How did you get in? We both know you're not the brightest. Your ACT scores were abysmal. Your SAT scores were even worse."

"Not anymore," said Robin, shaking her head. "I know you're always telling us those exams are intelligence tests, Mrs. Tucker. But you're wrong. They're just tests. So I studied over the summer and then I took them again."

"And your scores improved enough for you to get in to Princeton? I highly doubt that." Mrs. Tucker clicked her tongue as she spoke and her tone grew bitter. "In my experience, taking standardized tests more than once is simply a waste of time. You must have cheated. It's the only logical explanation. You must have copied the answers somehow or stolen them."

"No. I just worked really hard, that's all. I studied vocabulary lists. I took practice exams…"

Robin was telling the truth and Priela could sense her shock. Mrs. Tucker's accusations stung, instantly stamping out any joy she might have felt over her acceptance letter or any pride that should have followed years of hard work. It made Priela's throat fill with bile and her hands grow cold.

"Sure you did, Robin. It was always presumptuous to think a highly selective college would admit you, but I can't believe you would stoop to something this low. I bet you think you've outsmarted everyone. Is that it? Answer me."

"What? No."

"I have a mind to contact Princeton directly and tell them what a liar you are, although I'm not sure they'll care." Mrs. Tucker drew closer, stretching her neck so that it towered over Robin and tightening her jaw until veins protruded. "We both know the real reason you got in, don't we? Every school needs a token to trot around in brochures. You did absolutely nothing to merit this."

"That's not true, Mrs. Tucker. I'm the class valedictorian. I'm the student body president…" Robin's voice trailed off, but Priela could hear her thoughts resonate with growing intensity.

"Does Mrs. Tucker ever accuse the white kids of cheating?" she wondered. *"Does she force them to justify their successes?"*

Robin wished she could voice these questions, but she knew that broaching the topic of bigotry would only incite more of Mrs. Tucker's wrath. Robin couldn't even reveal her emotions, fearing the label of angry black girl. So instead, she just stood there and took the abuse, allowing the woman to dismiss her accomplishments and slash away at her self-worth, until Robin's temples were pounding and a sharp pain cut through her stomach.

"Do you honestly believe that you'll measure up to those prep school kids, Robin?" laughed Mrs. Tucker. It was a deep guttural sound. "Do you really think they'll accept you? That you'll ever fit in at a place like Princeton?"

"Well, I never said I was going there," said Robin, her eyes now teary.

"Good. Because your family can't afford it anyway. They can't afford for you to go to college at all." Then Mrs. Tucker crumpled up the acceptance letter and handed Robin one of the CSL College bumper stickers. "Take my advice and go to CSL where you belong. The school gives college loans to absolutely anyone. Even cheats like you."

Priela had heard about CSL. It was a for-profit institution and the place was run like a business that cared more about churning through students than about educating them. Apparently, less than a third of its students even graduated. Robin looked at the sticker as if the woman had handed her a grenade and her body started visibly shaking.

"Stop insulting Robin," shouted Anton, his braces glistening as he spoke. "She would never cheat on anything."

The awkward freshman was making his way back up the bleachers now and it was clear that he was trying to play the hero. But he was too late. Mrs. Tucker waltzed off and Robin fled in the opposite direction, her emotions ripping away from Priela like a band aid being torn from a wound. Anton was left alone on the steps, his head turning from side to side, watching both of them go.

Then suddenly a light shot downward, obscuring the room until it faded to nothingness. The muses were being whisked forward in time to the place where *"crazy tigers clad in stripes abound"* from Dion's poem.

Within the rays, Priela could see a house rising on a hilltop and constructing itself on its foundation. A frame grew first above a concrete slab with slants piercing upward in sharp, defined angles. Then massive limestones and panes of glass filled in the structure.

"Wow, that house is amazing," said Edessa. "I bet it was inspired by a muse."

"Indeed," said Lady Raymere, clearing her throat. "Now muses, we have arrived in the future. See the difference?"

Priela looked around, assuming that something had changed with the shadows but she couldn't really tell. Instead, she spotted Robin making her way up the front steps. Robin was wearing a tailored yellow dress. Her hair was blown out smooth and her lips had the faint sheen of lip gloss.

"Hello, I'm Richard," said an older man, noticing her through the glass and pushing open the door. "Congratulations on your acceptance to Princeton. Just head through those doors to the yard, help yourself to some lemonade, and be sure to grab a nametag. If you have any questions about the school, I'm here to help. We really hope you choose Princeton."

Priela recognized the man at once. She had always called him 'Uncle Richard' even though he wasn't technically a relative. Instead, he was an old college buddy and business associate of her father's.

Now Uncle Richard was dressed in a funny orange and black bowtie and matching trousers. His attire looked strange out of context, like a mismatched Halloween costume or something a person might wear in the circus. But Priela knew better. She had traveled with her father to his college reunions at Princeton University and she distinctly recalled the ridiculous outfits she had always been forced to wear.

"Did I miss something on the invitation?" asked Robin. "Was I supposed to dress in costume?"

Uncle Richard laughed. "Don't you know? These are the school's colors."

"Oh, of course," said Robin, but her posture had changed, turning inward uncomfortably as if she were trying to squeeze into a narrow enclosure. Then she ducked inside and headed toward the yard, with the muses following behind. But when she saw the crowd, she froze. Everyone was dressed in orange and black and they all seemed to know each other, with alumni swapping inside jokes, parents boasting about their kids, and students chatting as if they were the closest of friends.

"Jack," said a man in an orange vest, walking past Robin and shaking another man's hand. "Wow, it's been too long. Let me introduce my son, Mason. He wants to go the Woody Woo route too. Thought you could enlighten him."

A pair of young women in tiger-print skirts strolled by next. "You'll definitely have to bicker Ivy. Your dad was a member of the eating club, right? So you shouldn't have any problem getting in."

"How does everyone else know each other already?" thought Robin and Priela could hear the words pulsate through the air with precision. *"What are they all talking about? What's Woody Woo? What's an eating club?"*

Priela knew the concepts weren't all that complicated. Woody Woo was shorthand for the school's public policy program and eating clubs were basically coed fraternities with decent food. But to Robin, it seemed like everyone was speaking in code, like she had stumbled upon some secret society, some private club. Even the words themselves, 'eating club,' seemed emblematic of the school's elite nature. It's otherness.

Priela could feel Robin's discomfort grow. The emotions were brutal, closing in like a storm and thundering inside her, until she was visibly shuddering, her heart pounding with dread. Then Mrs. Tucker's words started replaying through her thoughts. They repeated like a mantra, over and over on a continuous loop, growing louder with each recitation.

"Do you honestly believe that you'll measure up to those prep school kids, Robin? Do you really think they'll accept you? That you'll ever fit in at a place like Princeton?"

Laughter followed. It was Mrs. Tucker's deep guttural laugh and it ricocheted through Robin's mind like a ghostly echo.

Robin's head tilted downward, her body turned away from the party, and she bolted back through the house and out the front door. She hadn't bothered to talk to a single person, or drink a glass of lemonade, or even put on a nametag.

"I don't understand," said Dion, watching her disappear down the steps. "Why is Robin so upset? What's Princeton?"

Priela looked from Dion to Lady Raymere, but no answer would be forthcoming. Did Lady Raymere understand what college was or why it was important? Priela studied her instructor's expression. She wouldn't blame Lady Raymere for not knowing. After all, muses had no need for higher education. They had no need for a skillset beyond the arts. Being a muse was a lifetime profession, a guaranteed birthright for those born with tensile wings, and certainly there were no shortage of humans to inspire these days.

Then suddenly, there was a lurching sensation. This time, the pressure from the whirling air was heavier and more deliberate, the rays of light thicker and spaced further apart. When the motion stopped, the muses were once again in the Muse Essentials classroom.

Priela felt drained and a bit ill, although her feelings had more to do with Robin than with the floating. But there was no point in talking about the girl's situation. The classroom was like a church or a funeral parlor, where certain discussion topics were simply off limits.

"Edessa, tomorrow we will visit your charge. Please come prepared," said Lady Raymere, tapping her nails against a desk. "And Priela, I know that you have yet to discover your talent. Please make good use of your time."

"I will."

Clio leaned in closer and sneered. "Good luck."

Chapter Sixteen
THE PHARMACY

Priela's father Daniel found her sprawled across the carpet, her head buried beneath a pillow, her room in disarray. Old textbooks were stashed in one corner. Abandoned art projects were scattered around the room in various states of completion. And random objects made from plastic and metal were everywhere as if Priela had sorted through a dumpster and brought it all home.

"Listen sweetheart," said Daniel, turning off the music. "I'm running over to the pharmacy. Keep me company?"

"No thanks."

"Come on. It'll be fun."

"Yeah, I'm sure that getting mouthwash and dental floss will be a blast."

He kneeled beside her and sighed. "What's going on, Priela? Talk to me."

"Dad, even if I wanted to go to the pharmacy I can't. I'm invisible now, remember?"

"Look, people can see your mom when I'm around because I love her. She exists in the human world as long as I'm there. And you know what? I love you too. Come with me. It'll be good for you to get out of this room for a bit."

"But what about my wings?"

"Yes. I'm aware that you have them now, but I honestly can't see them. I can't feel your mother's wings at all. Believe me, I've tried. I don't think it's something you particularly need to worry about."

"I just can't," she said, pushing aside the pillow and sitting up. "I have too much to do. I have this really important homework assignment and it's due Monday which my instructor thinks is plenty of time, but it's actually not enough because…"

"Yes, I can see that you're really breaking a sweat. Do you need a few more pillows or will that one be enough?"

Priela grabbed the pillow and threw it at him.

He caught it and laughed.

"I'm being serious, Dad. I know it looks like I'm just lying here. But I'm trying to channel my inner talent. It's like a Zen meditation thing. If I can get my breathing right then I'll be able to reach a state of enlightenment which is a higher level of consciousness, and then…"

"Uh, huh. And how's that working out for you?"

She gave him a sidelong glance.

"Come on sweetheart, we'll only be gone a little while. You can resume with your talent soul searching when we get back. Who knows, a quick break might even clear your head."

"Fine, I'll come. But only if I can figure out what to wear." She dragged herself off the floor and scanned her messy closet, looking for something remotely normal. "All of these spider-web dresses look like fairy costumes and my old clothes don't fit around my wings anymore."

"I remember when you used to love fairy costumes. We couldn't get you to wear anything else. Even grocery shopping."

"Yes, Dad. I was four."

Daniel held up Clio's raincoat which was slung behind the door. "What about this?"

119

Priela glanced over and cringed. She hated the idea of wearing anything that belonged to Clio, but the jacket would definitely make her look more human. She slid it over one shoulder and around her wings. Then she grabbed some linen flats that she hadn't worn in ages and glanced at her reflection in a mirror. She looked weird, but not too weird.

"Alright, I guess I'm ready. Let's go."

They made their way down the staircase, through the kitchen, and out the back door. Nightfall instantly surrounded Priela. It was only the human world but being there again in real time felt strange, different from floating practice at school. There was a higher concentration to the darkness, a tangible thickness to the gloom, as if her classroom trips were mere dreams and this was real. Priela knew that earth hadn't technically grown any darker. It was her senses that were changing, a little more each day, so that her street now felt like a cave. She backtracked through the door.

"Are you okay, Priela?"

"Yeah. I'm fine. I just, uh, forgot my cell. Would you mind grabbing it, Dad? It's in my room on the dresser."

"Sure." He swung the door shut and headed back upstairs, and Priela listened to the floorboards creak.

Then she took a deep breath and opened the door again. It was still nighttime but now the world had switched over to Gaia, and everything was visible again. It was as if all objects in the muse realm had a glossy sheen that reflected the light of the moon, while the earthbound objects had a matte finish.

Great. So Priela had to stay within twenty feet of her father to be inside of his love-range? Even ants could travel further than that before losing their way. She shut the door again and a wave of anxiety washed over her, making her throat dry and her forehead hot. She imagined it was the same feeling as having one's driver's license revoked as if a certain freedom she once possessed, her ability to navigate the human world at will, was now taken away, leaving her shackled to her father.

"I'm not sure why you wanted your phone, Priela," said Daniel, rounding the kitchen island and passing over her cell. "It's dead." Then he reopened the door, headed to the garage, and unlocked the car. She followed three steps behind, trailing him as if he were a guide dog.

But if the streets outside were unusually shadowy, then the pharmacy was its opposite extreme. Sensory overload. Ordinary sights and sounds were suddenly painful. The fluorescent bulbs were not only too bright, they now flickered like strobe lights. The air conditioning system had an irritating hum, and a woman's lingering perfume smelled noxious. Priela glanced down an aisle. The sheer volume of items cluttering the shelves seemed overwhelming so that her brain couldn't focus.

She took a few steps, noticing that her gait had changed. Instead of swinging by her sides, her arms were waving across her body and her hips were bouncing. It wasn't the graceful walk of a muse. It looked funny. She tried to correct her form but instead she stumbled sideways, knocking over a stack of tampons.

"Are you sure you're okay, Priela?"

"Yeah, Dad. I'm fine."

She bent down to pick up the boxes but then she heard a familiar voice. It belonged to a boy, but it possessed a certain tenor that suggested it was in flux, its tone on the verge of growing deeper and more resounding. Was it him? Priela poked her head around the aisle and she saw Noah standing at the pharmacy counter. He looked pretty much the same as before, although he was dressed in an ill-fitted suit and tie.

"Now get out of here before I call security," shouted the pharmacist. "This place is for paying customers only."

"Please sir."

"Get out."

Noah's back slumped, his shoulders dropped, and he turned around.

"Priela?" he said in a whisper, seeing her crouched on the floor. "Is that you?"

Priela was still holding boxes of tampons in each hand, her hair a tangled mess, her rain jacket odd, but their eyes locked and she felt a rush. The sensation was sharp and sudden, as though she'd been shot with an arrow, and her cheeks started burning. She stumbled to her feet, stashed the tampons back on a shelf, and laughed awkwardly.

"I'm warning you," said the pharmacist to Noah. "Get out of here."

"Wait a moment, son," said Priela's father in a firm tone that carried an air of authority. "Why don't you take a seat?"

Noah looked at Priela's father, bowed his head, and sat down on one of the small folding chairs that faced the pharmacy window. Priela took a seat too, although she kept her eyes focused on her father and tried not to move. She was afraid to make further eye contact with Noah but she was even more frightened of revealing her disproportionate reactions to the pharmacy's ambiance and her peculiar new mannerisms.

"I'm really sorry, Priela," mumbled Noah in a scarcely audible voice. Then he pushed his hair from his eyes. "You know, because of that stuff under the bleachers. I had no right to try and uh... I mean, I shouldn't have assumed that…"

"I know," she said, catching his gaze.

Priela's father watched them and frowned. Then he approached the pharmacy counter and placed his hands on its surface. He moved with the decisive manner of a man accustomed to control. "So what's the problem here?"

"Do you know that kid?" growled the pharmacist.

"What's the issue?"

"Well, he wants some medication but he can't pay for it."

"Right," said Priela, swiveling on her chair and reaching into her pockets. "Listen Noah, I got you something. But you need to understand that this isn't charity or anything. I just uh… here." She pulled out handfuls of money-tree leaves and dumped them in his lap.

Noah held up a brittle one by its stem and twirled it in a circle but it wasn't a hundred dollar bill anymore. It wasn't cash at all. It was just a leaf, nothing more. "Uh, thank you."

Priela laughed nervously. Then music swelled over the loudspeaker, but it wasn't the typical bland background noise that usually pumped through speaker systems. The song was bold and romantic, the voice curiously recognizable. It sounded like Clio.

Priela glanced around. Was she here? Was Clio watching them, singing a love song, trying to compel Priela to guide Noah somehow? Priela touched the buttons on her raincoat. Nobody else in Gaia wore anything like it. Had Clio given it to her so that she'd be willing to leave the house or was Priela just being paranoid?

Daniel cleared his throat. "So is it some kind of narcotic he wants? Some kind of sedative he's asking for?"

"No, nothing like that," said the pharmacist. "Nobody would take that stuff if they didn't have to. It makes you pretty sick. But he says his brother's illness is progressing. That he needs it."

"But he doesn't have a prescription, right?"

"No, he's got a prescription. Insurance too. Just no cash for the copayment. He was trying to talk me in to giving it to him for free, but I told the kid that's not the way the world works."

"True," said Daniel, glancing over one shoulder. There were a dozen folding chairs but his daughter had chosen the one right by Noah's side, and she kept giggling and touching her hair. He sighed deeply and turned back to the pharmacist. "Okay, so how much for the medicine?"

"Three hundred and thirty seven dollars."

Priela's father shook his head from side to side and grunted, but he whipped out a credit card and slapped it on the counter.

"I'll need a phone number to verify the prescription?"

Daniel glanced at Noah and he rattled it off. Then the pharmacist rang up the order and handed over the medication in a small paper bag. Priela's father passed it to Noah. "I didn't mean to question your character there, son. Please tell your brother I hope he feels better."

For a moment Noah just sat there in disbelief, looking down at the paper bag. Then he pushed aside the leaves, rose from his chair, and extended his hand. "Thank you. Thank you so much, sir. What can I do to repay you? Can I mow your lawn or maybe help out around your house?"

"Um, no," said Daniel, looking from Noah to Priela. "That won't be necessary. We really should get going." Then he took her arm and guided her out of the store, discarding his basket on the way out. "Come on, Priela."

"Didn't you need to get something, Dad?"

"I'll get it later."

Once they were back in the car with the doors shut, he turned to face her. "A friend of yours from your old school?"

"Yeah, something like that."

124

"Uh, huh. Good thing you're invisible these days when I'm not around, Priela. Now if I could bottle that and sell it to other dads I'd make some real money."

Priela playfully punched her father on the shoulder.

"You think I'm kidding? Sweetheart you're in such a hurry to grow up. It's okay to slow down a bit, you know."

Chapter Seventeen
THE LONG ROUTE TO CLASS

Priela opted to take a different route in the morning. She hoped the exercise would relieve her stress, or at least delay its inevitable onslaught brought on by knowing that she still hadn't found her art. She left early and headed southeast. The path would take her through a local shopping district and back around to the institute, adding about twenty minutes to her walk.

She found the main street with ease. It still existed in Gaia with the same intersections and narrow storefronts, although it was cleaner and quieter now. The antique store and small art gallery looked almost unchanged. The pastry shop and local bookstore were there too, as was a small theater. But the computer store was gone. So were the gas station, the McDonalds, the Starbucks. It was like someone had camouflaged the street and taken it back to an idealized earlier era.

Priela peered through a clothing shop window. The outfits looked practically human, although they were more stylized somehow. She leaned in closer and realized the items were only two-dimensional, like dresses made for paper dolls.

What was the purpose of having fake stores? She guessed some art teacher had created them, never intending for the stores to function. Instead the whole street was a giant still life, a full-sized replica of the human world designed to be painted by students, like those structures on film studio back lots that existed solely for the lens of a camera. It was disconcerting.

"What are you looking at?" said a creature, who appeared on the other side of the glass. She was a pixie, about the size of a Barbie doll, with delicate limbs, sheer wings, and sparkly eyes.

"Nothing. I thought this store was real."

"You expect me to believe that? Can't you see that I live here? How would you like it if I spied through your bedroom window?"

"Sorry."

Priela stepped away and a shadow fell across her face. A phoenix with fire colored wings, a long outstretched neck, and a halo-like glow was flying overhead. She watched it glide by in rolling waves and her eyes widened. How many mythical creatures existed in Gaia? Were there fire-breathing dragons too? Leprechauns? Unicorns?

The bird caught sight of Priela's gaze and it swooped back around, flying lower and slowing its stride. Then it pooped on her head and took off. Ugh. The goopy mess was disgusting.

"I told you to mind your own business," said the pixie, smirking. "You muses think you're so special. You think the rest of us only exist for your observation. Well stop staring all the time. We're more than just subjects for your art."

Priela bit her lip. Apparently, muses treated other creatures the way the paparazzi treated celebrities, ignoring their privacy to the point of driving them insane, all for the benefit of a photograph. "You're right," said Priela. "I promise, I'll never paint you."

"Good," said the pixie, buzzing away.

Priela continued east and turned a corner, finding an enormous fountain with multiple tiers that would have looked at home in Las Vegas. As she moved closer, music started playing with streams of water dancing in concert, and Priela's steps began to synchronize with the beat. Gaia was weirdly unnerving but it was magnificent too, so that the world possessed an amazing dream-like quality.

Why hadn't she spent more time exploring? When Alice fell down the rabbit hole into Wonderland she wandered around an awful lot. Wendy visited the far corners of Neverland too. But all Priela had done was travel to and from school in a continuous loop, selecting one route, in one city, in what was presumably an entire parallel universe. The thought was both inspiring and a little alarming.

But then, Priela wasn't like those fictional characters. She hadn't come to Gaia by accident or to avoid growing up. She'd never been a normal human girl. Instead, she was here because she'd felt like an outsider her entire life and she didn't want to be different anymore. She wanted to fit in. Besides, Priela couldn't just roam around. She had classes to attend, and homework assignments, and parents who'd probably go into anaphylactic shock if she ever went missing.

Priela rinsed the poop from her hair in the fountain and started jogging to make up for lost time, fluttering her wings as she ran. She still didn't know how to fly without jumping from a rooftop, so her efforts resembled a frightened chicken, scarcely lifting her more than a few feet off the ground. But at least she arrived to campus on time.

"We should just clip those wings of yours," said Clio when Priela reached the courtyard.

"I'm not in the mood, Clio."

"Oh, it's not an insult. Just an observation. Your wings have actually become quite lovely. It's just a shame that they're connected to such a worthless flier."

"I'm serious," said Priela, pushing past her and entering the classroom. "Leave me alone."

But Clio spied a damp spot on her gown from the fountain's splash and her lips curled upward. "I can't imagine what you must be going through. To be surrounded by so much talent while completely lacking in any. How it must eat away at you inside, causing you to wet yourself like an infant. Perhaps you should try diapers?"

Priela grabbed a piece of chalk and threw it in Clio's direction, but it smashed in to Lady Raymere instead, who materialized just at that moment between them.

"We do not throw things in this classroom. Honestly Priela, have some self-control."

"I'm sorry, I didn't mean for that to hit you."

"No. It was aimed at Clio, I see. And I'm sure she said something you found offensive, but that response was wholly inappropriate. There are already sufficient reasons to regret choosing you for this class. You do not want to add belligerence to that list."

"Sufficient reasons?" said Priela, her heart sinking in her chest.

"Indeed. It's come to my attention that you visited one of your charges last night."

Priela glanced at Clio and tensed her jaw. "That wasn't on purpose. Noah just happened to be at the pharmacy when I got there."

"Yes," sighed Lady Raymere. "Such is fate. You are meant to watch over that boy."

"Then I don't understand."

"Is the problem that she's trying to be his girlfriend and his muse at the same time?" said Edessa.

"I'm not trying to be either of those things. I haven't guided Noah. I don't even know how. And we're definitely not together."

"No, Priela," said Lady Raymere. "But you did give that boy money."

"Technically, I gave him leaves."

"That's not what I'm referring to. The medication was paid for."

"Yes, by my dad. I don't control him."

"True. Although your influence on your father is greater than you realize." Then Lady Raymere paced across the room and took a seat on the edge of her desk. "Priela, I know that you have undergone a dramatic transformation and that you are still learning to navigate this world. But if you wish to remain under my instruction, you must always keep the role of a muse in mind. Our influence is limited to art. We cannot go around fixing our charges lives in unrelated ways."

"Yes, I know."

"It is not a question of comprehension. It is a question of compliance. Are you certain that being a muse is what you truly want? Are you sure that Gaia is where you wish to remain?"

Priela swallowed hard and took a few steps forward. Her movements were as muse-like as ever, her steps graceful, her hands swaying with elegance, her posture poised. Even her wings now reflected the light, changing from pink to a shimmering gold. "Yes. I've never been more certain of anything in my life."

"Very well, then. I look forward to reviewing your art on Monday. Now Edessa," she said, rising from her seat and shifting her gaze, "please bring over your paintings."

Edessa lifted up two canvases and carried them forward. The first piece was Surrealist in nature with a stylized figure looking to the left at disembodied arms reaching through steel bars. The second work was a Cubist portrait of a man looking downward, and sideways, and a little over one shoulder at the same time. There was also a face in the foreground, although Priela couldn't make out the features.

The muses formed a line and Edessa held up her art and narrowed her gaze. Within moments Priela felt the familiar swirl of air, but Edessa's floating was smoother than Clio's and Dion's had been, the sensation softer somehow.

When the motion stopped, the muses found themselves in a waiting room. The place resembled an administration office with a reception desk and folding chairs lining the far wall. Were it not for the steel bars, the holding cells, off to one side and partially concealed from the entryway, Priela wouldn't have known it was a jail at all.

"Who is that?" whispered Dion, pointing to a man who was seated on one of the folding chairs and glancing over his shoulder, just like the figure in the painting.

The man looked an awful lot like Anton, Garrett's awkward younger brother and Edessa's charge, with the same square jawline and sloping shoulders. But it wasn't him. This man's eyes were a bit too close together, his brow a bit too pronounced, and his teeth a little crooked.

"I don't know," said Edessa, glancing from her art to the man and back again, the smile fading from her eyes. "Did I paint the wrong person?"

Chapter Eighteen
MR. STUART

The man in the waiting area had dark circles under his eyes, wiry hair that was going prematurely white, and nervous ticks that prevented him from sitting still. He kept cracking his knuckles, and clearing his throat, and shifting in his chair.

"Mr. Stuart," said a young police officer.

"Yes," said the man, rising to his feet and approaching the reception desk, a look of dread darkening his expression.

"Listen, we aren't pressing any charges. But this is the last time we cut your son slack." The police offer held up a sheet and waved the page in Mr. Stuart's face. "Trespassing. Public intoxication. If it happens again Garrett will be our guest for the evening and he'll have a record to contend with. Understand?"

Mr. Stuart nodded. "And what about Anton? Why did you bring him in?"

The officer pushed the paper aside and shook his head. "Just get them both home." Then he grabbed a set of keys, walked over to one of the holding cells, and unlocked the gate.

"Dad," said Anton, hurrying out. He looked a bit less awkward than before. His braces were gone, his pimples had cleared, and his hair was now cropped short. Although he was still plain-looking, possessing his father's square and somewhat unremarkable features, and his expression looked mortified.

"I'm sorry. I tried to stop Garrett but he wouldn't listen to me. He never listens to me."

"Let's not talk about this now," said Mr. Stuart with a grunt.

Garrett emerged next, stumbling forward and reeking of alcohol. But even in his dazed state he was handsome with those chiseled cheekbones and that perfect hair. He draped one arm over his father's shoulder and slurred his words, "Hey, Dad." Then he nearly collapsed.

Mr. Stuart hoisted him upward, dragged him out of the police station, and through a dark parking lot with the muses shuffling silently behind. Then he guided his son into the back seat of a vehicle, slammed the door, and swiveled around.

"What in the world happened, Anton?"

"My brother is an idiot," he said, yanking open the passenger door. "That's what happened."

"You know that I can hear you, right?" said Garrett, but his eyes were closed and a moment later he was snoring.

Mr. Stuart looked Garrett over and frowned. "This is just a phase. Garrett will get through it."

"Really? You still believe that, Dad?" said Anton, sliding into the car and pounding his fist on the dash. "Garrett got me in trouble this time and I wasn't even doing anything. I swear. The only reason I was even there was because I was trying to stop him."

"I know. You've always been the responsible one and your brother's always been…"

Mr. Stuart cleared his throat, opened the driver's side door, and got behind the wheel. As he moved, an image swirled through his thoughts and Priela could see it. The vision lacked color and it was dim around the edges, like an old photograph that had faded from excessive light or repeated wear. It revealed a woman, probably the boys' mother, lying in a hospital bed, her

133

body sickly. Along with the image, Priela could hear words broken into tired snippets.

"Garrett's not to blame," thought Mr. Stuart, the nervous ticks now returning in full force. *"This is all my fault."* He cracked his knuckles and shifted in his seat. *"I wish Sheila was still here. She would know what to do. She would know how to help our son."*

Then Mr. Stuart pushed the thoughts from his mind the way someone might clear off a desk, as if each sentiment were being carefully filed away, and the car sped off.

"Wasn't that handsome one your charge, Priela?" said Clio, gloating. "You must be so proud. He just exudes talent. I could smell it. Oh, no wait… that's what humans call liquor. Isn't that right?"

Priela glared in her direction but the wind had already begun to swirl. It wrapped around the muses in a gentle embrace, pulling them forward in time and then fading swiftly.

They arrived in an office with rich mahogany furnishings and rows upon rows of books. Dion slid her finger across a shelf and her eyes scanned the titles. "Wills. Estates. Trusts. These are all legal texts," she said. "You'd think they'd want more variety. Like books of poetry or literature."

"Um, I'm pretty sure this is a law office," said Priela, glancing around.

"So?"

Mr. Stuart was already there, seated in a leather chair, his head shifting from side to side uncomfortably. Priela looked him over. The man didn't appear much older and yet he had aged considerably. It was almost like looking at a photocopy, of a photocopy, of a photocopy, so that all of his features were intact but he was somehow a shell of his former self. His coarse salt and pepper hair had subtly thinned, his body was frailer, and his eyes were now so sunken that they resembled the pupils of a puppy dog. He looked exactly like the cubist figure in Edessa's portrait, where the colors were dark, the shadows were concentrated, and a face was turned in multiple directions.

"Do the boys know how serious the diagnosis is?" asked a man from behind a desk in a hushed tone.

Priela turned in his direction, recognizing him at once. It was Hank Hur, her best friend Kalista's father. He was dressed in his familiar grey suit and starched collar, and he hadn't aged at all. Clearly, the muses hadn't traveled that far into the future. Priela glanced at Hank's computer, making a mental note of the date. It was only a few months from now. Then her eyes narrowed on a framed photograph beside the monitor. It was a picture of Kalista, her head tilted to one side, her eyes smiling.

Priela's stomach churned. She had neglected her friend for a long time now, ignoring her texts, her emails, her calls. She simply hadn't known what to tell her. Still, seeing Kalista's image filled her with a sense of loss. It was like holding up a suntanned finger with a lighter band of skin where a ring once belonged, a visual reminder that something beloved was gone.

"I haven't told my boys anything," said Mr. Stuart. "I know that I look like crap but I haven't explained any of it. I just don't want them to worry."

Priela inched closer and she could feel something ominous, a sickness that was eating away at Mr. Stuart. It was growing quickly, instinctively, cruelly, leaving his body weak. Despite this, Priela didn't sense any fear. Only grief. The emotion flooded her body, draining her wings of color.

"Do you think we could finish updating my Will today?" said Mr. Stuart. "I don't have that much longer." Then he looked down at his hands, warily cracked his knuckles, and winced, as if there were once a time when he'd tried to control these spontaneous movements, to will them into submission, but that time was plainly over.

"Of course," said Hank. "We can stay for as long as it takes. You know, my wife passed away when my daughter was young too. I know how hard it can be as a single dad. I can't even imagine what you're going through right now."

Then Hank turned his attention to the monitor and scrolled through some pages on the screen. "Okay, let's see here. I know that your primary asset is the business. Before we make changes, remind me again… how did you come to own it?"

Mr. Stuart glanced out the window and sighed. "To be honest, it happened by accident. Buying the hardware store. I was heading to the bank, about to deposit my weekly paycheck, just like every other Friday. I remember that paycheck amounted to almost nothing. But instead, I bumped into this guy. Literally. He stormed out of the building and knocked me over. He was furious because he hadn't qualified for a loan and he offered me his hardware store right there for pennies on the dollar."

A bird passed by the window and Mr. Stuart followed it with his eyes. "I have no idea what came over me in that instant. I didn't know anything about running a business. I wasn't particularly handy. I don't even think I owned a wrench at the time. But I wrote that guy a check on the spot for his hardware store. It's probably the only risk I've ever taken in my life. And then I showed up the next morning at this tiny brick building as the store's new owner. I could barely even find the place. But it was a gift. And somehow I've managed to keep the place open all these years. I'm still its sole owner."

"Okay well, are you absolutely certain that you want to make this change and leave the store entirely to Anton? Garrett is your oldest, I would have assumed…"

Chapter Eighteen - Mr. Stuart

"Hank, you have to understand," said Mr. Stuart, shifting in his chair. "Before Sheila passed Garrett was this amazing kid. So imaginative. So capable. He was the real creative genius in the family and it was always my plan to leave the place to both boys. Garrett would be the visionary with the talent to take my little hardware business and turn it in to something great. And Anton, who's much more like me, would run the day-to-day."

He rubbed his eyes. "But now is not the time. Garrett's a mess. He can barely function. Maybe if I had more time I could get through to him, but at this point I'm not even sure that Garrett would show up to work. He'd run the business into the ground." Mr. Stuart's voice began to tremble. "I know that it'll crush him to get nothing. But this way, at least Anton can manage the store and support Garrett financially and it will all be okay. I just can't see any alternative, right?"

Hank shook his head, "I honestly don't know."

Then another image flashed through Mr. Stuart's mind. It sent a cold shiver down Priela's spine and turned her wings a shadowy black. There were Garrett and Anton standing side by side, dressed in dark suits. They were looking down at their father's grave in a state of dazed shock. They clearly hadn't known their father was ill and now he was gone. The grief was palatable.

Priela glanced at the other muses. Could they see the vision too? Probably. They all had pained expressions and Lady Raymere's skin had grown transparent, giving her the appearance of a ghost. Then suddenly the wind swirled up and around, pulling them back to the classroom. The tugging sensation was brisk this time and relatively benign.

"Edessa," said Lady Raymere, waving a nail at the portraits.

"I know," she said. "I painted the wrong human, but I studied the details of Anton's face at that jail. The spacing of his eyes. The shape of his lips. The depth of his brow. I won't make the same mistake twice. I'll paint Anton next time, not his father."

"Indeed you will," said Lady Raymere, her skin still ghostly. "Or you will not pass this course." Then she promptly vanished.

Priela yanked on a curl. Perfecting one's art seemed like such a minor task compared to the sheer discovery of any talent whatsoever. What had she gotten herself into? Why did she keep making promises that she probably couldn't keep? Priela avoided eye contact with her peers and hurried out the door. She'd better have the most productive weekend of her life, or this would all end very quickly.

Chapter Nineteen
SUNDAY NIGHT

It was late Sunday night, the weekend having slipped by without any artistic revelations. The only thing Priela still needed to decide was if she'd show up to class empty-handed and beg Lady Raymere for another chance, or if she'd simply stay home. There really weren't other options. But instead of feeling panicked, a serene calm had come over Priela. It was as if she'd gone through the five stages of grief – denial, anger, bargaining, depression – and now she had reached acceptance.

She wandered aimlessly through her house glancing at the brightly painted walls, the eclectic furniture, and Calliope's ubiquitous artwork. Priela now understood why her mother refused to sell her art. She painted things the way she saw them. Bold. Colorful. Stylized. From her perspective, the pieces were never abstractions. Instead they were a reflection of her altered perceptions, a window into her view of the world, and selling them would be like giving away a part of herself, as if she were peddling a lock of hair or a loose tooth.

Priela roamed into the home office which contained a beaten-up filing cabinet, her father's version of a scrapbook, and she impulsively opened one of its drawers. Then she thumbed through the file folders, noticing the words, *"Priela's Report Cards,"* on a tab. Just seeing the label caused her stomach to churn, snapping her out of her complacent mood and replacing it with a sense of longing.

Priela missed academic work. It was a strange thing to miss since some of her teachers were more miserable than shopping on Black Friday, but accomplishing things had given her a sense of purpose that she now craved. She grabbed the file, spilled its contents onto the desk, and took a seat.

"Physics: A+," she read. *"Algebra II: A."*

Priela had always been a pretty good student and the quantitative disciplines were definitely her strong suit. Could math be her talent? Was math even art at all? There was certainly an elegance to it, beauty in its stark perfection. And Priela had always believed that there was something creative in applying math to real world problems. It was worth a try.

She pushed her chair away from the desk and swiveled around. Clio and Dion had each specified their charges by name through their songs and poems, and Edessa had drawn portraits of hers, even if the facial features were slightly off. But Priela didn't know how to identify a human, any human, with numbers, let alone a specific individual.

Her eyes moved back to her report cards. In the upper left corner they contained her name, her student identification code, and her phone number. Humans had lots of numbers, lots of unique identifiers. Would a phone number work? If so, it wouldn't be enough on its own. She'd need to detail a moment in time in which to visit her charge too.

She pushed her feet against the floor, causing the chair to swivel again until she was spinning at a dizzying pace. Clio's song had specified that *'dank place on a stormy Tuesday'* which brought them to a basement. Edessa's painting had those steel bars which floated them to a jail. Would a date work to pinpoint a moment in time? The notion seemed almost too simplistic, like solving a maze with a single, straight path.

But even if dates would function, they couldn't be selected at random. Lady Raymere had been fairly clear that the moments needed to be important for the floating to work properly and Priela had no idea which dates from Garrett's life might be meaningful.

She stopped the chair abruptly and her eyes shifted back to the filing cabinet. She could definitely figure out which dates were important to her dad, at least in the past. Plus her father was human. He wasn't her charge, but right now she was only trying to test the concept, to figure out if using math was even feasible. Besides, visiting someone familiar, someone she loved, felt safer than snooping into the life of a stranger.

Priela rose to her feet, reached into the cabinet again toward the very back this time, and pulled out a couple of folders. One was marked, *"My original business idea!!!"* The sheets inside had printed text in a broad, simple font, a date in the corner, and faded notes scribbled around the edges. The second file contained a single receipt for a diamond ring.

She grabbed a blank sheet of paper and wrote down three math problems, opting to incorporate Greek symbols to make the equations more muse-like. Sigma. Pi. Delta. The solution to the first equation would be her dad's phone number. The solutions to the other equations were the dates from the folders. Then she penciled in the answers and thought of her dad.

A moment passed. Nothing happened. She looked at the math problems harder, narrowing her focus and trying not to blink, but the room remained unchanged. She closed her eyes but there was no swirling sensation, no whizzing breeze, no brilliant light from behind her lids.

She sighed deeply and opened her eyes. But she wasn't in the home office anymore. She was somewhere else entirely. Priela glanced around. She was in a small apartment now, about the size of a closet, and the room barely fit a desk, a bed, and a tiny refrigerator.

Her father was sitting in the darkness, his face illuminated by a computer screen, although he looked much younger than today. His cheeks were pudgier, his hair was a longish, disorganized mess, and he desperately needed a shave. This version of her dad was far from the polished man he'd grow to become. She moved closer and instinctively smiled in his direction, even though Priela knew she was invisible in the past.

Then her father started typing rapidly. There was excitement in his movements and a sense of urgency, as if his ideas would be forgotten if he didn't capture them right away. After a few moments, he printed off a page, grabbed a pencil, and wrote some more.

Dad's work was something they rarely discussed. Priela knew that he ran a software company, although she couldn't say precisely what the software was for. It had never been of interest. But now, as she watched her father feverishly scribbling, his eyes came alive. He was designing something, creating something. What had started as an idea had grown into a midsized business and there was a creative element to it all. An art. In that instant, it was as if Priela's father changed somehow, morphing into a new person, a talented person, before her very eyes.

Behind him, something moved in the shadows. Priela leaned in. The figure was faint, yet luminous with miraculous silver wings and long loose curls. Priela could only see her outline but it was definitely her mother, guiding him so long ago.

The vision didn't last long. After a moment, Priela switched to another period in time, in another place, and once again the experience was instantaneous, as if she were swiping through pictures on a screen.

Priela's father was there again, but now he wasn't quite as young. Her mother was there too, but she was dressed in human clothing this time and her body was fully visible. They were walking together down a crowded street, holding hands, and smiling.

"Would you wait here just a minute, Calliope?" said Priela's father. "I need to get something from across the street. I'll be right back, okay?"

"Okay, Daniel," she said, kissing him on the cheek.

Then he rushed away, deftly darting through a busy intersection until he reached the other side. He waited a moment until Calliope averted her gaze and slipped into a jewelry store.

But it was difficult for Priela's mother to stay perfectly in place. The sidewalk was packed and people kept bumping into her and pushing her out of their way, so that she looked like she was treading water against a river's raging current. Then someone shoved her directly into traffic and cars started honking.

"Get out of the street, lady."

Calliope spun around, her mouth opened wide, and her eyes grew wild. Priela understood why. Standing in the middle of a busy intersection was always scary, but for someone who had never experienced traffic or even moving vehicles it was terrifying. And her mother was probably new to the human realm, so her senses would have been greatly intensified. For her, each honk was as loud as a siren, each traffic signal flashed like a neon bulb, and every car was as threatening as a steamroller. Even the crowd likely resembled an angry mob.

Priela's heart sank. Her mother looked so confused and afraid. She clearly didn't understand what was going on. She couldn't process it all. And she finally went into panic mode, grounding her feet, covering her eyes, and screaming. It was a loud, piercing sound and it didn't help the situation. Now there were more frustrated people, shaking their fists from their car windows and blaring their horns.

"What are you doing?" yelled a uniformed police officer. "You need to get out of the street right now."

The officer waved his hands, stopping the vehicles in their tracks, and approached her. Then he tried to grab one of Calliope's wrists but she evaded his grasp and started running. Did law enforcement even exist in Gaia? Priela's mother probably didn't know what a police officer was. In her mind, this man was just some burly stranger who was trying to manhandle her.

She darted between the cars and down a narrow alley, while the police officer chased behind. "Stop right now. Put your hands up."

But she didn't stop. Instead, she spotted a fire escape and started to scale the ladder. Her movements were faster and significantly more fluid than the officer's, so she managed keep her lead, staying a full story ahead of him and finally navigating her way onto the roof, five floors up. Then she walked onto a ledge and spread her wings, although they were invisible to everyone except Priela.

"Don't jump. Stay right where you are."

The officer reached the rooftop and lunged forward, grabbing her forcefully with both hands and dragging her away from the ledge. Then he pushed her to her knees, yanked her arms behind her back, and cuffed them.

144

"Daniel," she started screaming. "Daniel. Daniel." The cries were deafening.

Priela watched her mother from the alleyway in horror. Until this moment, she hadn't realized just how high the stakes were for a muse living in the human realm. Could this happen to Priela too? She didn't want to believe it was possible. And yet, she was changing every day. Maybe she would never stand in traffic, or run from a police officer, or attempt to fly when humans were watching. But if she ever tried to rejoin the human world she'd likely do something erratic, or strange, or crazy.

Priela swallowed hard and gripped her chest with one hand, feeling it beat aggressively. Her desire to stay in Gaia had suddenly taken on a whole other dimension. It wasn't just something she wanted. It was more than that. She was like a tadpole transforming into a frog who once swam underwater but now could only breathe air. The human world might suffocate her now and there wasn't any simple way to reverse the process. Priela's mother was still something of a freak and she'd transitioned nearly two decades ago.

"Calliope," shouted a voice. It was Priela's father, standing a few feet behind her, and yelling up at the rooftop.

"Daniel," she screamed back.

He hurried his way up the fire escape, leaping from rung to rung, and Priela scaled the ladder behind him. As he moved, he continued to shout her name. "Calliope. Calliope." Then he maneuvered onto the roof, rushed to her side, and wrapped his arms around her.

"Take these handcuffs off immediately."

"How do you know her?"

"She's my fiancée."

"Well, your fiancée's completely lost it. She's a danger to herself. She was blocking traffic and she would've jumped off

145

this roof if I hadn't restrained her." He took a few steps forward and his belt rattled as he moved. "I'm afraid I'm going to have to commit her to a mental facility where she'll get the help she needs."

"Please don't. I'm sure Calliope had no intention of hurting herself. Can't you see that she's terrified?"

"I hate to break it to you pal, but she's more than terrified. She's unstable."

Daniel clasped his hands together. "Just let her go. I promise I won't let this happen again. I'll take care of her."

The officer gritted his teeth and shook his head. "Fine. I'm releasing her into your care. But I sure hope you know what you're signing up for. This mental illness stuff is a real nightmare. If I were you, I'd bail while I had the chance." Then he unlocked the handcuffs.

Calliope immediately collapsed into Daniel's embrace. Her entire body was trembling and tears were streaming down her face. The officer watched for a moment before opening a rooftop stairwell door and huffing away.

Priela moved closer and gently rubbed her mother's back. She didn't need any magical powers to feel her mom's profound sense of fear. But Calliope's breathing finally calmed and she lifted her head.

"Your fiancée?"

Daniel removed a small box from his pocket. "Marry me, Calliope."

"But you barely know me."

"I've known you my whole life. You're my muse."

"Daniel," she said clutching his hands, her cheeks still wet with tears. "I think you're amazing. You're passionate, and you're loyal, and you're far more talented than you know. But you need to understand… that man wasn't wrong. I am crazy.

I'll always be crazy. This world just doesn't make sense in my head."

"Yes, it's confusing. I'm human and there are times when I can't make sense of things either."

"That's not the same."

"Look Calliope," he said, pulling a torn sheet of paper from his pocket and handing it over. "I ripped this out of a book the first day that I saw you and I've been carrying it around ever since. It's from the Velveteen Rabbit."

Calliope unfolded the page, wiped the tears from her cheeks, and started reading aloud.

> *"What is REAL?" asked the Rabbit one day. "Does it mean having things that buzz inside you and a stick-out handle?"*
>
> *"Real isn't how you are made," said the Skin Horse. "It's a thing that happens to you. When a child loves you for a long, long time, not just to play with, but REALLY loves you, then you become Real. It doesn't happen all at once. You become. It takes a long time. Generally, by the time you are Real, most of your hair has been loved off, and your eyes drop out and you get loose in the joints and very shabby. But these things don't matter at all, because once you are Real you can't be ugly, except to people who don't understand."*

"This is very sweet, Daniel," she said with a sigh. "And I know that I only exist in this world because you love me, but…"

"No, don't you see, Calliope? You're not the rabbit in the story. I am. I'm the one who's changed. I'm the one who's become real. And it wouldn't have happened without you. I know it won't always be easy. But I meant what I said when I told that officer that I'd take care of you." Then he leaned forward on one knee and held out the box. "I love you so much. Marry me."

Calliope took the box and opened it. Then she looked into his eyes. "Yes."

Click. Priela was suddenly back in the home office, back in the present. She sat there for a few moments in silence, her chest tight, her emotions whirling, her mind picturing a stuffed rabbit that turned real when it was loved. Watching her parents had been overwhelming. But what had she actually experienced? Did she float? If so, the sensation was nothing like the prolonged, jolting motion brought on by the other muses. It was much more seamless.

At least Priela was pretty sure that she'd found her talent. Math. Of course. She'd always loved math. Why hadn't she thought of it before? It was like eating dessert before dinner, or putting milk in the bowl before adding cereal, or sleeping on her plush rocking chair instead of in her bed. She'd just assumed that things were a certain way, that math wasn't art, so she'd never bothered to consider the alternative.

She pulled on a curl and recalled that complicated equation on the glued-together pages of Mrs. Wilson's textbook. Solving it must have been the trigger that turned her invisible. Then her mind flashed to that absentminded fall down the stairs, the fall that had given her swollen bruises on her back, the fall that had given her wings. At the time, she was engrossed in a book about abstract mathematical theories. It was probably the discovery of her art, and not the distracted fall, that had caused her wings to grow.

Priela glanced out a window. The sun was already rising and she still had loads of homework to do. She looked up Garrett's profile online and quickly found his phone number but she'd need some dates too, ones that were significant to his future. How was she supposed to figure that out?

Priela opened a blank spreadsheet and started filling it in with thousands of dates, using a drag tool to auto-populate the cells. At least one of the dates would be meaningful, just statistically speaking right? Then she built the dates into equations, programming the cells to streamline the process, and she printed everything out.

She arrived to class just in time.

"I didn't think you'd show up," said Clio, her wings fluttering. "Does this mean you'll beg Lady Raymere for a second chance? I'd say that groveling was beneath you, but well… nothing is beneath you, Priela."

"No. For your information, I've found my art."

"Oh, really?" Clio stepped closer and glanced at the pages in Priela's hands. "So, you're good at math? How tremendous for you. Be sure to enjoy this feeling of accomplishment while it lasts because those equations aren't going to work at all."

"That's not true. I practiced already and the math totally worked."

"Yes. Math may work for floating purposes, perhaps. But how are you going to inspire someone? How are you going to lift a human's spirit or guide his soul? With numbers? What purpose does math serve in the human world anyway?"

Priela clenched her jaw. "Clio, you think you know everything but you know absolutely nothing. Humans need math. They rely on it."

"Uh, huh. Keep telling yourself that and one day you might actually believe it."

"It's the truth."

"Yes. I'm sure your talent is critically important. It's so crucial that you didn't even know what it was until now. Let me guess… you tried all of the other art forms and this was all you had left? You discovered it through a process of elimination, am I right?"

"No. That's not how it happened at all. The first time I found my art it was like… a revelation. It hit me so hard that I even fell down a flight of stairs."

"Uh, huh." Clio moved back to her chair now and eased into the seat. "Well, you'll want to be careful that your art doesn't injure you too greatly, Priela. We wouldn't want it to put you totally out of commission. It would be such a tragic loss."

Priela's face turned red, but at that moment Lady Raymere arrived and she looked her over as if she were some foreign creature intruding in her class.

"I'm glad to see you," she said, now eyeing the pages. "That's your art, I presume?"

"Yes."

Lady Raymere glided closer, reached for the sheets, and started paging through them with a long fingernail as if they were butterfly wings that could shatter with any sudden movements. She even examined the margins, although they were blank.

"We haven't had a mathematics muse at the institute for some time," she said, although her tone was difficult to read. "And you've printed these pages? I haven't seen that tried before. Calligraphy is such a lost art."

"Uh, yeah. It was just more efficient to do it that way. I have at least five thousand equations there. I would have had more, but I ran out of time."

"No matter. We wouldn't have time for over five thousand visits to the human world anyway." Then Lady Raymere selected two math problems seemingly at random, underlining them with her golden chalk, and she handed the pages back. "These should suffice. Shall we begin?"

The muses linked their hands together and Priela read her equations, solving them quickly and blurting out the answers, and the worlds promptly transitioned.

"What just happened?" said Dion. "Did we float? I didn't feel a thing."

"Indeed," said Lady Raymere. "Math is a very precise art form, so the light and air knew exactly where to go. Some have even argued that math is the pinnacle of artistic expression."

Priela shifted her gaze to Clio and pursed her lips. Clio glared back, fuming.

Chapter Twenty
GARRETT

A white neon sign reading, *"Mr. Stuart's Hardware Store,"* snapped into view and the muses looked around. In Gaia, there was a hardware store too, but it was only a quiet façade, its tools blunt and unusable, while this place was chaotic. Oversized signs marked each aisle reading, *"Hardware," "Plumbing," "Electrical," "Tools,"* and merchandise with sharp edges and whirling parts was everywhere.

Edessa was drawn to the paint samples. "So many shades," she said gliding over. "The blues alone have a whole section. But I don't understand why they need such large canisters. Do humans use these paints for wall murals?"

"Uh, I'm sure some do," said Priela. "Mostly, people pick one color and then paint a whole room the same."

"Why would they do that?"

Dion scanned a display of building manuals. "*How to Build a Deck in Five Easy Steps*," she read aloud. "'*How to Design Custom Cabinets*.' Such strange titles and the prose… it's so pedantic. 'Secure the beam to the joist.' Honestly? It should say, 'The beam is a boat tossed at sea that must be secured to its joist like an anchor in harrowing waters.'"

"Um, yeah," said Priela, shaking her head. "I'm sure people would find that much easier to follow, Dion."

Then Priela caught sight of Garrett. He was moving through the aisles in a relaxed stride, but he was no longer a teenager. He was a man now, in his late twenties perhaps, and his features were even more chiseled than before.

Priela watched him and her eyes widened. Something had shifted in the way she perceived him. She imagined it was the same sensation coworkers might experience when one was promoted to be the boss of the other. She'd never cared before if Garrett was talented. She'd never cared if he was ambitious or lazy, responsible or reckless. But now suddenly, she cared very much.

Would Garrett be good at math or did he have other artistic gifts? She moved closer, trying to connect with the guy, trying to hear his thoughts and feel his emotions, but all she sensed was his strong cologne.

"Hey, bro," said Garrett, throwing open a door to a small business office in the rear.

"Ever hear of knocking? I'm in the middle of something here." It was Anton, sitting at an immaculately organized desk. He resembled his father now more than ever.

Garrett sashayed into the room and his hands grazed across the back of a chair, the edge of a filing cabinet, and the top of a lamp, touching things as if he were a dog marking his territory with his scent. Then he approached a corkboard that was pinned with old photographs. "You should really digitize these pictures of Mom. They're falling apart."

"You're the one with the free time," said Anton, pushing his chair away from the desk and shutting a drawer. "Go for it. But when you're done, I want them back. I don't have duplicates."

"I know, genius. That's the whole reason they need to be scanned." Garrett unpinned the images, slipped them into a blue folder, and tucked the folder under one arm. "So listen, I need some money. Just like five hundred bucks."

"Uh huh, I figured you weren't here to say, 'hi.'" Anton straightened his posture. "I've given you almost two thousand dollars already this month. I have no idea how you go through it so fast but you're not getting another dime."

"You don't even know what the money is for."

"And I don't care. I'm done supporting you, Garrett. It's time you got a job."

"Doing what? It's not like I've been holding back some hidden talent all these years. And don't tell me that I can work for you at the store. I'm not interested."

Priela bit her lip and pulled on a curl. Just because Garrett wasn't aware of his talents didn't mean they didn't exist. Still, it wasn't the best of signs.

"Fine, Garrett. Whatever. The answer is still, 'no.'"

Garrett slumped down in a chair, pulled a Gateway Credit Card from his wallet, and began flicking it between his fingers. "Lucky I have this as backup, huh? Do you remember getting these cards in high school? What was that girl's name who sold them to us? Rachel, Riley…"

"It was Robin and yeah I remember. She was smart enough to reject you." Anton rose to his feet, circled the desk, and snatched the credit card from his brother's hands. "How much are you using this thing anyway?"

Garrett shrugged.

"Just tell me. What do you owe?"

"I dunno. Twenty five thousand, maybe thirty."

"What? How can you have that much credit card debt?"

"Honestly, I have no idea," said Garrett, rolling his eyes and kicking his feet up on the desk. "I never pay attention to that stuff. It's probably all the interest. They're charging me like twenty percent."

"Are you serious? We got our cards at the exact same time and my rate doesn't even approach that."

"Well congratulations on always being the responsible one. Good thing Dad gave you the store and left me with nothing when he had the chance, right?"

"And whose fault is that?"

"Oh, so because I got drunk as a teenager I deserved to be disowned for life?"

"Garrett, you act like the whole world owes you something because our parents died. But guess what? The world doesn't owe you crap. I don't owe you crap. So you need to stop believing that you have some right to take my money forever."

"Your money? Really? Do you ever hear yourself?" Garrett stood back up, yanked the credit card away, and clenched his jaw. "You're so self-righteous. You haven't earned a penny of the money that you've taken from here. You're slowly destroying this place. I can't believe you don't need duct tape just to hold it together."

"Yes, Garrett. You're such a business expert."

"And you know the worst part? You're sacrificing your entire life for this dump and you don't even realize it. Do you know that Dad never went on a single vacation? He never lived at all."

"Don't you dare say that about Dad," said Anton, grabbing his brother by the collar with one hand. "Running a business is living. You couldn't possibly understand the pride that comes with hard work. You're such a pathetic parasite."

"Uh, huh. And you're really living the dream." Then Garrett pushed his brother away and stormed off.

155

Priela watched him deflated. Clearly math wasn't Garrett's talent or he would have known how much he owed on that credit card. He didn't seem to exude any artistry at all. But even more troubling was his lack of ambition and his bitterness. It wasn't a good recipe for success. She glanced at Lady Raymere.

"Does every human have a talent?"

But Lady Raymere didn't answer her question. Instead, the muses shifted timeframes, floating instantaneously to a small apartment. Garrett's face had now morphed into a withering replica of his former self, so that his collarbones protruded visibly and his chiseled features looked eerily skeletal. He was sitting on the floor, tearing through a stack of envelopes, his once perfect hair glued flat against his scalp.

Priela looked at the envelopes. On one of them, she recognized the Gateway Credit Card logo with the words, *"Final Notice,"* printed in bold red letters. On another, she could see the phrase, *"Service will be shut off."*

Someone started knocking on the door.

Garrett glanced up and rose to his feet, but he didn't approach the door. Instead, he grabbed a cardboard box and began throwing things inside. He shoved in a pillow and a blanket. He emptied his drawers of socks and boxer shorts. He snatched a package of beef jerky, a container of ramen noodles, and a bag of trail mix, gathering items as if he were expecting to live out of that box.

The knocking turned in to thunderous pounding now and it didn't stop until the door flew open, cracking on its frame and popping one of the hinges, and a man in a sheriff's uniform stepped inside.

Garrett stumbled backward. "Are you here to kick me out? I thought I had until the end of the month before I had to leave the apartment. The eviction notice said…"

The sheriff crossed his thick arms over his chest and grunted.

"But I don't have anywhere to go. I'm going to wind up sleeping on the street. Is that what you want? It's freezing out."

The sheriff sauntered closer until his shadow loomed across the space.

"Hold on. Don't I know you?" Garrett angled his jaw and his eyebrows shifted together. "Yes… you're that guy. It was years ago. I was drunk and stupid. I probably deserved to be taken in, but you brought in my brother too and he was just a kid. He hadn't been drinking. He hadn't been doing anything. You could have just driven him home but instead you shook him so hard that he nearly passed out and then you threw us both in a cell."

The sheriff's face contorted like an angry cartoon character and he reached for Garrett's shoulder, but Garrett shuffled sideways and dodged his grip.

"Don't worry, I'm not going to fight you this time. I just need to find something really quickly and then I promise I'll leave."

Garrett rushed over to the desk and started pushing things aside until he located a blue folder, but the sheriff yanked it away.

"Hey, what're you doing?"

Then the sheriff pulled out a photograph of Garrett's deceased mother and ripped her face in half bit by bit, as if someone had hit a slow motion button on his movements.

"Stop… Don't."

The sheriff reached inside the folder again, selected another picture, and crumpled it this time.

"Please," he said, shuddering. "I'm begging you."

157

Clearly, Garrett had never bothered to scan the images and an intense loneliness swept over him. Priela could feel it, detecting the isolation and sadness that was buried deep beneath his casual veneer, as if she'd unearthed a haunted tomb and released the ghosts inside. Finally, Garrett grabbed the folder back and kicked the box through the door.

"Alright you win, you maniacal jerk. See? I'm going."

The sheriff followed Garrett into the hallway, slamming the door behind them, and in that instant the human world was gone, replaced by the Muse Essentials classroom.

Lady Raymere nodded in Priela's direction before disappearing, as if to say, *"Good job on the floating today,"* although she didn't actually verbalize the compliment. Dion and Edessa looked her way too and smiled before leaving.

It left Priela with a dull aching sensation. She hadn't expected a parade or anything for succeeding with her art, but the mild nods made her achievement seem trivial, especially after visiting Garrett.

What was the point of being good at math if she couldn't fix his real inner pain or his outward devastation? The guy was utterly lost. He needed debt relief. He needed therapy. But most of all, he needed a far warmer blanket than the one in that box. She pictured him, shivering in an alleyway, terrified and alone. And she felt disillusioned, as if she were Dorothy seeing behind the curtain and realizing the wizard of Oz had no powers.

Chapter Twenty-one
BENJAMIN

"Smile, Priela," said Clio, after Lady Raymere and the other muses had left the room. "After all of that treacherous effort, you should be elated that you've finally accomplished something. Mathematics. The pinnacle of artistic expression. How fantastic for you."

"Goodbye, Clio."

"It's just too bad that handsome one is such a disaster. Do you think he's an exception or are all of your charges equally wretched?" Clio grabbed a piece of chalk and began scribbling math problems on the board. "I've never been trained in mathematics myself, as I'm sure you can tell from these crude equations. But they should suffice to visit that boy you're always obsessing over. What do you think? Should we float to see if Noah's a loser too?"

"I know what you're trying to do Clio and I'm not falling for it. I'm not getting myself kicked out of class."

"Such paranoia. My time is far too valuable to waste it on some inane plot to discredit you." Then she put the chalk down and strutted directly in Priela's face. "But don't worry. Even with your newly discovered talent, I'm still fairly confident that you can fail all on your own."

Priela broadened her stance. It was obvious that Clio was trying to bait her, to entrap her in a bad situation, and she'd had enough. Priela raised her fists to her chin, angled one shoulder forward, and jutted out her jaw. Her fighting posture resembled the exaggerated pose of a comic book character, but her anger was real.

"Back off, Clio."

"Do you really want to fight me, Priela? Violence isn't worshiped here, like in the human world. Everyone will think less of you." Then she snickered, in a slow, exaggerated laugh. "And you're already considered so pathetic."

"Say one more word and I'll just have to risk it."

"Yes, your mother took risks too. And look how well that turned out? She's an embarrassment to the ancient Calliope's lineage. A disgrace."

Priela took a swing. Her fist was aimed directly at Clio's face and its momentum was backed by weeks of sweltering fury. But it didn't make contact. Instead, it whooshed through the air and Priela's shoulder banged against the chalkboard, bruising it instantly. She spun around, but Clio was gone. Did she disappear, or turn invisible, or was it something else?

Priela took a deep breath and tried to rein in her emotions. Clearly, this feud with Clio couldn't continue to escalate. Insults would never defeat her and violence was even more pointless. The only way for Priela to win was to become an accomplished muse, to meaningfully inspire humans, and to gain the respect of her peers. She rubbed her shoulder, more determined than ever to succeed.

Then her eyes shifted to the equations left behind on the board. Clio's math entailed simple algebra and she could solve the problems in her head. The answer to the first equation was Noah's phone number, the one he had rattled off at that pharmacy. The answer to the second equation was the current date.

Priela shook her head, annoyed, and grabbed a thick eraser. But she couldn't bring herself to wipe away the math. It was a weird compulsion, like some people had for washing their hands multiple times, or for rearranging objects in a ritualized manner, or for repeatedly making certain that a door was shut. She had to solve the problems. She *had* to.

Hopefully her action would have no floating effect, but even if it brought her to Noah it wasn't the worst consequence. After all, she was his muse and she was supposed to watch over him. It wasn't like she was stalking the guy and she certainly wasn't planning to inspire him or anything. Priela grabbed the chalk, pushed her hair behind her ears, and solved the problems.

Click.

She wasn't in the classroom anymore. She was in the human world now with its dust and its shadows, in a dimly lit bedroom. A woman was there who resembled Noah with the same dark hair and blue eyes. Although she looked tired, old beyond her years, and her expression was pained. She must have been Noah's mother. That phone number he'd rattled off at the pharmacy was hers.

"You still awake, Benjamin?" she said, keeling beside the bed.

A boy rolled over. He looked a lot like Noah too, but he was younger and he didn't seem well. He must be his brother.

Priela approached the boy and placed a hand on his shoulder. Numbness instantly engulfed her fingertips. Then the numbness spread across her arm and down her torso, until it consumed the entire left side of her body. Weakness came next, making her joints stiff and her limbs heavy. She attempted to move her left foot, to take a step forward, but her leg was weighted down now as if it were in quicksand.

She glanced at her wings. One was still pink, but the other had lost its color. That had never happened before. She tried to jerk her hand away, but it didn't want to respond. The hand just remained still. Motionless. She used her right arm now to pull her left one off the boy. It worked, but the heaviness persisted and a strange electric current ran down her spine. Clearly, Noah's brother was still very ill. Why hadn't that medicine from the pharmacy helped?

Priela fluttered her wings until the left one regained its pale pink hue and the numbness in her hand gradually subsided. But for Benjamin, it wouldn't be so easy. She sensed that something was eating away at his nerves, a little more each day, disconnecting them from his brain so that the signals couldn't pass through.

Priela had known for a while now that Noah's brother wasn't well, but she didn't really get it until this moment. She didn't understand Noah's desperation or his sense of urgency.

A door swung open and Noah entered the room. Priela observed the shape of his jaw and the breadth of his shoulders. His hands were pale but strong. His frame was still scrawny, but it moved in a manner that was masculine and deliberate. And his hair was so dark, his eyes such a deep shade of blue in the dim light.

"Listen, honey. I've got to go to work now," said Noah's mother, kissing Benjamin on the cheek. "But I'll be back before you wake up. Your brother is going to stay here in case you need anything, okay? Try to get some sleep."

"I'll be fine, Mom," said Benjamin.

"Noah, I should be back around five in the morning. There are some leftovers in the fridge in case either of you get hungry." She rose to her feet, gave Noah a quick peck on the cheek, and left the room. "Thanks, dear."

Benjamin watched his mother go and propped himself up on one elbow. "So, were you able to find her, Noah?"

"Not that it's any of your business… but no," he said, glancing at his hands. "I've looked everywhere. She's stopped showing up at school. She's not posting stuff online anymore. I got her number from the school's directory and tried texting, but the messages bounced back like her number's been shut off. And her best friend won't even talk to me. It's like she's just disappeared."

Priela felt her face flush. Was he talking about her?

"What about, you know…" said Benjamin, glancing over one shoulder as if he were afraid of being overheard. "The rumors?"

"I don't believe them. I mean, she was wearing this strange jacket the last time I saw her, and it was a little weird that she gave me those leaves, but otherwise she seemed fine. Totally normal."

Priela's muscles tightened. What rumors? What were they saying about her?

"She seemed fine, huh?" said Benjamin, laughing a little.

"Okay, better than fine. She was…" But Noah didn't finish the thought. Instead, he reached into his pocket and pulled out a bracelet. It was the one he'd given her under the bleachers. The one she'd thrown back in his face.

Now he turned it over and the colorful stones glistened as they slid across the silver chain. Maybe it was because Priela was a muse now, or perhaps the lighting was a factor, but the stones didn't look cheap anymore. Instead, the jewelry reminded her of a necklace she once wore. Did Noah know about that necklace when he bought the gift? Did he buy it to match?

Noah glanced in Priela's direction now and his eyes widened. Then he rubbed them and looked at her again. Could he see her? Was that even feasible? She felt her face turn red, her body become warm, and her wings involuntarily flutter.

"Don't you have to go?" asked Benjamin, looking at a small clock on his nightstand.

Noah checked his watch. "Uh, yeah," he said. Then he shoved the bracelet back into his pocket and turned around. "I can't be late. Are you sure that you'll be alright on your own, Benjamin? Did you want me to bring you some of those leftovers before I go?"

"No, I'm fine."

"Okay. I'll be home before Mom gets back. Goodnight." He nodded in his brother's direction and darted out the door, closing it behind him.

Priela watched in disbelief, her mind racing. Noah had just agreed to look after his brother. To stay home. Where was he going? What was he doing? The last time Noah snuck out at night, he'd attempted to rob a house. And his brother was still sick. Was he planning to rob someplace else so he could afford more medication?

Priela needed to follow him. She still wasn't planning to influence Noah or fix his life in any way. Lady Raymere had been pretty unequivocal on that topic, so Priela would save her assistance for sudden mathematical emergencies. But in the meantime, she needed to make sure he was safe.

She rushed to the door and tried to open it, but nothing happened. The knob didn't budge. She tried again, with both hands this time. Still nothing. She kicked the door a few times. It looked hollow and its hinges were missing a few screws. In human form, she would've been able to easily knock it down, but she wasn't in human form now.

Priela could walk around the cramped bedroom, and smell the musty air, and feel the doorknob's cold, smooth surface. But she wasn't really there. Floating to the human world was like watching a three dimensional IMAX film. She could observe events unfold in a tangible, visceral way, but she had no means to effect the action. She had no ability to transport herself to the other side of that door.

She moved toward an open window and peered down. She was about a dozen stories up and she could see Noah's mother below, walking down a brightly lit street. A few moments later she saw Noah too, bolting out the door and heading down a narrow sidewalk. He was hurrying in the same direction as his mother, but he was using an alternative route one block over.

Priela climbed into the windowsill and braced herself. She'd only flown once and it wasn't a particularly successful endeavor. But what other choice did she have if she wanted to follow him? She glanced back at the door. Even if she could pass through it somehow, she'd be too far behind now. She'd lose Noah for certain.

She glanced out the window again and her eyes scanned the street below. The vehicles looked like matchbox cars, the streetlamps were dollhouse-sized, and the signs were illegible from this height. Then her self-preservation instincts started to kick in and her body trembled. If she didn't do this now, she'd lose her nerve. She spread her wings, bit her lip, and jumped.

Priela started flapping vigorously but there was no wind, no breeze, and it wasn't working. She flapped harder, flexing her muscles and stretching her wings until she could feel the air's friction pushing them upward. But it still wasn't enough. She began waving her arms and kicking her legs, as if she were treading water. Nothing.

She lunged forward and pushed one arm outward, like Superman. But it didn't have the desired effect. Instead, her stomach dropped and her body began to tumble head over feet. It was all happening so fast. She was out of control. In freefall.

She tucked her wings inward and the spinning happened faster. Think. Think. She forced them back out, but it didn't slow the force of her descent. She straightened her body until she was shooting downward like an arrow, feet first. Her eyes searched for something to grab on to, something to catch her fall, but it was all a blur. She looked down. The pavement was zooming toward her. Closer. Closer.

Was this how it all ended? In a grotesque mess of splattered blood and crushed bones. Would it be painful? Would her invisible remains ever be found? She felt fear. Panic. There was only one thing left to do. She closed her eyes and screamed.

Then her feet bumped abruptly against something solid and the falling seemed to stop. She opened her eyes. She was back in the classroom, in front of the chalkboard, standing perfectly upright. She was safe, but Noah was gone.

Chapter Twenty-two
THALIATION

"Excuse me. Pardon me," said a giantess while squeezing her way through the upper balcony of a recital hall. She probably measured twelve feet tall, not including her high heels, and her head grazed against the ceiling as she ambled forward.

Priela edged sideways to make space, but the creature's pointy stiletto landed on the bridge of her foot, piercing hundreds of pounds of weight into her skin with a razor's edge. Urgh! Priela winced from the sting and yanked her foot away, causing the giantess to stumble forward.

"Are you okay?" said a pixie.

"I'll be fine," said Priela, leaning over and rubbing the sore spot.

"I wasn't talking to you. I was talking to Bertha," she chirped. "How could you trip her like that? You muses think you're so superior. Well let me tell you something, just because we don't have your artistic training doesn't mean we can't enjoy these performances too. We have every right to be here."

"I didn't trip her on purpose."

"Sure," said the pixie, flicking her hair over one shoulder and escorting the giantess to her seat.

Priela bit her lip and sunk into a velvety chair. She was there to watch a dance performance featuring Edessa's younger sister, but she had trouble paying attention. Her foot was throbbing, its skin turning purple in a thumbnail-sized bruise, and that pixie kept huffing in her direction.

Priela avoided her gaze, but she had a nagging sense that something was off in Gaia. Muses were like an elite class of beings who looked past the creatures that crawled, and scuttled, and flew around them, like someone ignoring a yapping dog, and the creatures seemed to resent them for it.

When the performance was over, Priela kept her head down, hobbled through the aisle, and headed to class.

"Today, we will practice thaliation," said Lady Raymere, watching her limp into the room.

Then she waved a glittery sleeve and a series of doors appeared. There was a standard wooden door, similar to those inside a home. There was also a rod-iron gate, a disembodied car door, and a set of elevator doors, none of which were connected to a wall or secured by a frame. Instead, the doors floated in place, surrounded by air.

"Thaliation is a form of intangibility. It is a method for passing through closed doors in the human world."

Priela yanked on a curl and swallowed. Did Lady Raymere know that she'd attempted to follow Noah through a door, just the other evening? Was she trying to protect her from needlessly jumping out of windows? Or was this particular lesson just a coincidence?

"The process was named after Thalia, the ancient muse of comedy. Most believe she discovered the skill by accident, although I believe it was something she thought about for quite some time. You'd be astonished at how compulsive humans are when it comes to closing doors."

Dion and Edessa giggled, but Priela nodded in agreement.

"I take it the experience sounds familiar, Priela?" said Clio over one shoulder. "People slamming doors in your face. Were you that unpopular in the human world too?"

Priela shot her an irritated glance.

"Muses, please understand that the use of proper thaliation technique is imperative. You must always push your thoughts away. You must always keep your mind clear."

"Oh, this should be a breeze for you, Priela," laughed Clio. "Tell me, does it require effort to be so ignorant or does your empty head just come naturally?"

"Clio," said Lady Raymere, glowering. "Thaliation is not something to be taken lightly. We are not discussing splinters here. A muse can become stuck to a door irrevocably, her skin fused to the wood, the metal, the glass, her wings broken or crushed. Even her heart can be impaled. Are we clear?"

Clio nodded and Lady Raymere began passing out pieces of shimmering chalk.

"Please begin."

Dion rose from her seat, approached the rod-iron gate, and started writing letters in a tiny font along the rails, most likely a poem. Edessa chose the car door and started sketching, while Clio began writing musical notes on the wooden door.

Why hadn't Priela thought of using math to follow Noah? It was so obvious. She stood on one foot, hopped to the elevator doors, and scribbled an equation. As she wrote, her hand began to vanish, so that her skin resembled a sheet of waxed paper that had caught on fire, disappearing without any smoke or sound. The sensation didn't hurt although her hand tingled as it faded away.

She glanced at the other muses. They were disappearing too, the invisibility creeping down their arms, across their bodies, and through their wings, coating their skin until they resembled ghosts.

Priela turned back to the elevator doors and blinked at her barely-there reflection in the metallic surface, catching only glimpses of her outline when she moved. Until this moment, she'd always been able to see her own mirror image. It was creepy.

"Muses, you are now intangible," said Lady Raymere, narrowing her gaze. "Please clear your thoughts and pass through your doors."

Priela pressed one finger into the metal, allowing it to sink beyond the surface. But it wasn't so easy to push her thoughts from her head. She couldn't help from questioning the physics of thaliation. Had the glittery chalk spurred some kind of chemical reaction inside her? Would the matter in her body really disperse and then reassemble, the way ice cubes could melt and then reform? And why did her mindset even matter?

She attempted to channel a Zen-like state, held her breath, and walked forward. The sensation was bizarre. The elevator's surface fought against her movements as if she were wading through those thick pools of tar that once ensnared ice age wooly mammoths and saber tooth tigers. The more she struggled, the firmer the substance became.

Stop thinking. Stop thinking.

She inched ahead at a glacial pace until she made it to the other side. Then she breathed a sigh of relief. Her body had arrived intact, although the fine hairs that once dotted her arms felt like they'd been ripped away, and her skin sizzled as it started flickering back into view.

"Help me," shrieked a voice from across the room.

It was Dion. She'd managed to pass halfway through the gate, but now her body was reappearing in a zebra-like fashion with stripes of skin visible between the rails. If the rest of her rematerialized she'd be stuck, her torso forever skewered by the iron rods, like a victim of medieval torture.

"Clear your mind, Dion," said Priela.

"I can't," she wailed.

"Yes, you can," said Lady Raymere firmly.

Dion furrowed her brow. She looked like she was struggling internally, a writer trapped inside her own head, her thoughts unaccustomed to being shut down. Then her eyes took on a deathly stare and she made it to the other side. Not a moment later, her missing stripes of skin reappeared, although they had a blistery singe.

"Are you okay?" asked Edessa.

Dion nodded but she was clearly shaken and she leaned against a wall to support her weight. "Will we have to thaliate again?" she asked.

"No," said Lady Raymere, waving the doors away. "Thaliation is merely a navigational tool. Nothing more. You may use it at your own discretion. But understand, Dion. Not everyone is fit to work as a muse, to traverse the human world, and to inspire charges. You may wish to consider alternative career endeavors."

"But I have to work as a muse. My whole family is counting on me. When I was born with these wings, the very first in my line, my parents were so proud. They named me 'Dion' after an ancient city where muses were honored. They even threw me a party when I first discovered my talent for writing at three years old. This is all they've ever wanted for me. I can't disappoint them."

Lady Raymere took a seat on the edge of her desk and exhaled. "Then your next assignment will be crucial. You'll need to determine your charge's talents. If you cannot discern them, you cannot work effectively as a muse."

Dion nodded but the task sent a shiver down Priela's spine. Garrett didn't appear to possess any artistic gifts at all. He was the opposite extreme of a prodigy, like Mozart who composed a minuet at five, or Picasso who completed a Post-Impressionist painting at nine. Garrett had reached adulthood without a hint of talent and even if there were something buried deep inside him, the guy was apathetic, unfocused, and listless. Priela would have trouble bringing his gifts to the surface, just to know what they were.

"Violet's talent is clearly singing," said Clio, crossing one leg over the other. "So I've already completed the next assignment."

Priela raised an eyebrow. The last time the muses had seen Violet, she was singing in a dusky bar. Her voice was pretty awful and the whole experience left a foul taste in Priela's mouth. Had Clio sensed something in Violet that had escaped Priela, or was her faith in the girl's vocal abilities only wishful thinking?

"If singing is indeed her art..." said Lady Raymere extending her arms, "then it should be easy enough to verify. Shall we?"

The muses assembled in a line and Clio began to sing. Swoops of air encircled them, slowly at first and then marginally faster, but the floating sensation was strangely dark this time, the blinding light gone. After a moment, the air came to a halt and the muses found themselves in a hallway.

Violet was walking through the narrow passage at a brisk pace. Her features had matured, becoming more angular and refined, although it was hard to place her age with all the dark makeup. In one hand, she clutched a shopping bag. Priela recognized the Palomar Boutique logo on its surface, the store where she'd once bought that expensive coral dress.

"What's this?" said Edessa, dragging her finger along a wall.

"Oh that's dust," said Priela.

"Why do humans put dust on things?"

"Humans don't put the dust there. It just kind of exists in their world."

"Really? How utterly revolting."

Then Violet stopped suddenly, waved a key over a lock, and pushed open a door. For a moment it seemed like the muses would need to thaliate, but Violet left the door open and her jaw dropped.

"What're you doing here?"

"I didn't think you'd be back until tomorrow," said Damien, the tattooed guitarist, who was there along with the rest of the band.

"That doesn't answer my question. This is my apartment. Why are you here?"

"We were just about to rehearse," said an older woman with a partially shaved head. "Damien said we could use your place until we found a new studio. Said you gave him permission."

"Yes, I said that because I assumed I'd be invited to the rehearsals."

The musicians' eyes collectively turned to a closed door and Violet's eyes shifted in the same direction. A toilet flushed, a knob turned, and a girl of maybe sixteen stepped out. Violet had been about the same age when she'd first joined the band.

"Who's that?" said Violet, pointing.

"Um, I'm Samantha. The new singer."

"The new… what?"

"Look, I didn't want to say anything," said Damien, sauntering up to Violet and draping an arm over her shoulder. "Nobody wanted to blame you. We all know how sensitive you

173

can be. But we used to be able to fill a nightclub and lately we can't even get bookings…"

"So what exactly are you saying?"

"I'm just saying that we need to make some changes to the band and Samantha's special."

"Oh, and I'm not?"

Violet pushed his arm away, stiffened her back, and locked her knees together. It was the same stance she'd once used in Mrs. Wilson's algebra class, a stance of bewilderment, a stance of distress. But Violet was older now and Damien wasn't some distant authority figure trying to intimidate her at random. She'd clearly trusted the guy for years and now he'd betrayed her. His duplicity ignited a long-suppressed anger inside Violet and Priela could feel her rising fury pounding like a drum on a battlefield.

"You jerk," she said, smacking him hard across the face.

"I knew you would overreact," he sneered, rubbing his cheek. "You take everything so personally, Violet. We're just doing what's best for the music."

"Seriously? You think you're doing what's best for the music? You wouldn't know talent if it hunted you down, Damien. You're a bloodsucking leech. You've been using me since the day we met. First because I was a gullible kid and you thought that image was all that mattered to make the band famous. Never mind that the music was trash. And when it didn't work out, you kept up the stupid charade because I was the only one in this band with a job. I had some cash… money that I was willing to share and that you were all too happy to take."

"Just calm down, Violet."

"No. Stop telling me what to do, Damien. I've listened to you for long enough. Believed in you. Given up everything because of your promises. I even dropped out of school for you."

"Whoa, don't put that on me. You've made your own choices." He reached for her.

"No. Don't touch me," she screamed. "You want me out of the band? Fine. I want you out of my apartment. All of you. Never come back here again." She gritted her teeth and pointed. "Now get out. Get out."

Damien's expression contorted into a scowl and he leaned inward until his shoulders loomed over Violet. Then he spat in her face and stomped out the door. The other band members quickly followed.

Violet wiped the spit from her cheek, slammed the door behind them, and collapsed onto a faded grey sofa. But in that moment she seemed changed somehow, as if someone had gutted her insides and left her skin, like those stuffed deer heads that hunters mounted on walls.

"Don't worry, Violet," said Clio, kneeling by her side. "I'll make you the greatest singer the world has ever known. Damien couldn't do it. But I can. I will."

"I'm not sure that singing is what she really needs," said Priela.

"Well fortunately, what you're so sure about isn't a priority," said Clio, her tone vicious, her wings turning blood red. "Violet is my charge. Mine. You can mess up your own humans if you want, Priela. But leave her alone."

"I was just trying to…"

"I know what you were trying to do and you'd better back off."

"Clio is right," said Lady Raymere, stepping between them. "She needs to focus on Violet's talents. To strengthen them. To set them free. That is our role and nothing more."

175

"But what if singing isn't Violet's talent? Her voice isn't that good."

"Enough, Priela."

At that moment the wind whipped upward, sweeping the muses away in a jolting motion and pulling them forward in time, further and then further still. When they arrived they were in the very same apartment, although it was a handful of years into the future and something about the place was horribly off.

The room still had the same grey sofa, now faded more than ever, but the clothes that were once confined to a few piles of laundry and some shopping bags in the corner were everywhere. Clothing draped across the furniture. It heaped in giant lumps on the floor. It filled the closet to capacity such that its door wouldn't close.

Some of the clothing looked expensive. Many pieces still had their tags. Other items were old, worn, and even threadbare. There was a grotesquely stained shirt and a shredded pair of jeans. There were a pile of purses stacked to the ceiling and crushing one another from their weight. And there was a uniform, pale green overalls and a matching cap, hanging on the back of a door. Priela could tell that the getup was Violet's current work outfit because it had sweat stains that were still wet.

A tiny mouse rushed by Priela's foot. The animal had gnawed its way through a mountain of clothes, creating a network of tunnels that allowed it to dart through the apartment. Violet didn't seem to notice the creature. Instead, she was sitting on the floor, rocking back and forth, and her expression was filled with dread.

Priela didn't have to listen in on her thoughts to understand what had happened. She remembered Violet's emotions on that day at the Palomar Boutique. Purchasing something expensive, something she couldn't afford, had given her a rush. It had filled a void and sparked a compulsion that replaced Violet's innate love for fashion with a simple, yet unrelenting need to hoard clothes.

Resting in Violet's lap was the torn, indigo-blue dress that Damien had ripped apart so long ago, a dress she once wanted to sew back together and rebuild anew. Now, Violet stroked its fabric as if she were petting a cat. Clearly, the material represented more than just silk and chiffon. It signified Violet's younger self, so alive and full of creativity. She began to sing.

> *"Where has all the time gone?*
> *I was supposed to be a star.*
> *Where has all the time gone?*
> *Still driving the same old car.*
>
> *In this city, where the sun shines,*
> *it is awfully dark and cold.*
> *And I don't know if I'll make it,*
> *but I'm too proud to go home."*

The song sounded like something Clio might have composed, its melody sweet, yet sad. And Violet's singing technique was stronger than before. Her voice was on key. Her pitch flawless. But her tone was far from beautiful. Instead, it was gruff and throaty. Violet cried as she sang, although her sobs were muted, as if her tears were rising up from the core of her being.

Priela glanced at Clio. Her wings had now faded to black, matching the night's sky, and her eyes had a curious, yet pained expression. Still, it was difficult to tell what Clio was thinking. Was she proud of her charge for singing such a wistful melody, or did she understand that Violet was miserable?

Chapter Twenty-three
MORIELA

Priela had developed a pattern. Every night she'd roam through her house and peek behind her mother's art in search of dates. When she found them, she'd jot them down on Post-it notes. Then she'd gravitate toward her father's rusted filing cabinet in the home office, rummage through the drawers, and write down more dates.

Priela wasn't sure what she'd do with the information. She had no intention of visiting her parents on all those occasions. But just knowing when important events occurred gave her comfort. It was like an emotional escape plan, reserved for times when she felt unhappy or overwhelmed, and enabling her to withdraw into the past.

Now, Priela reached into the filing cabinet and pulled out a grey image. She turned it over in her hands a few times, unsure which way was up. The picture was basically a blob with a date in the corner from three and a half months before she was born. A sonogram print-out?

Priela imagined her parents on that day. They'd both wanted a girl or at least that's what she'd always been told. So it must have been a happy time. She could almost see their smiling faces. Almost.

She touched her pencil to the Post-it pad but instead of jotting down a date, she wrote an equation. Should she visit her parents now? She tilted her head to one side and shrugged her shoulders. Sure… why not? Then she solved the equation and the lighting changed instantly, the smells intensifying in wisps of ammonia and disinfectant.

She was now in a small medical examination room and a younger version of her mother was lying on a table, dressed in a patient's gown. Her father was there too and they were both listening to a technician who was pointing to a monitor. On the screen was a fuzzy creature with an alien-sized head and a rapidly pounding heartbeat.

"The baby's head circumference is 256 millimeters," said the technician. "Perfectly normal for the gestational age. And I'm counting ten fingers and toes. Do you want to know the baby's gender?"

"Yes," said Daniel, reaching for his wife's hand.

"It's a girl."

Priela's parents exchanged glances and smiled.

"Just a few more measurements now. Let's see, the femur length is within the normal range. The abdominal circumference looks fine." Then the technician's eyebrows narrowed. She appeared to be counting something. She counted again and again, leaning forward and scratching her scalp.

"Is something wrong?" asked Calliope.

"No, everything's fine," she said, but her tone was far from reassuring. "I'm going to ask you to wait here for just a moment. I'll be right back." Then she rushed out the door.

Priela's parents exchanged glances again, and he squeezed her hand firmly.

The woman returned a moment later with another technician, a man wearing identical white scrubs. They whispered something and he moved to the monitor and started counting, although he was much more obvious about it, writing little check marks on his pad with each count. Then he printed out a scan.

"What's going on?" said Daniel.

"It'll be just another minute. Wait right here."

Both technicians scurried out the door and Priela's parents stared at one another in silence. Minutes passed. With each tick of the clock, Calliope's teeth clenched, so that her face looked like a living wrench squeezing her jaw tighter and tighter. Finally, another woman entered the room. She was older and dressed in blue scrubs instead of white ones.

"Hello, my name is Dr. Fredman. I'm a Maternal-Fetal Medicine Specialist."

"Could you please just tell us what's going on?" said Daniel.

The woman rolled over a stool and breathed in deeply, "I'm afraid your baby has extra vertebrae."

Daniel shook his head, "What does that mean?"

"Having one extra vertebrae in the lumbar region is relatively common. But your baby has six extra vertebrae in the thoracic section, the upper back, right here." She touched the screen with one finger and traced a curve around the moving image.

"I don't understand," said Calliope. "Will she be okay?"

"Well, your daughter has a spinal deformity. I can't really speak to its seriousness at this stage."

"Try," said Daniel.

"Uh, there's a possibility…" she said, her eyes shifting from Priela's father, to her mother, and back. "That your daughter will have difficulty standing up straight. Walking. She may suffer from pain. She may need surgery."

Tears welled in Calliope's eyes.

"Could you give us a moment?"

The woman nodded and left the room.

"Do you think she might grow wings, Daniel? Do you think that's what's really going on?"

"I don't know." He touched the screen with one hand as if he could glean something from its feel. Then he moved his palm to his wife's belly and rubbed it. "Have you ever had your vertebrae counted?"

"No, never," she said, wrapping her arms around his neck, her face turning pale. "I'm so scared."

"I know, I am too."

Then they both started crying. The sobs were deep and gut-wrenching.

Priela fluttered her wings, feeling them brush against her back. She knew that she'd been born a healthy human girl. She'd learned to crawl at the normal age, learned to walk at the normal age, and her posture had always been fine. Her parents must have been so relieved. And yet, they must have always wondered if she'd become a muse someday. The thought made Priela shiver.

Then the vision snapped away and she was back in the home office, back in the present, but now she wasn't alone. Someone was watching her.

"La la, are you okay?" asked Priela's sister. "You just appeared out of nowhere, like Mom does sometimes."

"Yeah. I'm alright, Morgie."

Moriela took a seat but her body was stiff, her movements rigid. It wasn't so long ago that she'd followed Priela around like a shadow, hanging on her every word, gossiping for hours, sharing secrets. But something had shifted in their relationship.

These days, Priela didn't pay much attention to her sister and it wasn't because she was particularly busy. Moriela still thought she was human which contributed to the current dynamic, but there was more. Priela's worldview had grown increasingly dark, causing her to question her belief system, her perceptions, even her sanity. It wasn't something she particularly wanted to discuss, especially not with Moriela who might herself become a muse someday. The truth might terrify her and Priela didn't want to do that to her sister. At least not now, while there were still so many things Priela didn't understand, so many questions she couldn't answer.

"Will you tell me what's going on, La la?"

Priela shook her head and sighed. "Things have just been rough at my new school. That's all."

"Mom said they would be. She said you'd talk about it when you were ready and I've been waiting, but it's been so long. We used to tell each other everything and now it's like you've totally shut me out. Please tell me what's going on, La la."

"It's complicated, Morgie."

"Does it have something to do with your wings?"

Priela's stomach dropped. Did she hear correctly? Could Moriela see them?

"They're very pretty, La la. I like the pink color. Would it be okay if I touched them?" Priela bowed her head and Moriela traced one finger along the edge of her wing. Her hand was warm. Her touch soft. "Oh, they're so smooth. Not at all like Mom's."

"You can see Mom's wings too? Since when?"

Moriela shrugged. "I dunno. I guess I've always been able to see them. Hers are so sparkly, like shiny silver crystals, but I like yours better."

"I couldn't see Mom's wings until I grew my own," said Priela, her hands instantly clammy, her breathing suddenly shallow. "So all of those times we talked about how she was nuts… her sneaking around… her talking to herself. You've known all along that she wasn't human? That she wasn't really crazy?"

"Well, she is a little bit crazy. Aren't all moms?"

Priela started pacing back and forth. Years of conversations were replaying through her head. Moriela had always been truthful. She'd always discussed things as they were, explaining their mom's behavior from a magical perspective, while Priela had always tried to rationalize her conduct and explain it away, dismissing her sister's perceptions as mere childhood fantasies. How could Priela have been so dense? Why didn't she ever truly listen?

She pivoted to face Moriela now, suddenly seeing her sister for who she really was. Astute. Perceptive. Capable. Priela may have possessed a sixth sense, but it was Moriela who had the real clairvoyance, the real gift of understanding.

"La la, do you think I'll grow wings too, someday?"

"I really don't know, Morgie. But either way, I want you to know that you're beautiful. I'm sorry that I've been so distant lately. I promise I'll tell you everything that's going on from now on. Promise."

Moriela jumped up and embraced her sister, making Priela suddenly aware of just how much she'd missed their closeness.

"So, what's it like? Flying."

"Well, I'm not very good at it, but you could help me practice."

"Really?"

"Absolutely."

Moriela grinned ear to ear and without another word the sisters rushed to the backyard. Once outside, Moriela started pushing aside the patio furniture, stashing away some old toys, and scattering pillows across the lawn. "Those wings need space," she muttered. Then she walked around her sister in a wide circle. "So why don't you think you're good at flying?"

"Well, I'm supposed to be able to launch straight upward from a standing position, but I don't know how to lift off the ground that way."

"Show me."

Priela stretched her wings and began flapping vigorously, but she only rose upward a few feet.

"That's a good start," said Moriela, rearranging some pillows. "But I don't think your legs are quite right, La la. You need to space them more when you're taking off, like this. It should give you more power."

Priela did as instructed and this time she rose noticeably higher, almost to the roofline, before gliding back down. But she'd needed to flap at a hummingbird's pace to achieve the lift.

"It's supposed to be much easier than this. My wings feel like they're straining."

"I think it's because your wingtips are pointing inward. It doesn't look right." Moriela repositioned one of her wings, grimaced, and then adjusted it again. "Yes, that looks better. And I don't think you need to flap so hard, La la. Just try and relax."

Again, Priela did as advised. But now she rose beyond the roof and past the power lines that crisscrossed above, flying to a height where the wind was stronger, where she could stop flapping and begin to glide.

"You're doing it, La la!" said Moriela, jumping up and down and applauding. "You're really flying."

Priela allowed her body to swoosh downward, rounding a chimney, whizzing between two trees, and soaring just over Moriela's head. She waved at her sister and Moriela waved back.

But then, the wind stopped abruptly and Priela thumped down, landing on a stack of pillows.

"Are you okay, La la?"

"Yeah, I'm fine. But can we work on my landing next?"

Moriela nodded.

"I love you, Morgie."

"I love you too, La la."

Chapter Twenty-four
THE CRIB

The money tree stretched even taller these days with branches that twisted in a repetitive pattern, like fractal art, and leaves that had turned from green dollar bills to red, orange, and yellow currencies from around the world. It resembled autumn but in a less organic way.

Priela caught a falling leaf and turned it over. It was burnt orange with a Romanesque arch on one side, a bridge on the other, and a shiny hologram along its edge. She shook her head and allowed the note to drift to the grass. It was upsetting that the money only existed in Gaia. It could benefit so many people.

"You have to help me, Priela," said Dion, seeing her and rushing over. "I need to figure out Robin's talent. You knew her when you were human. What was she good at?"

"Uh, we went to the same school," said Priela, wrapping a curl around one finger. "But I didn't really know her."

"You must know something. Did she dance? Did she paint? Was she a good writer?"

"Well, Robin was the student body president."

"Yes, I already knew that. Remember how she mentioned it when we floated to see her?"

"Right," said Priela, recalling that uncomfortable day. At the time, Mrs. Tucker, the school's college counselor, was berating

Robin on the bleachers. The woman's insults were pointed and cruel.

"Do you honestly believe that you'll measure up to those prep school kids, Robin? That you'll ever fit in at a place like Princeton? Take my advice and go to CSL where you belong. The school gives college loans to absolutely anyone. Even cheats like you."

It wasn't particularly surprising that Robin later fled from that Princeton reception, overcome with self-doubt. But none of it had anything to do with her talent.

"I'm sorry," said Priela. "But I don't think I can help you."

Dion's shoulders slumped forward and her wings turned a bluish-grey. Then they both shuffled to class.

When Lady Raymere appeared, she looked Dion over. "Is everything alright, Dion?"

"Um," she hesitated, twisting one foot behind the other. "Would it be okay if I visited Robin again?"

"I presume you're still trying to discern her talent?"

"Well, I'm sure that she's creative. I can feel it. But as far as knowing her exact art… if I could just see her one more time… I really want to get this right, to help her."

"Very well," said Lady Raymere with a sigh.

A moment later, the muses were floating into the future. Although this time, it felt like they were traveling in the back of a pickup truck, with the air rushing in a single direction, a steady bumpiness, and a sound that hummed. They landed in a small pharmacy. It was the same one Priela frequented with her father on occasion, the same one where she once sat beside Noah, her cheeks flush, her heart pounding.

"Does this place remind you of anyone?" asked Clio with a sneer.

"I don't know what you're talking about," said Priela, although she couldn't help from picturing Noah's quiet eyes, his longish hair, his strong hands.

"Uh, huh," said Clio, handing Priela a slip of paper with that same math problem she'd written on the chalkboard the other day. "Here. This is just in case you forgot my equation. I know how you yearn for that boy."

"Whatever," said Priela, turning away and heading down an aisle.

Edessa glided behind her. "Why are humans so obsessed with signage? They've labeled every single one of those containers. Aspirin. Cough medicine. Sleeping pills. It looks so cluttered. Why can't humans just remember what's inside those little boxes?"

"Uh, you think that medicine packaging should be blank?" said Priela.

"Well, not blank necessarily. Pill bottles could be ceramic masterpieces or maybe they could just sparkle."

"Yeah, I'm not sure that would be the best idea."

Then a young man with an injured leg stumbled past them, his brace thumping against the floor as he moved.

"Robin," he said. "You work here?"

Priela turned her head and spotted Robin behind the cash register. She looked similar to before. Although her hair was shorter, her cheeks were narrower, and her eyes carried a certain detached maturity.

"Why would you lie to me about working here?" said the man, reaching the counter now and lowering his voice. "I thought you were busy sending out resumes and going on interviews? Looking for a real career and not just some crappy job."

188

There was something about the man's familiar line of questioning and his hurt expression that suggested he and Robin were more than friends.

Robin shook her head. Then she locked the cash register and called over one shoulder. "I need five minutes, Hal."

"Fine," said a voice from the rear. "But plunge the toilet when you come back. It's stopped up again."

"Got it," she said, propping open a side door to a parking lot and walking through. The man followed, his injured leg causing him to grimace with each footstep, and the muses slipped behind.

"You have to understand, Jay," said Robin, turning to face him now and biting her lip. "I wanted to tell you but I just didn't know how. You're always saying that the only way to get ahead is to have a career that values my education and allows me to grow. Everything else is just treading water, right? And believe me, I wish that I could quit working here and search like mad until I found something better. But I can't. I just don't have a lot of options right now."

"Come on, Robin. You have plenty of options. Did you even go to the job placement office at your college, like I told you?"

"Yes, Jay. But the job placement office at CSL is practically nonexistent. It's not like where you went to school, with those alumni networks and those recruiters who show up on campus."

Priela winced. So Robin would attend CSL? She knew the college's reputation. The for-profit institution supposedly left graduates with an education that employers didn't value and a mountain of debt.

"That's just an excuse," said Jay, waving his arms through the air. "We're supposed to be saving up for a wedding, but we'll never have enough cash if you're stuck in this minimum wage job."

"It's not an excuse. I'm buried in college debt, okay? I never told you, but I took out these private loans to pay for CSL with interest rates that were just insane and Grandma Dee is the cosigner. She used her home as collateral and everything. So if I default now, if I miss a single payment, they'll literally take my grandma's house away."

Then her eyes dropped to the ground and her expression darkened. "That's why I have to keep working here, no matter what. Even if it means I'll never have the time to search for something better. But it's okay. I mean, we could just elope or something. I never wanted a big ceremony anyway."

"How much debt are we talking about? Five thousand? Ten?"

"More."

He stomped in a circle now, dragging one foot, and the hair on his arms bristled. "When were you planning to tell me all this?"

"If you love me, it shouldn't matter."

"This isn't about love, Robin. And it's not about the wedding ceremony either. How are we supposed to build a life together? How are we supposed to buy a house and start a family? You're the one who wants kids so badly. But there's no room for them in my studio apartment and there's no way that any bank will give us a mortgage when you have thousands of dollars in debt."

"I know," she said, quivering now. "It isn't fair, Jay. I was only eighteen when I took out those loans. I had no idea they would affect my entire life."

"Well, you can't go back in time, now can you?"

Robin reached for him but he pulled away and a moment passed in silence. Priela could feel Robin's emotions welling up inside. There was regret, and shame, and an overwhelming sense of being trapped. It felt like she was confined to a prison with invisible shackles that silently limited her choices and quietly controlled her autonomy. It was a prison made even more restrictive because its bars couldn't be seen, the way some puppies feared the outdoors after a single zap from an invisible fence.

"So what happens next?" she whispered.

"I don't know," he said hobbling away, his foot banging rhythmically against the asphalt. "I have to think about all this."

Robin watched him go and a tear rolled down her cheek.

"I don't understand," said Dion. "What are college loans? What's debt? Does it have something to do with Robin's talent?"

"Um, not exactly," said Priela. "But sometimes debt can stand in the way of a person's dreams."

"Really? Why?"

"That's quite enough," said Lady Raymere, her glare biting. "Dion, you do not need to inquire about such things. We are not tooth fairies. We do not fret over coins. Money and art simply do not intertwine."

Priela gulped. The notion that pursuing one's artistic passion and having a measure of financial security were unrelated topics seemed ludicrous. But then, she couldn't exactly tell Lady Raymere she was wrong. If muses couldn't understand the logic in labeling a container of sleeping pills, they'd never understand concepts relating to money.

At that moment the wind swept around, carrying the muses forward in lurching gusts of air and landing them in a small, carpeted room. Its walls were painted yellow, a rocking chair sat in the corner, and along the far wall was an alcove with a desk.

191

Robin entered the room, approached the desk, and ran her hand along its surface. She looked significantly older now and her hair was loose and wild. As her hand moved, the edges of her lips curled downward.

"Jay," she called out. "Come here."

"What?" he said, appearing at the door. Jay looked older as well and thicker around the waistline.

"Why is this desk here? You know that I'm saving this alcove for a crib."

Jay paced the length of the room, took a seat in the rocking chair, and rested his elbows on his knees. "Let's face it, Robin. We're too old. We just waited too long. We're not going to have a baby. I was thinking we could turn this room into an office."

"But the doctor said…"

"I know what the doctor said, but I'm done trying. I think we need to be realistic here and move on with our lives."

"There are other options. I've always been open to other options. Adoption. Bringing in a foster child."

"You aren't hearing me," he said, lacing his fingers beneath his chin and rocking the chair on his heels. "I'm tired. I can't deal with all the tears anymore. If it was going to happen for us, it would have happened already."

"But you promised me that if I got a decent job and paid off those stupid college loans, we could buy a house and start a family."

"Yes, I made those promises fifteen years ago when I had no idea how long it would take."

"So that's it? After everything we've been through, you're just done?"

He looked away and Robin's body began shuddering until she sank to the floor, folding her legs toward her chest in a fetal position. Priela could feel her yearning and her emptiness, and she could hear Robin's thoughts ricochet around the room like rubber bullets.

"Why is this happening? If only there was some way… everything is so pointless now… this wasn't supposed to be my life."

"I wish I could help you," whispered Dion, her eyes glossy. She'd clearly embodied Robin's emotions too and she reached for her charge, but at that moment the air rose up and yanked the muses away.

Chapter Twenty-five
THE DOLL IN THE PURPLE BOX

Priela never threw away Clio's slip of paper. Instead, she'd kept it in the folds of her gown, occasionally peaking at the equation that could take her to Noah. It wasn't the only note Priela had saved, although it was the only one stashed in her dress. Other scraps littered her bedroom.

There were Post-its stuck to her walls, and scattered across her desk, and wedged behind her mirror. There were even a few taped to the ceiling in an elaborate collage. Most were marked with dates from her mother's art or her father's filing cabinet, although some referenced Garrett, and others had random equations that simply popped into her head.

She jotted down numbers the way an author might write about dreams in a journal. Priela had even created a code for keeping track of everything, a system of symbols and string lines. Although she couldn't really articulate her rationale for doing it all, even to herself. The process had simply become second-nature, a thoughtless mechanical endeavor, like brushing one's teeth or washing one's hands.

She scanned her bedroom now, her eyes darting from one note to the next. It all made sense in her head, but if anyone ever saw the place they would think she'd lost it. It resembled those stalker-walls from detective movies where two plain-clothed investigators crept into a room, waved their flashlights, and exchanged a meaningful glance, knowing they had found their predator.

The chaos was even more fanatical than Calliope's art studio, a space Priela once viewed as proof of her mother's insanity. The thought gave her goose bumps and her eyes turned reflexively to the one piece of her mother's art hanging in her bedroom.

The small square portrait was less than a year old. But it showed Priela as a human, dressed in jeans and combat boots with a cellphone gripped in one hand. She'd been so different back then. So normal. She approached the art now and touched its surface. Something about the piece filled her with a sense of mourning, like she'd lost a part of herself.

She grabbed her thaliation chalk, stepped on a stool, and wrote a math problem in the corner of the painting. Its solution was her own phone number. She'd never written an equation to visit herself before, but something about it was strangely comforting. It was like a quiet acknowledgment that she wasn't that same girl anymore. A version of goodbye.

She adjusted her weight and the stepstool tilted sideways, throwing Priela off balance. She grabbed onto the painting with both hands to catch her fall, but it didn't work, instead yanking the art from the wall as she crashed to the carpet. One knee bent uncomfortably. She reached for it and realized that her skin was now invisible with the top half of her body inside her closet, divided from her bottom half by the door's wooden plane, like a magician's assistant who'd been sawed in half.

Priela pulled her legs inward, just as her skin snapped back into view. What was going on? Had she thaliated somehow? If so, the process was much more instantaneous than her classroom experience, the chalk having transferred over like a stamp from the painting to the closet door, and whisking her through.

Was her mother's art some kind of magical accelerant that had hastened the thaliation chalk's activity the way gasoline ignited a fire, or did the speed have something to do with the math equation itself? Whatever it was, Priela could now chase Noah. She could follow him rapidly through that door.

She pulled Clio's slip of paper from her gown and thought of him. Noah was in possible danger. Or at the very least, he was doing something he wasn't supposed to be doing, sneaking out instead of staying home with his sick younger brother. And Priela was charged with watching over him. She had saved Noah once before, stopping him from committing a robbery. She could do it again.

She gripped her mother's art firmly with one hand and solved Clio's equation. A moment later she was back in that small bedroom, watching the scene with Noah's family play out a second time. Although now, Priela positioned herself near the wooden threshold and when Noah rushed past, swinging the door shut behind him, she followed him right through.

He darted next across a small den and out the apartment's front entryway. She thaliated a second time. But this door was fire-safe, thick and heavy, and completely sealed around its edges, and the metal slowed her movements. She waded through, just barely missing Noah as a set of elevator doors sealed shut. She could thaliate one last time, but the elevator car was already heading downward, creaking loudly as it moved. She'd be entering an empty shaft. There was no point. She'd lost him again.

Priela rubbed her eyes, leaned her mother's painting against a wall, and took a seat on a windowsill. What was she doing? Why was she so intent on following Noah anyway?

196

Her dreams had turned to him more and more. And they were the kinds of dreams that one only spoke of in a diary, kept under lock and key. But dreams were capricious things that didn't necessarily carry greater meaning. She didn't truly like Noah in that intimate way that made some girls behave irrationally. Did she?

She looked out the window at the quiet street twelve stories below and spotted him running out of the building. Even from this distance, she could see his distinctive eyes. He tossed his hair and glanced in her direction, and she felt a rush. Her cheeks grew warm. Her arms prickled. Her heart beat faster. Without giving it another thought, Priela grabbed onto the sill, hoisted herself into the window's frame, and jumped.

The last time she'd tried this it didn't work out so well. And like before, there was no wind, no breeze. But she'd had more flying practice now, training with Moriela almost every night. So she kept the tips of her wings pointed outward, and instead of flapping wildly, she allowed herself to fall awhile before fluttering in a deliberate and even tempo. Her body lunged downward and then rose back into the sky in a curved swooping motion. It was working.

She leaned northward, pushing her wings to flap harder and accelerating until she soared at a speed she'd never achieved before. She whizzed over the shadowy street, swooping over power lines, and through the narrow spaces between buildings. Her eyes darted around, searching for Noah.

Priela sensed that she was heading in the right direction but he was hidden now by the alleyway's wide awnings and its darkness. She turned left and left again, carefully rounding a telephone pole in a gradual half twist that prevented her from spiraling into a tailspin. But instead of finding Noah, she spotted his mother.

Priela watched from above as the woman joined a line that snaked into a massive warehouse, placing a cap on her head as she inched forward, and removing her coat to reveal pale green overalls. It was the same uniform that was hanging on Violet's doorway in that cluttered apartment, suggesting this would be Violet's future too if Clio couldn't change it. Something about the thought made Priela's stomach queasy, churning her insides and recoiling her body until she felt herself falling.

Priela watched the pavement zoom closer and she stretched her wings, angling them slightly in an attempt to slow her momentum, just like she'd practiced. Then she extended her legs and when her feet hit the concrete, she forced them to run forward, slowing her motion like an airplane decelerating down a runway. It wasn't the way other muses landed. They could perfectly stick their landings, like elite gymnasts. But at least Priela wasn't injuring herself anymore.

She took one final look around in search of Noah and then watched his mother disappear into the warehouse. Something told her to follow the woman and these days Priela trusted her intuition more than ever. She walked inside and glanced around.

The place was some kind of sorting facility with no natural lighting to provide a sense of time. Instead, florescent bulbs glared brightly and an air-conditioning system pumped out ice-cold temperatures at an unrelenting pace.

Hundreds of workers scurried around in an organized rhythm, barely saying a word. Noah's mother joined them, lifting a box off a pallet, scanning it, and placing the box onto a conveyor belt. She resembled a tiny ant in a massive colony, virtually indistinguishable from the other workers. But then something caught the woman's eye and she let out a startled gasp, dropping a box to the floor.

"Lady, if that merchandise is damaged at all, it's coming out of your paycheck," yelled a supervisor, approaching.

"I'm sorry," said Noah's mother, picking it back up. "But you need to understand…"

"No, you're the one who needs to understand," he said, grabbing the box away. "We're not running a charity here. This is a place of business. You need to pay attention and do your job."

He turned the item over in his hands. It was a winged doll in a purple box, the same type of doll Priela's father had once given her. "You see this ding over here?" he barked, pointing to a mark on the packaging that was barely visible. "This item is ruined. Now get back to work."

"Wait. That's my son over there. I just need to talk to him."

Priela turned around and saw Noah rounding a stack of pallets that reached to the ceiling. He was lifting boxes and sorting merchandise, just like his mother. The supervisor glanced in Noah's direction too and wiped his shiny brow.

"Lady, you know there's no socializing here. You can talk to your boy on your own time."

"But he can't be working here."

"Why? Is he a convicted felon or something?"

"No, he's… underage."

The man looked back at Noah and his lips twisted into a snarl, "Come here, boy. Are you eighteen? This isn't a joke."

Noah looked up, saw his mother, and the color drained from his face. "Um, no sir," he said, moving closer. "But you don't understand. I need this job."

"Everyone here needs this job. You think anyone's at this place for personal fulfillment? You're fired, effective immediately."

Then he yanked the scanning device from Noah's hands and swiveled around to face his mother. "And as for you, lady. Some kind of mother you are. You should know better. We can't have children running around this place. Can you imagine the threat to our reputation?"

"And it's so dangerous."

"Uh, huh. What are you, a full time worker or a temp?"

"Well, I'm scheduled to work twenty five hours this week, but…"

"Ah yes, the new normal. If you know what's good for you, you'll sign every document they put in front of you. Or I can guarantee that next week we'll no longer need someone with your, uh, particular qualifications. Now both of you, go to the conference room and I'll have someone meet you there."

The supervisor pointed to the far side of the warehouse and Noah and his mother headed in that direction, with Priela on their heels. They kept their heads bowed as they moved and the other workers looked past them, as if they weren't even there.

When they reached the bleak, empty conference room, Noah's mother closed the door and spun around. Her face was red. "I can't believe you, Noah. Who's watching your brother?"

"Benjamin doesn't need a babysitter, Mom. What he needs is a real doctor, not those people at the clinic who won't even give him five minutes of their time. Their diagnosis was wrong. That medicine didn't work at all. Benjamin can barely walk anymore. That's why I got this job. To help him."

"You think that dropping out of school and working at this place is the solution to our money problems? Believe me Noah, all it will do is limit your future." Her arms were waving wildly now and her knuckles were white. "I know you love your brother. I know you want to help him, but you need to stop being so impulsive and listen to me. Your job is to stay home and babysit when I tell you. I'm the one who'll take care of Benjamin."

"How? By writing another letter to the health insurance company? You're not a lawyer, Mom. Those depressing letters aren't going to convince them of anything."

"I'm doing everything I can. You need to trust me."

"No," he shouted. "Your everything is not enough."

Noah's mother gritted her teeth but his words had clearly struck a nerve and her expression changed from frustration to grief. Then suddenly, she grabbed at her chest and her body started shaking uncontrollably.

Priela absorbed the panic, soaking it in like the roots of a tree. Ice shot through her veins, sharp pains pricked at her skin, and pressure pushed inward on her chest, compressing it until she was hyperventilating. She steadied herself on the back of a chair, but the sensation only intensified. Her wings changed from a pinkish hue, to a shade of purple, to red, and her body buckled to her knees with debilitating swiftness.

"Mom," screamed Noah. "Mom, what's happening? Are you okay?"

Priela didn't have a chance to see what happened next. When she lifted her head, she was back at home, back inside her closet, alone in the darkness. She stayed there for several minutes, quivering in silence, until the panic finally subsided.

What was Priela doing? Why was she so compelled to keep visiting the human world? Every time she went there it was like she'd entered some horrible nightmare. Did she really believe she could help anyone?

She rose to her feet and turned to exit the closet, but her eye caught sight of a purple box stashed in the corner. It was that same winged doll from the warehouse.

Priela's father had given her the gift on the day she became a muse. He must have thought the toy would make her feel better, special even. After all, most people fantasized about such things. They dreamed of magical worlds and magical powers, about having wings and becoming invisible. But she hadn't appreciated the gesture at all, carelessly tossing the present aside, not even bothering to open the packaging.

She lifted the box now, exited the closet, and removed the figure. The doll wasn't really a children's toy. It was more of a collector's item, with a porcelain face, hand-painted eyelashes, and delicate braids woven into a mass of soft nylon curls. She smoothed the doll's silky gown and straightened its pale pink wings, adjusting the wisps and spirals. It looked just like her.

If Calliope's painting represented the human Priela, marking a time in her life that was over, then this doll was the Priela of today, finally coming out of its box, a symbolic gesture that she couldn't hide who she really was anymore. But as Priela propped up the figure on her nightstand, she felt a certain hollowness. Much like this inanimate doll, Priela possessed a sort of mythical beauty, and yet she was absolutely powerless. If she couldn't help Noah and his family, then what was the purpose of it all?

Chapter Twenty-six
ANTON

Edessa's paintings were massive, stretching from the grass to the roofline, with strokes as thick as tire treads, and colors that were saturated and bold. From a distance Priela could decipher the details, but as she moved closer the images blurred, softening into stray blotches of paint.

"What are you doing?" asked Priela.

"Uh… you know how we have to declare our charges' talents today?" said Edessa, her long black ponytail whipping around as she dipped her brush and continued to paint. "I just wanted to visit Anton one last time before class."

"So you haven't figured out his art yet? I still don't know Garrett's either."

Edessa looked over and frowned. "I thought… maybe if I made my paintings bigger… but this was the largest canvas I could find… I don't know. Do you think it'll help?"

"Um, it can't hurt."

Edessa continued painting and Priela stepped backward to soak in the image. It revealed some kind of formal event with hundreds of people milling about in a massive banquet hall. Anton was in the foreground and his depiction was perfect this time, revealing his square jawline and his sparse eyebrows and not his father. Although Edessa had painted him as older man, with wisps of grey around his temples and a relaxed posture, giving him a certain mature sensibility, as if he'd finally grown into his large head and narrow shoulders.

"Do you mind if I float with you, Edessa? Just in case Garrett's there too."

"Oh, he's there… hold on, I'll show you."

Then she moved to the edge of the piece and started sharpening details until a shadowy figure in the background resembled Garrett. But Garrett wasn't dressed in formal attire like everyone else. His shirt was filthy, his face badly needed a shave, and above one eye was a cut, dotted with what appeared to be blood. But even more jarring was his frame. Garrett looked emaciated with sunken cheeks and jutting collarbones. The once handsome brother was now the ugly one.

"Did you really have to paint Garrett like that? Couldn't you make him a little healthier?"

"But that's how he'll look."

"Could you at least repaint his clothes? Everyone else is wearing tuxedos and evening gowns. Where are they, anyway?"

"Hold on, I think that white square is a sign." Edessa moved to a void in the painting and started filling it in with block lettering in a handwriting style that wasn't her own.

"Annual Charity Benefit. Fifth Street Homeless Shelter."

"How do you know what's on that sign? How do you know any of this?"

Edessa tilted her head and pursed her lips, and Priela sighed. After everything that had happened, it was still difficult to accept that muses just knew stuff.

A few moments later, Edessa and Priela were floating into the future with the air pulling them forward like a string tugging a kite. They arrived in that crowded banquet hall.

Garrett emerged from the shadows and sauntered closer, swinging his arms as he moved. Then he tapped his brother on the shoulder.

Anton swiveled around. "What are you doing here, Garrett?" he said, his contented demeanor immediately collapsing into a sense of dismay. "You look terrible."

"It's great to see you too."

Anton leaned in, lowered his voice, and held out a key. "Listen, why don't you go to my place and wait for me? Grab something out of the fridge. Take a shower. I'll be home soon and then we can talk."

"Why?" asked Garrett, grabbing the key, tossing it into the air, and then flinging it back at his brother. "Am I embarrassing you?"

"No, it's just. Well, this isn't a good time."

"Uh, huh." Garrett's tone was bitter, his posture aggressive, and people were starting to turn in his direction. "I used to believe all this charity stuff could actually make a difference. What a joke."

"Enough," said Anton, taking his brother by the sleeve and dragging him aside with Priela and Edessa following behind. When they reached a restroom, Anton checked the stalls and spun around. "What are you thinking, Garrett? You know how important this fundraising event is to me. How could you humiliate me like that in front of everyone?"

"Oh. Did I bruise your precious reputation?"

"You're so pitiful. Let me guess, you need money again? How much is it this time?"

Garrett smirked. "Fifty thou."

"What? No. Absolutely not. I'm not bailing you out anymore." Anton slammed down his fist on the countertop and shook his head in disgust. "You've never done anything productive your whole life. You just mess around while I finance your lifestyle and then you have the audacity to spit in my face."

"Uh, huh. You're so impressed with yourself, Anton. Always bragging about that tireless hard work. But inheriting the hardware store because Dad dropped dead isn't an accomplishment. Taking a dying business and keeping it on life support isn't an accomplishment." Garrett turned to face the mirror now and examined the wound above his eye. "Too bad nobody's going to die and leave me with anything."

"Yes, you're always the victim."

"And you're always a hypocrite. You'll raise money for all those people at the homeless shelter, but you expect me to work for mine?"

"That isn't the same thing at all and you know it. Do you realize what other people would give for the privileges you've had?"

"Some privileges. Dead parents who thought I was a screw up and a brother who's an entitled idiot. Yes, I'm sure they're all lining up to take my place." The gash above Garrett's eye opened up now and blood began streaming down his face.

Anton grabbed a paper towel, ran it under the sink, and handed it over. "Fifty thousand. Really, Garrett?"

"Yeah, I owe most of it on that stupid Gateway Credit Card."

"Let me guess. The collectors are finally coming after you? Time to pay up?"

"Something like that. I was evicted. They took my car. They took everything. But I'm sober now. Clean. I swear it. I've been clean a long time. I just don't know how those debts ever got so out of control."

"Uh huh, it's a real mystery."

"Look, Anton. I'm trying to make it right, but no matter what I do I still owe them a fortune. They're bleeding me dry." Another trickle of blood ran down Garrett's cheek and he wiped it away.

"Yes, quite literally, I see."

Garrett gritted his teeth and steadied his arms on the counter. "Okay, fine. You were right all along. I shouldn't have wasted so much cash. I shouldn't have let my debts get so insane. There. I just admitted it. Are you satisfied?"

Anton sighed deeply. "How about this. Give me your statements and I'll call the Gateway Company. I'll see if I can work out some kind of payment plan. Then you can work at the hardware store and I'll cover your costs for a while. We'll get you back on track, okay?"

"Yeah, sure. Stocking shelves? Taking inventory? No thanks."

"It's honest work."

"It's pathetic work." Garrett swung his arm through the air, punching the mirror and cracking it slightly.

"What? You want some fancy job title? I can't even rely on you to show up half the time. Maybe if you'd ever tried pulling yourself together…"

"Oh, so if I wore a suit I'd be worthy of your pity? You don't get it, do you? It's not about the title. It's about the business. Do you really think the place will survive much longer with all those big chain stores expanding? Wake up. The store has maybe two years tops before it implodes. But I have this idea…"

"Always the genius, right Garrett? Always the brilliant one. This isn't a partnership. It's a job."

"I don't need your pity."

"I think you do."

"Whatever." Garrett tossed down the paper towel, allowing the gash to bleed, and stormed out the door. "I'll find another way. Thanks for nothing."

Anton watched him go. Then he turned to his own reflection in the cracked glass and Priela could feel his regret building to a crescendo and then receding backward, like a wave lapping on the shore.

"What will happen to Garrett?" he thought. *"How did I fail him so badly?"*

At that moment the wind rose up, catapulting the muses into the future. Months passed. Then years. When they arrived, they were at Anton's hardware store. Although now, the windows were boarded up and the place was virtually empty.

Priela glanced around and her skin grew cool. The store looked haunted, as if its livelihood were gone, replaced only by memories. There were no racks of tools, no colorful paint samples, no dynamic displays with beeping noises and whirling parts. One sole employee, dressed in an apron with the hardware store's logo, was moving around a dolly while Anton looked on, his lips tensed in a wide straight line.

"So what's next for you?" asked the young man.

Anton dropped his eyes and scratched his head, dragging fingers through hair that had grown coarse and grey. "I really don't know, Joe. Every day since I was a teenager I've opened up this place. I can't believe it's all over now. Without this store, I'm not sure what I'll do."

"At least you had a good run. My cousin tried to open a business and it failed in six months."

Anton smiled at the young man, but there was an emptiness in his gaze. "Yeah. There was a time when this place was worth something. It used to have a niche. Specialty paints. High-end fixtures. Locally sourced lumber. Designers loved it here. I even had a few offers to buy the store. But everyone wanted to change the business somehow, to tear down my father's shop and remake it. And I just couldn't see the vision." He sighed deeply and tightened the muscles in his jaw. "I should've listened to Garrett. My brother understood what was going on and he wanted me to make changes, but I refused to hear him."

"Well, everything happens for a reason, right? Maybe it's time to take a vacation?"

"You sound just like him," said Anton, shaking his head. "Garrett always wanted me to travel too, said that I was wasting my life away. But I'm not in good health anymore. It's too late."

The young man wheeled the dolly out the door and Anton's expression grew dark. Priela could feel his emotions intensify. He felt humiliated. Desperate.

"I've failed Dad's legacy," he thought. *"I've failed Garrett. I have nothing left. But I don't want pity. I refuse to become a burden on anyone."*

Anton grabbed a sharp blade off a shelf, one of the few remaining tools in the store, and Priela sensed that he was about to do something rash, something to harm the one person he most despised. Himself. Edessa must have sensed it too and her face grew pale, her wings draining of their beautiful lavender hue. She reached for him, but the wind pulled her away until the air grew wild, sweeping them back to Gaia.

When the light faded, Edessa was shaking, her expression bewildered. Clearly, their visit to Anton hadn't illuminated his artistic gifts, only making her task harder. But they'd run out of time.

They headed to class, where Dion was shifting in her chair uncomfortably. "Priela, what did you say your dad did again?"

"Uh, my dad runs a software business."

"No. You said something about writing?"

Priela shrugged. "Well, my dad always says that computer programming is like a form of writing, just more structured in some ways and more limitless in others."

"And your mom inspired that when she was his muse?"

"Yeah, why?"

"I just feel like Robin's talent is similar to my own gift of writing, but it's also different somehow."

"That's how I feel too," said Edessa. "Like Anton's gift is art, but not art."

"Uh, huh. So by that logic Garrett's talent is math but not math?" said Priela. Her tone had a hint of sarcasm, but both Dion and Edessa nodded as if she'd said something extremely profound.

Clio just sat there stone-faced, staring straight ahead. Was she unsure of her own charge's gift? Was she at risk of doing poorly for once? Priela should've felt vindication, but she didn't really want Clio to fail and she certainly didn't want Violet to suffer. Priela just wanted to silence her insults by becoming a successful muse herself. Although the closer she came to her goal, the more improbable it seemed, the way a mountain appeared larger and more difficult to climb the nearer one was to its foothills.

Then Lady Raymere appeared and a hush fell over the muses.

"Today we will identify your charges' talents," she said, gesturing toward the chalkboard. "Please write their skills in these blank spaces with your thaliation chalk. Dion, you may begin."

Dion stiffened her shoulders and rose from her seat. Then she wrote, *'Robin's gift is programming,'* in swirling pink letters and her wings changed from a muted purple to a brilliant fuchsia hue.

There was something ritualistic about identifying a human's art, like exchanging rings at a wedding ceremony, where a simple act held far greater meaning. But Priela looked at the board and pulled on a curl. She hadn't realized that Dion would take her programming comments to heart. Did Dion have any clue what she was doing?

"Edessa, it is time," said Lady Raymere.

Edessa's body was still quivering and her expression looked muddled, but she approached the board and wrote with a steady hand, *"Anton will bring architecture to the world."*

Was Edessa just guessing too, picking Anton's talent at random because architecture was art, but not art? Priela hadn't sensed any design instincts in the guy, but maybe Edessa magically knew something the way she knew precisely how humans would look in the future?

"Priela, it is your turn."

Priela swallowed forcefully. Then she rose from her chair and angled through the desks, taking as much time as she could to reach the front of the classroom. She removed her thaliation chalk in a deliberate manner and pushed back her sleeves, hoping that Garrett's talent would miraculously pop into her head. But she felt nothing.

"Garrett will be involved in engineering projects," she wrote in messy block letters.

Priela wasn't convinced that the words represented the truth. Garrett wasn't analytical at all and engineering required a certain mastery of applied math mixed with an artistic flair. She'd only selected the art because it was sufficiently similar to her own talent to be plausible and she was afraid to admit that she really didn't know.

But unlike human coursework, where students received a grade and moved on, this particular assignment could have far reaching consequences. What if her guess turned out to be wrong and it doomed Garrett to a lifetime of frustration, like marrying him off to a mismatched spouse? She ran her fingers through her frizz and returned to her seat. At least she could console herself in the knowledge that Garrett's future wasn't so great from the outset.

"Clio," said Lady Raymere with a nod.

Clio rose to her feet and glided forward, but her hand shook as she wrote, obscuring her handwriting's normal elegance. *"Violet's artistic gift embraces her fully, from her outermost layer to her heart deep within."*

Really? Were muses allowed to be that vague? If Priela had known, she would've been less specific about Garrett's talent too. She looked over at Lady Raymere to gauge her instructor's reaction, but there was none.

"Muses, you have now identified your charge's gifts," she said, clasping her hands together. "Tomorrow, we will commence with glimmer practice. Glimmers are how you'll inspire your charges and change their lives forever." And with that, she was gone.

Priela stared into the empty void where Lady Raymere had been standing and bit her lip. The upcoming lesson should have been a source of excitement, but she felt only dread.

Chapter Twenty-seven
GLIMMER PRACTICE

Priela had grown accustomed to the vibrant sky, the warm pavement, and the echoes in the air, so that she no longer shielded her eyes when she left her house or felt strange walking barefoot. The eerie store facades were now familiar. She even recognized the same handful of muses flying by overhead, a flute instructor, two theater muses, and a younger muse with wings of pale blue. Sometimes she joined them in the air, particularly when she was running late. But on most days Priela preferred to walk because it required less exertion.

Now, she turned a corner and spotted a familiar Minotaur with bull horns that twisted like coarse rope and hairy human feet. The gentle creature, Walter was his name, was always polishing the parked vehicles until they possessed a glossy sheen, as if he were preparing them for a television commercial. But the cars would never go anywhere. They lacked gas pedals, and gear shifts, and fuel gauges. Priela waved at Walter now and he nodded in reply.

These days, Priela had become so adapted to Gaia that when she entered the Muse Essentials classroom, it took her a moment to register that the room had changed completely. She peered back through the door to make sure she was in the right location. Then she glanced around with awe.

The space now resembled a narrow tower, its walls stretching perhaps thirty yards into the air with randomly arranged windows and a myriad of odd furnishings, while the building's exterior retained its low, flat roofline. The effect reminded her of Mary Poppins when she pulled oversized oddities from her handbag, or of a circus vehicle when it released dozens of clowns, where the inside of a space seemed disconnected from its exterior.

"How tall would you guess this building is?" asked Priela, meeting the other muses outside the door.

"What a ridiculous question," said Clio. "Everyone knows that classrooms are flexible. Well, everyone of significance. The angles in the singing hall adjust based on each singer's voice to optimize the acoustics."

"The lighting in the art studio does the same thing," said Edessa. "I always know when we'll be painting a still life with a banana because the room turns yellow."

"Well, this change is much more incredible than all that."

"Be careful how you toss around words like 'incredible,' Priela," said Clio, removing her scarf in a slow, deliberate manner. "Some might say it makes you seem simple. I'm not speaking for myself, of course. I formed my opinion of you long ago."

Then Clio sashayed inside, swiftly rounding a piano, squeezing between a coat rack and a marble statue, and taking a seat on a canopied bed, as if navigating between furniture was the standard daily protocol.

"No, this will not do," said Lady Raymere, appearing suddenly, her voice echoing through the chamber. "Much too advanced for beginners."

Then she clapped her hands and the furniture began to disappear in rapid succession. A chaise lounge sank into the floor, a buffet piece melted away, and a row of windows snapped shut and vanished into a wall. Then the ceiling began to fall, plummeting quickly as if it were a flyswatter about to squash its prey, and Priela crouched down reflexively. It halted just above Lady Raymere's head.

"Ah, much better," she said, taking a seat on an antique credenza and smoothing her golden robes. "Muses, it is time to commence with glimmer practice. A glimmer is a glowing sphere of light containing your thoughts. You will direct these orbs toward your charges, who will hear the words inside. Humans experience these thoughts as if they are hearing their own conscience, but in a manner that is more sudden and vigorous. It is a moment of insight, a rare spark of inspiration that can shake a human to her very core and motivate her to great artistic achievements."

"How do we put our thoughts inside the orb?" asked Dion.

"The mechanics of glimmers are simple enough. All you must do is think a few words with intensity. You may even voice the words aloud, if you wish. But for glimmers to form effectively, you must truly connect with your charge. You must have focus. Conviction. Passion. Time typically slows during the process, often coming to a standstill before moving forward once again."

Lady Raymere gestured toward a massive clock and its secondhand began ticking loudly. Then she pointed at a greenish mannequin and it rolled to the center of the room. The thing had a head and a body, sort of. But no clothing. No real face. Nothing to make it feel particularly human.

"Priela, you've had some experience creating glimmers. Please demonstrate the process."

"Huh, what do you mean? I've never done this before," said Priela, rising to her feet, but Lady Raymere just held her gaze.

215

"Uh, okay. So, I'm just supposed to think something? Anything?"

"If your charge were standing there, what thoughts would you have? How would you inspire his art?"

Priela looked from her instructor, to her classmates. They were all watching her, their wings fluttering. Even Clio seemed intrigued. Priela shrugged her shoulders and turned to face the mannequin.

"Um. Garrett, you should become an engineer," she said, although it was difficult to garner too much emotion. "Become an engineer," she said louder, but the clock continued to tick away, the mannequin remained motionless, and nothing discernible happened.

Clio snickered.

"You are not connecting," said Lady Raymere.

"How am I supposed to connect with a mannequin? That thing doesn't even look like a real person."

"Priela, there are times when humans will disappoint you. If you cannot create a glimmer here, with a figure such as this, then you will not succeed in the human world where faces can be cruel."

Priela bit her lip, swiveled back around, and closed her eyes. But this time, she visualized Noah. After all, he was her charge too. She pictured him under the bleachers, waiting to kiss her, and she imagined what might have happened if she hadn't panicked that day.

"I like you too," she thought now with a certain concentrated intensity. *"I like you, Noah… I like you."*

She repeated the mantra over and over, sharpening the thoughts in her mind until beads of sweat dotted her forehead. The clock started ticking slower, slower. Her knees grew weak, her breathing quickened, and suddenly a glimmer rose up from her thoughts, rising slowly like a bubble lifting into the air.

The sphere was roughly the size of her head, perfectly rounded and shining. It bumped against the ceiling, bounced to the floor, and then ricocheted around the room like a slow-motion ping pong ball, until it eventually landed on the mannequin and dissolved away. The process didn't look quite right, but Dion and Edessa let out a cheer.

"What were you thinking about?" asked Dion. "Did you tell Garrett to become an engineer again?"

"Um, yeah," said Priela, looking at her instructor and gulping audibly. "An engineer."

"Indeed," said Lady Raymere, although it was difficult to interpret her tone. "Priela, we'll have to work on your directionality. Had there been an open window, that glimmer would have escaped the room for certain. But your form was nearly perfect. Your brightness intense. You've clearly established a connection with your charge. Nicely done."

Priela nodded and took a seat.

"Congratulations," said Clio, clapping her hands in an exaggerated fashion. "Was it a challenge to connect with that mannequin Priela, or do you just naturally relate to dummies?"

"Why are you always so awful, Clio?"

"At least I'm not a liar. Engineering? Really? Dishonesty is the most horrible of traits, wouldn't you agree?"

Priela gritted her teeth and looked away.

"Can I go next?" asked Edessa, jumping up and approaching the green figure. Then she whispered something into its ear and a glimmer appeared. Her orb moved quickly, bee lining to the mannequin in a precise, controlled manner, although it wasn't as bright as Priela's had been.

Clio had success too, her glimmer softly tinkling as it moved, like wind chimes on a breezy day.

But Dion struggled terribly. "Robin, your gift is programming," she said, but nothing transpired. "Robin, humans will value your art," she said more forcefully, but her words didn't elicit anything.

Was it nervousness that hampered Dion's attempts? Had she selected the wrong art form? Or was it simply more difficult for a literature muse, whose heart was in her head, to feel an emotional connection?

"Robin your future is bright," she shouted directly into the mannequin's ear and a glimmer finally emerged, but it was dark and shapeless, and it rolled down Dion's shoulder and scattered to the air like a lump of ashes.

With each attempt, Priela, Edessa, and Clio showed progress. Their glimmers became increasingly vibrant and directional, and the ceiling rose higher, windows opened, and more furnishings began to appear, until they were all using an advanced configuration of the classroom. But Dion's orbs scarcely improved. They remained dim and diffuse, never casting a shadow, never landing on the mannequin, only spinning in circles or falling apart.

The room itself seemed to know this. Whenever it was Dion's turn, the space would adjust on its own. The ceiling shifted downward. The furniture neatly rearranged itself or disappeared altogether. It all happened so quickly that Priela had to jump out of the way to avoid flying coffee tables. But Dion just stood there in silent frustration, allowing the occasional vase to smack against her, until her arms were black and blue.

"Don't worry, Dion," said Priela. "It will be different when your charge is real. More than just a green figure on wheels."

"That's not true. Lady Raymere said that if we couldn't create a glimmer with that mannequin, then we wouldn't succeed in the human world either."

"Well, maybe your choice of words is wrong?"

"Okay… so what have you been thinking, Priela? You aren't saying anything out loud. Is it still that engineering stuff each time?"

"Uh huh," she said, pulling on a curl. But Priela hadn't been thinking about Garrett at all. Her thoughts had focused entirely on Noah and her inner dialog had grown increasingly intimate, using words taken directly from dreams and fantasies.

"You just need more practice, Dion."

"I wish that were the case," said Lady Raymere, drawing closer. "But unfortunately, practice is not always sufficient. Dion, you are a great literary talent. But as I've said before, not everyone is fit to work as a muse, to traverse the human world, to inspire charges. It is particularly challenging for those who are first in their line."

"So, what are you saying?" asked Dion, her wings flickering to a murky blue.

"I know it is a difficult thing to hear, but sometimes we must accept who we truly are."

"I know exactly who I am. I'm a muse."

"Dion, muses guide humans. If you cannot create a glimmer then you cannot be of service in the human world. I'm afraid it makes you…"

"Useless?"

Lady Raymere strained her neck. "Perhaps your daughter or your grandchild will be born with a muse's wings. After a few generations, our gifts typically…"

"No," said Dion, stomping down one foot and quivering. "That can't be. I know I'm a real muse. I know I can help people. I'm sure of it."

Then she burst into tears and fled from the classroom, tripping over a lantern on her way out the door and leaving behind a trail of shattered glass.

Chapter Twenty-eight
THE LETTER

Priela found Dion under the money tree, crouched beneath its shadow. Her arms were wrapped around her knees, her head was slumped forward, and she seemed so lost.

"Are you okay, Dion?" asked Priela, taking a seat on the grass by her side.

"No. I'll never be able to create a glimmer."

"That's not true. We've only just started practicing. You'll get the hang of it. Remember how long it took me to find my art?"

"That's totally different. Once you tried using math, it all just clicked for you. It wasn't something you had to learn, to study."

"Maybe. But there are plenty of things I've had to work at, like flying. And I'm still worse than everyone else."

Dion's eyes locked with Priela. They were wide and dark. "You just don't get it. The institute doesn't allow for slow learners. There are no beginner tracks here. Either I keep pace with the class or I'll lose my spot. If I'm lucky, Lady Raymere will give me another week to practice, but then she'll just move on." Dion glanced away and exhaled in a long, slow breath. "I have no idea what I'm going to say to my parents. They'll be so disappointed."

"I'm sure they'll be proud no matter…"

221

"You're wrong, Priela. I'm not like you. I don't come from a long line of muses. My mother is a water nymph and my dad and brothers are all sprites, which means they've never been to school. There's no need for woodland creatures to have an education. But muses are special. We can learn about literature and art, and we can share our gifts with the human world. It's elevated my family to a different status, like they're part of a privileged group."

Then her body shuddered and she pulled her knees closer to her chest as if she were trying to shrink herself, like a flower closing its petals at night. "If I can't work as a muse… it'll be over. It'll be like my whole life was a waste."

"Dion, even without glimmers you can still share your talent. You can still work as a muse."

"Yeah? How?"

Priela dug her fingers into the cold grass and glanced up at the tree. The autumn leaves were falling quickly now and the money was landing in scattered piles around them.

"Do you remember when I saw that face in the Pool of Polly when I almost drown?"

"Uh huh."

"Well, he's the person I was picturing when I practiced my glimmers. His name is Noah and he needs help. He needs to write a letter. One that's brilliant. Inspired. And I wouldn't even know where to begin. I can create the glimmer myself, but maybe you can tell me what to say?"

Edessa was walking toward them now, her feet stomping on the leafy piles of money. "Dion, are you okay? I've been looking for you." She took a seat on the grass too and observed Dion's confused expression. "What? What's going on?"

"Priela wants me to help her charge. She wants me to write a letter. And I appreciate it, really. I know you're trying to make me feel better but…"

"Yes, I'd like to make you feel better, but this isn't about you. It's about Noah. He's desperate."

"He's desperate?" said Edessa, inching closer. "Why?"

Priela brushed her hair behind one ear and hesitated. She wasn't sure how to explain Noah's situation, the severity of his brother's illness, the intensity of his mother's anxiety, and the utter indifference of the insurance company. It was such a human problem, so remote from a muse's artistic sensibilities.

"So you see, Noah's brother is really sick and his family can't afford to help him. It's tearing them apart. His mom wrote a few letters to an insurance company, but she's not a lawyer. The letters didn't work."

"And you think I can do better?"

"Yes Dion, you can write anything. And I was thinking that if you used some legal terms then maybe the insurance company would be afraid of getting sued, and then…"

Dion shook her head, "Priela, using legal terminology won't make a letter sound professional. Legal writing is a craft. There's a certain way to phrase the arguments, to lay out the facts, to build a case."

"Which is exactly why I need your help. You know this stuff. You know everything about writing."

"It sounds like a horrible idea," said Edessa, leaning in. "Lady Raymere said that we can only guide our charges for the sake of art. If we use our glimmers for anything else, we'll be kicked out of class."

"I know, but we'd be inspiring Noah to write a letter. A wonderfully crafted one. And what's more artistic than that? Besides, Dion already thinks she's in danger of failing. Maybe this will convince Lady Raymere that muses don't need glimmers of their own to help humans?"

Dion picked up a leaf and twirled it between her fingers, as if she were rolling over the idea in her mind. The currency was yellow and green with an illustration of cherry blossoms in the foreground, a mountain in the distance, and an emblem in a Japanese script.

"Please, Dion. Noah's family is in a lot of pain and I can't help them without you."

"Okay, fine. I'll do it. But I want to be there when you guide him."

"I want to come too," said Edessa. "I mean, if this letter is going to work at all, it can't be written on ordinary stationery. He'll have to use some kind of professional letterhead with a logo, or an emblem, or something. I could design it."

Priela's eyes brightened and she removed a post-it from her gown and scribbled down a math problem that would take them to Noah at the present date and time. Then she solved the equation and the worlds transitioned instantly.

Now, they were in that small apartment and Noah was seated at a banged up computer, probably working on homework, his hair partially blocking his face. Priela's eyes flickered across the screen and she sighed. Human homework was so straightforward. She missed it.

"Okay," said Dion, looking him over and raising an eyebrow. "He needs to write a letter to an insurance company, right? So the first thing I need to know is… what's an insurance company?"

Priela swallowed hard, but she did her best to explain the concept and Dion started writing. At the same time, Edessa sketched a logo, integrating Noah's last name into a scales-of-justice emblem. Technically, the logo didn't use the words, *'law firm,'* anywhere. And nothing about Dion's language openly threatened a lawsuit. Although it certainly hinted in that direction, using veiled threats and overt legal language.

When the muses were done, Priela looked at Noah and focused. Then she read the letter out loud and tried to visualize the logo as clearly as possible. Nothing happened. She read it again, more slowly this time, and Noah's fingers stopped typing, until he was sitting perfectly still. She kneeled beside him and blew the hair from his face, seeing his quiet eyes. Then she put her hand on his arm, felt the warmth of his skin, and her heart started pounding. She read the letter once more, enunciating each syllable.

Suddenly her vision blurred, her ears started ringing, and her scalp began to burn. The sensation was far more visceral than her classroom experience, as if her skull were opening up and her thoughts were being wrenched from inside, the way a dentist extracted teeth.

She looked up and saw the glimmer. It was perfect in its roundness. Its light brilliant. It rose to the air, stopped short of the ceiling, and then fell like a shooting star onto Noah's forehead, quickly absorbing away. And instantly, the burning sensation was gone, releasing all pressure from Priela's head and making her thoughts feel light, as if she'd removed a weight that she hadn't even known was there. She looked into Noah's eyes and squeezed his arm, feeling a strange oneness with him, a mystical connection that made her wings glow.

Then the worlds transitioned again, returning the muses to that shady spot under the money tree. But now, Clio was there. Great.

"And what have you all been doing?" she asked, her arms crossed, her glare threatening.

"Nothing."

"You realize that you're a horrible liar, Priela?"

"Uh huh. Just add that to my list of inadequacies."

"Oh, I'll do much more than that. You've just guided someone. I can tell. It was that boy, wasn't it? The one you're obsessed with. Let me guess, you sent him a love song so that he'd fall for you?"

Priela rolled her eyes.

"It's a shame that we won't be able to enjoy your company anymore, Priela. Having you as a classmate has been so... entertaining. But I'm afraid I have no choice." Then she flapped her wings and rose to the sky.

"Where is she going?" asked Dion.

"She's going to tell Lady Raymere," said Priela, pulling on a curl.

A moment later, Clio reappeared with Lady Raymere by her side, but her instructor was dressed in a bathrobe now, her hair wrapped in a towel with dripping wet strands poking through. Priela saw her attire and cringed.

"Tell me it isn't true, Priela."

"I don't know what Clio just told you," she said, shuffling her feet from side to side. "But all I did was help Noah to write a letter."

"A love letter," said Clio.

"No, that's not true. The letter was addressed to an insurance company."

"An insurance company?" said Lady Raymere, shaking her head. "That is far worse, Priela. I specifically forbid you from using your powers beyond art."

"I know, but the letter was very well written, so..."

"So you think it will transform your charge into a brilliant novelist?"

"Uh, probably not, but..."

226

"Then what was the letter's purpose?"

"Well, I was trying to get the insurance company to pay for Noah's brother to get the treatment he needs. His brother's really sick. He can barely walk anymore and…"

"I see," said Lady Raymere, pacing beside the money tree now. "Priela, you have a kind heart, but it is not our role to help humans however we see fit. You know this. We are limited to inspiring poems, manuscripts, song lyrics. Muses do not venture into the mundane."

"But that doesn't make any sense. We have all this knowledge, this magic. Why limit it? Why not do everything we possibly can to help our charges?"

"You've fought this premise for long enough," she said drawing near, her lofty stature appearing to grow taller as she approached. "And now, you've consciously disobeyed my instructions. I cannot sanction your behavior any longer. Do not return to my class."

"But what if I promise never to do it again? What if I promise…"

"Your promises are meaningless, Priela." Then she whipped around and was gone.

Priela stared straight ahead for a moment, then her eyes shifted to Clio and her expression hardened. "Congratulations, Clio. I guess you've won. I guess I'll be leaving this place after all. Are you happy now? Are you going to celebrate? Or maybe you'll just write a victory song about how you've destroyed my entire life."

"Yes, it's so easy to deflect blame," said Clio, striding around her. "I suppose you think I've caused all this?"

"You've been out to get me since day one. You insult me constantly. You pushed me toward Noah with that raincoat and that math equation because you knew that if I saw him enough,

227

I would help him eventually. This whole thing has been one giant plot to get me kicked out of class."

"Uh, huh. Such convoluted logic. Despite what you may believe, I don't hate you, Priela. Did I nudge you in that boy's direction? Perhaps. It was certainly amusing to watch you fall for a human, just like your pathetic mother. But in the end, you've made your own choices. This wasn't my fault. It was yours."

Priela's hands balled into fists and her wings turned bright red. "What did you call my mother?"

"Come on," said Dion, rising to the air and motioning for Clio and Edessa to do the same. "Let's give Priela some space."

"Yes, let's give her all the space in the world," said Clio, lifting to the sky. "Go back to where you came from, Priela. You're not welcome here." Then she swiveled around and flew over the classroom building, disappearing beyond its roofline with Dion and Edessa trailing behind.

Priela didn't bother watching them go. Instead, her eyes followed the last remaining leaf as it drifted down from the money tree and landed silently on the grass, leaving the tree barren. Then she collapsed to her knees, put her face in her hands, and began to sob.

Chapter Twenty-nine
THE CULT OF TALENT

It was late when Priela finally returned home. She had stayed under the money tree until the edge of the sky had turned from gold, to orange, to black, digging her hands into the grass while she sat there, not wanting to let go.

Priela's reluctance to leave the muse world was stronger now than ever. There was no way to hide what she was from humans anymore, no way to avoid dancing on the edges of sanity in their world. But what was the alternative? Remain in Gaia, expelled from class and branded as a failure? The thoughts were overwhelming, filling her with guilt and shame.

The next several days passed by in a blur. Priela continued to leave her house every morning, saying goodbye to her mother as if she were still attending school. But instead she wandered aimlessly, taking no joy in the remarkable sightings around her. Sometimes she broke into the empty store facades, slipping behind the lavish window displays and into the barren spaces beyond. Then she'd curl into a ball and sleep on the floor.

She was so tired now. Barely eating. Her body aching with joints that were stiff and feet that felt weighted down. Even her sleep was fitful, her dreams frightening and bizarre.

On one occasion, Priela ripped down the notes from her bedroom walls, tearing away some paint in the process. Then she gathered the crumpled scraps, carried everything to the fireplace downstairs, and set the papers on fire. She watched the flames burn until the debris had turned completely to ash, eying glowing embers as they floated up the chimney and disappeared into the darkness. But her heart didn't mourn for the lost math equations. She just felt empty.

Evenings were the hardest. Priela said little to her family, instead spending hours just staring at her mother's art. It wasn't so long ago that the pieces looked abstract, the brushstrokes disjointed, but now the images seemed shockingly real. She'd gaze at the works glossy-eyed, trying to suppress any thoughts about her own situation.

Now, she stared at a portrait of her mother that was hanging in the narrow hallway outside her bedroom. Calliope was pregnant with Moriela in the piece, and something about it stood out from the rest. Its brushstrokes were fragmented, not long and smooth, and it was painted in greyscale, not color. Priela focused on her mother's eyes. They stared back at her with a strange mix of contemplation and yearning, as if Calliope were trying to reach her through the portrait and tell her something.

Priela hadn't floated in a while, but now she longed to know what her mom was trying to say. She located a date on the back of the frame, scribbled down a math equation, and found herself a moment later in a room that was strangely familiar, yet off somehow.

The coffee table was identical to the one they had in the den. A few vases on a shelf were identical too, and Priela naturally recognized her mother's art. Although the sofas were different, the television was much smaller and fatter, and the family room looked onto a small patio instead of opening directly into the kitchen.

Calliope was seated on the sofa, but her hair was wilder than how she wore it today. Her cheeks were flush. Her belly was very pregnant and her eyes looked tired.

"Richard came through," said Priela's father, bouncing into the room with a white binder in his hand. "We've got the funding." He looked younger too and thinner than today, although he was dressed the same as always, in his usual crisp shirt and tie.

"Congratulations, honey. That's wonderful," said Priela's mother, leaning forward and smiling. "I told you Richard was the right person to ask. He knows you. Trusts you."

"Yeah, I'm not sure why I ever believed that strangers would give me money for my company," he said, pouring himself a glass of wine from a makeshift bar in the corner and taking a seat by her side.

"You know, I used to be so intimidated by Richard. On our first day of college, I was in the dormitory setting up this ancient computer, and Richard shows up with his entourage. My new roommate. He had so many clothes, they wouldn't fit in the closet. And he had these golf clubs, and tennis rackets, and skis. But mostly, I remember his computer equipment. Thousands of dollars of professional quality stuff. All still in boxes. And I just panicked. I remember thinking, how am I ever going to compete with these rich kids? My scholarship barely covered tuition and he had everything."

Priela's father took a long sip of wine, savoring the flavor, and leaned backward on the sofa. "I mostly avoided him for weeks, and then one day I see Richard trying to write an essay by hand. Turns out, he had no idea how to set up all that equipment and he was intimidated by me too. Thought I was some kind of computer genius. I helped him get set up…"

"And now, he's returning the favor," said Calliope, tilting her head sideways. "I'm sure he still thinks you're a genius, Daniel. He's not wrong."

"Well, he doesn't know that I have a muse as a secret weapon."

"Uh, huh."

Daniel flipped through the binder now, furrowing his brow, and pointed to a page. "Listen, there's something I need to show you."

"Just tell me," she said, pushing the binder away.

"So, um…" he said, hesitating. "One of the contingencies of the funding is that we have to move our company's headquarters."

"What? You said that was only a possibility. You said, maybe someday."

"I know, but circumstances have changed."

Calliope looked away and took a few deep breaths. "When?"

"As soon as this deal closes. A month, maybe two. I realize it's sudden."

"Sudden?" Calliope's tone was measured, but her body was stiff and her left eye began twitching. Priela recognized the look. Her mother was trying to restrain anger.

"I don't know why it should make any difference where we live?" he said, taking another sip of wine. "You can fly and you can teleport through space and stuff. So you can always come back here, if you want. Besides, we should be able to afford a bigger place. So you can have that art studio you've always wanted, and Priela won't have to share a room with the new baby, and I can finally have a home office, and…"

Calliope rose to her feet and clenched her jaw. "You don't get it, Daniel. Priela won't be able to fly. This new baby won't

232

be able to fly. And I'm trying to become human too. To fit in here. I haven't flown in ages."

"Okay. So you can fly like a human, if you want. On an airplane."

"This isn't about transportation, Daniel," she said, her face turning red. "It's about our children. Where are they supposed to go to primary school? Have you even thought about that?"

"Calliope, it's not like we're moving to the middle of nowhere. There should be plenty of schools…"

"You're missing the point. I spent three years trying to get Priela off the waiting list at the fine arts academy, practically from the day she was born. And now, she's finally been accepted. She's supposed to start classes in the fall."

"I know, but I'm sure there are other art schools."

"Not like this one. Anyplace else, she'll be lucky if she winds up with an art class or two. Do you know what a mainstream education will do to our daughter if she ever transforms into a muse someday? Have you thought about her at all? It would be terrible."

"Yes, this will impact Priela," he said, standing up and placing a hand on her shoulder. "But why is that such a bad thing?"

Calliope narrowed her gaze and brushed his hand away. "After all these years, you still don't understand, do you? Talent is everything in Gaia. It's like a cult. All they care about is a person's natural gifts. But they're wrong. Do you know how I became the youngest muse ever to graduate from the institute? Practice. Dedication. Persistence. Yes, I love art. And I'm good at it. But it didn't all just come on its own. Hard work is so underrated in the muse world."

"So maybe you could practice… what do you call it? Culinary arts? Maybe learn how to cook a little?"

"You didn't just seriously say that," she said, balling her hands into fists and stepping into his face.

"Whoa. Calm down. I'm sorry."

"You have to understand, Daniel. I still remember those auditions like they were yesterday. I struggled with them myself. But for Priela, it will be awful. She'll be so far behind."

"Okay, I get it. But we don't even know if she's a muse yet. And you realize this isn't a choice, right? I didn't want to relocate either."

"I know," she said, softening her tone and glancing away. "And I want your company to succeed, Daniel. I really do. It's what we've been working toward for years and I'm so proud of you. It's just… it's not all about you and me anymore. It's about Priela and this little one." She put her hand on her belly and rubbed it.

Priela's father took another sip of wine and sighed. "Well, you're always saying that they teach the wrong stuff at that muse school anyway."

"I know."

"Okay, so what should they be teaching?"

Calliope shrugged her shoulders. "Well, someone should really teach your talent, computer programming. It's such an amazing art form."

"What else?"

She reached for the white binder which was now resting on the coffee table, and traced her finger along its slick cover. It read, *"Company Valuation and Financing Proposal."*

"This," she said. "Someone should teach muses about this."

"My business?"

"No, don't you see? Someone should teach muses life skills. Like how money works and why it's valuable. Most muses think they can help someone paint a picture and call it a day. But what

234

are humans supposed to do next? There is so much great art that is unseen and unknown. Unpublished manuscripts, paintings hidden away in dusty attics, singers whose voices have only been heard by a few. Art for its own sake is not enough when a person is struggling financially."

"True."

She returned to the sofa now and gazed forward in a wistful stare, as if she were looking into the past. "You were my test, Daniel. My experiment. I knew what was at stake. I knew the risks. But I wanted you to succeed and my guidance wasn't helping at all." She shook her head and pursed her lips. "So I rejected the cult of talent. I broke my oath. Instead of guiding your art, I helped with ordinary things. Mundane things. Like keeping you in school and securing that first job. I stopped you from wasting money. I steered you away from debt. And your art flourished all on its own. Giving humans financial freedom is the real way to set their talents free."

"You did much more than that, Calliope," he said, sitting back down beside her. "You gave me hope when I was broken. You believed in me when I was alone. Without your support, your love, I wouldn't be where I am today." He took her hand in his and squeezed it, and she rested her head on his shoulder. "We'll figure this out with Priela and the baby. I promise."

The sight faded from view, and Priela closed her eyes to extend the moment a little longer, allowing Calliope's words to echo through her thoughts. *"Someone should teach muses life skills… someone should… someone should."*

Her mother's passion was tangible and her ideas made so much sense. Calliope had risked everything to prove she could help humans thrive and she had succeeded, but the muse world rejected her anyway. Maybe Priela could fulfill her mother's vision and carry on her legacy? Maybe she could teach muses life skills? Priela's mother had sacrificed so much, she owed it to her to give it a try. Besides, she had nothing left to lose.

Priela twisted a long curl between her fingers and opened her eyes, finding herself back in the present, back in the hallway. But Calliope's self-portrait was no longer painted in shades of grey. It was in color now with vibrant greens and specks of gold. Her mother's expression was different too, the yearning now replaced by hope.

Chapter Thirty
THE HEADMISTRESS

Priela didn't know if the headmistress had another name. Everyone just referred to her as the headmistress, quieting their voices and stepping out of her way when she passed by, as if she were an ambulance whose mere appearance demanded the right of way. She'd been in the audience that first day of auditions, and despite her petite stature, she drew attention at even the most crowded of concerts with her authoritative air and her mass of silvery-white curls.

Now, Priela hesitated as she headed toward the headmistress's office, shuffling her feet and weighing her idea's merits one last time before knocking on the door.

"Come in."

Priela stepped inside and glanced around. The office was in the same location as the principal's office at East High and its dimensions were roughly equivalent, but instead of having straight walls, the space was now arched like the inside of a cave and paintings adorned every surface, even the curved ceiling. Priela looked at an image immediately to her left and her eye twitched.

"That piece is a fine example of Romanticism," said the headmistress, pulling on a silver curl. "Your mother painted it when she was about your age."

Priela didn't need clarification to know it was her mother's art, as identifiable as a fingerprint, with smooth brushstrokes that tilted to the right. But it was strange to see one of her mom's paintings outside their home, as if she'd stumbled upon an essay written in her own handwriting without having any memory of creating the piece or any knowledge of its subject matter.

She stepped back from the art to take it in. It revealed the institute's courtyard with its engraved monuments, its grassy lawn, and a far younger Lady Raymere standing alone in the shadows. There was something intimate about the piece, something deeply personal.

"Your mother and Ray were quite close back then," said the headmistress, rising from her chair and approaching. "They grew up together, you know. Discovered their talents together. Took the oath standing side by side." She narrowed her eyebrows now and pointed to the far wall where words were etched in a delicate font. "Are you familiar with the oath?"

"No," said Priela, scanning the inscription.

> *"I give my oath to the nine muse sisters, that my guidance will inspire music, and literature, and art. That I will advise my charges to set their talents free, in a manner that enriches the spirit beyond the commonplace and the mundane.*
>
> *Whatever humans I may visit, I will appear for the benefit of art alone, remaining unencumbered by other pursuits and aspirations. If I keep this oath faithfully, may the effects of my inspiration be great, and if I transgress may I leave Gaia forever."*

"Why did you come here, Priela?"

"So, I came to your office because…"

"I'm not asking why you came to my office. I'm asking why you came to Gaia."

"Oh, well…" she said, gulping down a lump in her throat. "I guess that all of my life I never really fit in, and I thought that here I'd finally belong."

"And do you belong?"

"Um, that's what I wanted to talk to you about. I'm not sure if you know, but I've been struggling with things. But I was thinking… maybe it's not just me. Maybe it's the institute."

"The institute?"

"Yes, this school teaches muses to inspire art which is great and all, but it isn't enough. Humans can't reach their full potential with art alone. But what if we started guiding our charges with ordinary tasks, like writing resumes or making smart choices about money? Just think of the possibilities… because you see when a human has financial freedom…"

"What exactly are you proposing, Priela?"

"Well, maybe I could be the one to teach muses life skills? After all, I'm half human. I know this stuff. Maybe it's been my destiny all along to connect the mundane with the magical."

"Have you learned absolutely nothing?" said the headmistress, her tone growing bitter. Then she waved an arm through the air, cutting it brusquely, and Lady Raymere appeared.

"Ray, I told you to put an end to this nonsense, to explain the truths of our world so that Priela wouldn't succumb to her mother's fate. But you've failed. She's even worse than Calliope. She still doesn't understand a muse's proper role."

Lady Raymere stiffened her jaw and eyed Priela. "I've only done precisely as you've instructed."

239

"Then why isn't this fixed?"

"Because Priela can see right through your logic. She understands that muses can help people, that we can change lives beyond art. Calliope believed it too and she begged you to change the rules, to release her from her oath. But you refused, choosing instead to make her the ultimate sacrifice to your worldview."

"My plan would have worked, if she hadn't fallen in love with that wretched human."

"You're wrong, Headmistress. Sending Calliope away didn't change her mindset. It only hardened her views. She didn't reject Gaia for a man. She rejected it because she disagreed with you. It wasn't until later that she finally found love."

The headmistress crossed her arms over her chest and began pacing in a circle, stomping her feet as she moved. "And I suppose you think I'm making the same mistake with Priela?"

"I know you want to protect the great lineage of the ancient Calliope. And Priela is the last direct descendant in that line. But you cannot mold her into someone she's not any more than you could change her mother. You cannot force Priela's obedience by expelling her from my class. You will only succeed in making her miserable. I'm surprised she's come to you at all."

The headmistress's wings flickered from silver, to pink, to green. "So what would you propose, Ray?"

Lady Raymere took a long look at Priela and sighed deeply. "I believe we have an opportunity here. Calliope's choices sent reverberations through our world that still can be felt to this day. And Priela is continuing her legacy."

"That's precisely what I'm afraid of. It is my responsibility to protect the sanctity of art and Calliope's actions went against every rule, every precedent. I'd rather have a muse leave this world, in disgrace if necessary, than have her turn it upside down, no matter how painful that may be."

"Yes, Calliope broke the rules, but she only did so to help her charges and Priela is doing the same. But it's not causing chaos like you predicted. It's not destroying art. It's making things better."

"That's not possible."

"It is," said Lady Raymere waving one arm and suddenly there was a blinding light and Priela felt her stomach lurch, as if she were falling from a great height. Then the light was gone.

Now the muses were standing on a rickety fire escape in the human realm where a window looked into Noah's small apartment. They could see him through the glass chatting with his brother, Benjamin. But the boy wasn't sick anymore. Priela could tell by the way he moved effortlessly across the small space.

Noah's mother was there too, holding up an envelope to the light. She was dressed in those unflattering green overalls from the warehouse. At least she'd managed to keep her job.

"Mom, is that another letter from the insurance company?" said Noah, grabbing the envelope away. "Don't open it."

"We can't just ignore them."

"Yes, we can. I don't know why those vultures don't just do the right thing? We shouldn't have to prove that Benjamin really needs a specialist or his new medication. We shouldn't have to prove that these treatments are finally working. His condition is chronic."

"Stop talking about me like I'm not even here," said Benjamin, taking the envelope from his brother's hands, ripping it open, and scanning the page.

"What does it say?" asked his mother.

"I think your letter worked, Noah."

"Why? Because I pretended we'd sue them?" He moved closer and looked over Benjamin's shoulder. "That's just another bill. I told you they'd never read what I wrote and even if they did, I knew they'd never take it seriously."

"No. Look at the bottom of the page, right here."

Noah glanced at the sheet again and there was a pause. "That can't be right. It says, *'Paid in Full.'*"

"Does it say why?" asked Noah's mother.

"No," said Benjamin, leaping with ease. "But what else could it be? The letter totally worked!"

"I'm so proud of you. Benjamin's going to be just fine. We're all going to be just fine."

Noah's mother wrapped her arms around her sons in a tight embrace and her eyes welled up with tears. Priela could feel her emotions emanate through the glass, radiating a joy so deep that it had a gravitational force all of its own.

"You did this?" said the headmistress, turning toward Priela now and softening her tone. She'd clearly embodied the emotions of Noah's mother too, and there were tears in her eyes.

Priela nodded.

"I cannot deny that you have helped your charge," she said, tapping one foot against the metal grate. "I cannot deny that there are things humans need to understand, things of value that extend beyond art. But just because humans should learn certain life skills does not mean that muses need to know them too."

Lady Raymere crouched down until her eyes were level with the headmistress. "I know you regret what happened with Calliope. I know it broke your heart. It broke mine too. Please, I implore you... do not make the same mistake with Priela."

"Ray, I simply cannot support her objectives. I simply cannot permit the teaching of mundane subjects at the institute.

The school has a certain reputation cultivated over millennia, a certain legacy…"

"What if my lessons weren't a part of the official curriculum?" said Priela, stepping forward. "What if I just found an empty space and my own students, and you didn't endorse anything?"

"Priela, I am responsible for the sanctity of art whether I choose to endorse such endeavors or not."

"But I'm not trying to harm art. Really. I just want to help people."

There was a long pause and the headmistress peered into the distance. "And would helping people give you what you've been searching for? Would these lessons make you feel like you finally belong?"

"I honestly don't know," said Priela, her voice cracking. "All I know is that I can barely get out of bed in the mornings. I've almost completely stopped eating. I've been having these horrible thoughts. Thoughts of going away. Thoughts of ending it all. I just feel like such a failure. I have to do something."

The headmistress sighed and a tear rolled down her cheek. "I will give you some leeway here, Priela. But if anything goes awry, your lessons will be shut down immediately."

"I understand."

"Good. Please tell your mother that she is deeply missed." And with that, she was gone.

Lady Raymere edged closer and pulled a bracelet from the folds of her gown. It was the same bracelet that Noah had given to Priela under the bleachers all those months ago, with tiny stones that glistened in the light.

"You like that boy, don't you?" she said, clasping the bracelet around Priela's wrist and waving a glittery sleeve. The motion transformed Priela's dress from a shimmering pink gown into ripped jeans and a loose fitting t-shirt, with ratty sneakers appearing on her feet, as if she were Cinderella in reverse. "Please remember that I'm watching over you." Then she tilted her head and disappeared.

Priela put her hand to her chest, unable to wrap her thoughts around everything that had just transpired, and the bracelet brushed against her heart. At that moment, Noah looked up and saw her. His expression was confused, as if she were merely an illusion. Still, he ambled toward the window and pulled it open.

"Priela? What are you doing here?"

"Quick. Come in, come in," said Noah's mother, grabbing her by the arm and dragging her forward. "That fire escape is dangerous. You realize we're a dozen stories up?"

"Yes, I know."

"Don't ever do that again. Do you understand me?" She raised an eyebrow. "Wait. You're that girl from the painting."

Priela followed her gaze, glancing over one shoulder. Hanging by the window was the human portrait of Priela, the one she'd used to thaliate and left behind.

"Um, yeah. I guess that painting looks kind of like me," she said with a nervous laugh.

"I'd think you were stalking me," said Noah. "But I haven't been able to find you anywhere."

"You were looking for me?"

Noah's cheeks turned red. "I was just, you know, worried. That's all. I haven't seen you around in a really long time. Are you okay?"

Priela glanced down at the bracelet.

"Is that the bracelet I gave you? How did you…"

"Mom, why don't we run to the grocery store?" said Benjamin, yanking on his mother's sleeve and pulling her toward the door. "You said we're out of milk? I'll go with you. Come on."

Noah watched them leave and then turned his attention back to Priela. His eyes were wide, seeing her every move, her every gesture. He ran his fingers through his hair and stepped forward, and Priela could feel his emotions with intensity. The interest. The attraction. All of it was there.

She closed her eyes, leaned in, and kissed him. It was a delicate touch, her lips meeting his, her hand lightly grazing his cheek. He kissed her back. The kiss was soft and she could feel his heart beat faster. His energy. It made her stomach flutter and her body warm.

She moved away. "I have to go, Noah."

"No, wait. Um, are you hungry? I could make you something to eat?"

"I'm fine, Noah. I need to go."

"But when am I going to see you again?"

Priela didn't answer his question. She just smiled and headed out the door.

Chapter Thirty-one
NEPTUNE BUGS

The funny triangular room with its miniscule window and slanted ceiling was empty. In the human world, it had been Mrs. Wilson's algebra classroom. The memory was not something Priela chose to dwell on. At least here, the cramped space had the potential to grow, and no one seemed to mind if she used it.

After bringing in a few stray chairs, a wipe board from home, and some school supplies, Priela pinned a signup sheet to the trials board that read, *"Learn the secrets of the human world from Calliope's daughter. Discussions held afterschool in the room beside the money tree. No auditions required."* Then she watched from behind a monument as muses read her notice. But hours passed and nobody signed up.

Even Dion and Edessa seemed uninterested, whispering something before walking away and leaving the page blank. The rejection stung, making Priela feel like her friends had slapped her in the face, and she ripped down the sheet.

Still, she didn't give up. The handwritten notice probably hadn't done enough to communicate the value of her lessons, so the next day Priela printed out a series of elaborate flyers and posted them on walls, and trees, and along stairwells. But they started to disappear. Either Gaia was vanishing them somehow, which wasn't implausible in a world that eschewed messiness, or it was Clio's handiwork, a thought that made her stomach churn.

Priela needed a method that couldn't be overlooked or sabotaged. She needed to talk to muses directly.

"Would you like to enroll in my discussion group?" she asked a group of orchestra muses as they waited outside a recital hall. "You could just give one lesson a try."

The muses were polite, listening patiently as Priela described possible lesson topics. Then the questions came.

"Is it a required course?"

"Uh, no."

"Will it improve my art?"

"Well, not exactly. But you see…"

"Who else is signed up?"

"You'd be the first!"

"Sorry," said one muse, wringing her hands. "It sounds really interesting, but I'm just too busy right now to take on anything else."

"Maybe in the fall," said another muse, shuffling her feet. "Good luck, though. Let me know how it goes."

Then the muses turned away, the first of many failed pitches where Priela's lessons were mocked, or misunderstood, or simply dismissed. She couldn't really blame anyone. After all, it was nearing the end of the semester, most muses were overwhelmed with their existing course load, and anything that didn't specifically focus on art was thought to be of little relevance. She needed a different approach, something radical.

Priela glanced at the money tree and allowed her mind to wander. The leaves were still gone, but flowers had sprouted now, made from clusters of coins. The penny flowers were prettiest, having a shimmering copper hue that set them apart from buds made of nickels, or dimes, or quarters. A buzzing insect leaped from one flower to the next.

"What do you think I should do?" she asked the bug, not expecting a response. But it stopped moving and nodded in her direction. Something about the insect seemed oddly sophisticated, even wise, and it gave Priela an idea. She should invite other magical creatures to her lessons.

Priela knew that sprites, and pixies, and minotaurs did not take classes at the institute. Although she wasn't sure if the exclusions were a clear-cut rule or a matter of choice. Either way, her lessons stood apart from the school's official curriculum and maybe if these creatures liked what she had to say they'd spread the word?

"Hi. I'm Priela and I'm going to be leading a discussion group," she said to a satyr. "I'd love for you to come."

"Baaaa," said the half-man, half-goat creature, scratching a pointed ear with a hoof that poked out from behind its blazer.

"We'll be talking about the human world. I'm kind of an expert."

"Baaaa."

Priela crouched down until she was looking the satyr straight in its eyes. Its brown irises lacked any white around the edges and its lashes were long. "I know that you can understand me," she said. "I know that you can talk. You gave a speech once by the administration building. I was there. I heard you. You can even play the flute. You're really good."

"Baaaa," it said again, wrinkling its snout and snorting.

"You realize that goats say 'Ma,' not 'Ba,' right? Sheep say, 'Ba.'"

"Maaaa," it said this time, flinging its snot in Priela's direction. The sticky mucus narrowly missed her. Still, she backed away.

Priela approached Bertha next, the giantess who had once stepped on her foot in a pointy stiletto. She reasoned that giants were basically tall humans, so the creature wasn't likely to feign ignorance or speak in animal noises.

"Hi. I'm Priela and…"

"Aren't you Calliope's daughter?" said Bertha, pulling up a white glove until it stretched the length of a hockey stick. "Your mother left Gaia in disgrace, right?"

"Um, yeah. So listen, I'm going to be leading this new discussion group and I'd love for you to come."

"And aren't you the muse who failed all of your auditions, except one?"

"Uh, yes."

"And then you were kicked out of that class too?"

"Right, me again. But…"

"So you're saying that the biggest loser in the history of the institute is now teaching classes? Don't you find that a little suspect?"

"Uh, well," said Priela, trying to restrain her irritation, but she could feel the hair on her arms bristle and her muscles grow tense. "My lessons aren't really affiliated with the institute, so…"

"And that's supposed to be a selling point?" Bertha placed her hands on her hips and grunted. "I know you think that I'm just some talentless oaf, unworthy of an artistic education. I know this is all an elaborate joke to make me look stupid."

"No. That's not what I'm doing at all."

"Well, I refuse to be mistreated," she said, spitting on the ground and stomping away.

Priela didn't watch her go. Clearly there was an undercurrent of mistrust in Gaia, a simmering of inter-species dynamics that eluded her, making her efforts pointless.

She bowed her head, walked to the triangular room, and shut the door, feeling defeated. But she didn't cry. She just collapsed to her knees and stared out the window, watching the clouds drift across the frame in silent repetition as if they were trying to lull her into a state of hypnosis.

After what felt like hours, the door swung open. Dion and Edessa were standing in the threshold.

"What are you doing here?"

"Isn't this where you're holding your discussion group?" said Dion, walking inside and taking a seat. "I thought the first lesson was now?"

"Yes, but you guys didn't sign up. I watched you read my notice and walk away."

"Does that mean we can't attend?" said Edessa. "We just wanted to ask Lady Raymere's permission first, but when we went back to the trials board the sheet was gone."

"No, it's fine. What did Lady Raymere say?"

"She told us what happened with that letter we inspired. She said it helped your charge."

"Really? Was Clio there? Did she say anything?"

Dion and Edessa exchanged glances. "Does it matter?"

"I guess not."

Priela pulled over a chair, cleared her throat, and rubbed her hands together, but she hadn't bothered to create a lesson plan believing that no one would show up, and now she wasn't sure what to say. There was an awkward moment of silence.

Dion tipped her head to one side and bit her lip. "Can I ask you something, Priela?"

"Yes. Anything."

"Do you remember when we visited Robin? You said that debt could stand in the way of a person's dreams. Is that what happened to her? Because I keep floating to see her and she has so many regrets. Robin wants to take career risks, but feels like she can't. She wants to start a family, but keeps waiting. None of it makes any sense. How can someone's life pass them by?"

"Yeah," said Edessa, her eyes growing wide. "Is debt some kind of dark human secret?"

"Um, I'm not sure I'd call it a secret," said Priela, running her fingers through her curls. "But it is something that causes a lot of unnecessary suffering. It is something that can put a human's life on hold."

"So what is it?"

Priela stretched her neck. How could she explain debt to muses? It was something a lot of humans didn't understand. The only reason she'd grasped the concept was because her father left financial statements around the house and she'd studied the math the way some kids poured over comic books, knowing every superhero, every villain.

"Well, debt is basically when a human borrows money and then she has to pay it back. Robin borrowed money to go to college."

"But that can't be right," said Dion, shaking her head. "Robin was still a teenager when she went to college."

"I know."

"So I don't understand why she waited so long to pay it back? I mean, Robin is unhappy for decades. Why didn't she just get rid of the debt and move on with her life?"

Priela scooted closer. "Dion, you have to understand that college is expensive. Very, very expensive. And Robin was working at that register in the pharmacy, so she probably wasn't earning much for a long time. It would've taken her years to pay back those loans and the debt would've ballooned."

"What do you mean?" said Edessa. "How can debt get bigger? Is it magic?"

"No, it's math."

Edessa shrugged, "I don't get it."

251

Priela sighed, glancing through the doorway at the money tree, her eyes resting on the peculiar insect that was still buzzing around. Then she rose to her feet, walked outside, and extended her hand. The tiny creature crawled onto her palm.

Priela had never been afraid of bugs, although this one was particularly ugly, even as insects go, with short thick legs and dark spots across its back. She carried it inside and shut the door.

"I don't think you want to mess with that Neptune bug," said Edessa. "They're kind of like cockroaches, but much smarter."

"Yeah, you have to be very careful what you say around them," said Dion. "They take everything literally."

Priela raised her palm up to her nose and looked directly at the creature. "Are you smart enough to solve a math problem?" she asked the bug. "Let's say your eggs could hatch every minute... how many Neptune bugs would there be in half an hour?"

Priela didn't actually believe that the insect could grasp her question. She was just trying to distract Dion and Edessa from the mathematics and then she'd explain the concept herself. But the Neptune bug didn't hesitate. After precisely one minute, it dropped a tiny yellow egg which hatched instantly, releasing another fully formed insect. The new bug looked identical to the first, but this one didn't pay much attention to Priela, darting rapidly from one side of her hand to the other.

"Uh, okay," she said, holding out her palm for Dion and Edessa to see. "So in this example, the first bug is like the money that Robin borrowed to pay for college. It's called the principle. And this second insect is like the extra amount that Robin had to pay back on top of what she borrowed. It's called interest."

"Does all debt carry interest?" asked Edessa, scrunching up her nose and inching away.

"Pretty much. It's the reason that Robin was able to get a college loan in the first place. Because she promised to pay back more than what she borrowed. Money isn't free."

Another minute passed and both insects laid eggs which swiftly hatched, releasing two more bugs. These new insects were also fully formed adults, but they were even wilder, jumping fitfully. One leaped onto Priela's other palm. Then all four insects laid eggs and there were eight bugs. A minute later, there were sixteen. Then thirty-two.

Priela cupped her hands in an effort to restrain the creatures. "You see, the thing about interest," she said, shifting her weight. "It's not just a flat fee. It's a rate. So in the same way that these new bugs are laying eggs of their own, interest also grows on itself. It's a process called compounding."

The original insect was still watching Priela and it lowered its head now as if it were signaling the others. Then there were sixty-four bugs, and a minute later one hundred and twenty eight. The bugs started crawling along Priela's arms like moving sleeve tattoos.

"This is repulsive," said Dion, gathering up her bright pink dress and rising to her feet. "Is this really what happened with Robin and her college loans? Did she really have to pay interest on the interest?"

"Uh, huh," said Priela. "Robin's debt grew out of control. It can happen whenever a human doesn't pay what she owes right away. It happened with Garrett too and that Gateway Credit Card. It's why he was evicted."

"And I suppose it also happened with Violet and those clothes she bought with that Palomar Boutique Card?" said Edessa.

"Exactly."

"Okay, we get the point," said Dion. "Now could you please put those gross things outside?"

Priela moved to the door and twisted the knob, but it wouldn't budge. She tried it again. Nothing. Why wasn't it turning now? Was the room itself magical and trying to reinforce her lesson? Were the bugs in some way responsible, or was the sudden stubbornness of the knob just bad luck? She placed one foot against the wall to amplify her strength and yanked aggressively, but her fingers slipped, hurling her to the floor and scattering bugs everywhere.

She tried to scoop them back up, but with each passing minute their numbers multiplied. The ninth minute ticked by. Five hundred and twelve bugs. Twelve minutes. Four thousand, ninety six. Fifteen. Thirty-two thousand, seven hundred and sixty eight. The bugs now carpeted the floor in a revolting mass.

"I've never seen anything so disgusting," screamed Dion, flying to the ceiling to get away. "Make them stop."

"I told you not to mess with those things," shrieked Edessa, joining her in the air.

"Stop," yelled Priela. "Stop. Stop. Stop."

But the bugs didn't stop. Instead, they continued to buzz around and lay eggs relentlessly, until mounds of insects were crawling on top of each other like a rising tide. Their wings twitched. Their eggs smelled putrid.

One bug leapt onto Priela's dress, then another, until her outfit was teaming with creatures. Next they invaded her hair like giant-sized lice, and one even crawled into her ear, buzzing with the irritating pitch of a dentist's drill. She shook her head frantically and the insects rained back down, but it was only a temporary fix.

Why had Priela used a half hour in her original equation? She knew this growth process was exponential, not linear. She knew that thirty minutes equaled over a billion bugs. A billion. The room couldn't hold that many. Not even close. The cockroach onslaught would trample their bodies and crush their bones, if it didn't smother them first.

"This is the most horrible thing ever," wailed Edessa.

Then Priela spotted the original creature. It was the only insect standing still and it was watching her carefully. "Thank you," she said, forcing a smile. "We really appreciate the demonstration, but you can stop now."

The bug dipped its head and all at once the other insects were gone. Priela picked up the original creature and raced it out the door, which swung open now without incident.

"I'm going to be sick," said Dion, rushing outside behind her and clutching her stomach.

"I'm so sorry about the bugs. Does the debt stuff at least make sense now?"

"Uh, huh. You've helped me to understand that Robin shouldn't go to college at all."

"What? That's what you took away from my lesson? No, no, no, no, no. That's entirely wrong."

"How can it possibly be wrong?" said Dion, her body buckling forward. "I need to save her from those miserable college loans." Gasp. "So that her life won't be put on hold." Gasp. "She'll be free." Gasp.

"Please don't give Robin that guidance, Dion," said Priela, stepping closer. "Please let me show you that college is worth it, even with all the debt."

Dion's wings turned lime green. Then she vomited, splattering bile across the grass. "Thanks, but uh…" She puked again. "I think one discussion was enough."

Chapter Thirty-two
TIGERS CLAD IN STRIPES

Priela was sitting on her bedroom floor, her legs crossed, her eyes staring straight ahead with an almost catatonic stillness. But behind her blank expression, her mind was racing, the thoughts coming to her in broken gusts as if they were being translated from Morse code.

Although Priela wasn't thinking about her own situation. She wasn't thinking about her failed efforts at teaching a class, or how she was completely out of options now with nothing left to do, nowhere left to go, and no world in which she belonged. Instead, she was thinking about Robin.

Dion was about to stop Robin from going to college and it seemed like a huge mistake. Priela knew that college was important, that it opened doors and helped people start a career. She even understood that college was supposed to pay for itself because college graduates made more money. And yet, Dion's logic made sense. None of those good things had happened for Robin. Her education hadn't helped her to secure a decent job, so her school loans lingered for decades making her miserable. But why? Was there something wrong with her school?

Priela rose to her feet as if her joints were stiff and her bones were frail, holding her back with one hand, steadying her weight as she moved, and clutching a handrail to lower herself down the stairs. Then she took a seat at the computer in the home office and started researching different colleges online, entering graduation rate data, and job placement figures, and incomes for degree holders into a spreadsheet.

She organized the schools by type, grouping together public-sector schools, and private colleges, and places designed to make a profit, and sorting the institutions from the most selective schools to non-selective ones. Then she graphed everything.

What she found was unsettling, sending a cold shiver down her spine as if she'd opened a cursed tomb and released something ugly. Yes, the graduates of some colleges earned plenty of money, but not all schools were the same. Students who attended for-profit institutions, like CSL where Robin ended up going, were actually worse-off than before getting a degree. They tended to earn less money, with the added burden of debt, and most students dropped out of their programs long before finishing.

"Really?" said Priela out loud, her demeanor instantly revitalizing as though she'd been shaken aggressively. "Robin needs to go somewhere else." Then she jumped out of her chair, rushed through the door, and flew to the institute with uncharacteristic speed.

It was possible that the headmistress had already vanished her classroom since her first lesson definitely went awry. And even if the room was still there, she didn't think that Dion or Edessa would show up. But she felt compelled to go anyway, just in case.

Fortunately, the triangular space was exactly how she'd left it and about ten minutes after she arrived the classroom door pushed inward.

"We're just going to keep this thing open," said Dion, propping the door in place with a stack of books. "You know, because of the bugs."

"I'm really glad you came back."

"Well, we weren't planning to," said Edessa, tiptoeing inside. "But Lady Raymere kind of forced us."

"Yeah, she didn't care at all that we were almost smothered to death. She said there was only one factor that mattered."

"What?"

"She wanted to know if we learned anything."

"Oh," said Priela nodding, but she could feel her stomach flutter. She longed for Lady Raymere's approval and for her peers' respect, and it felt good to finally receive a little even if it was reluctant in nature. "So listen, I have a plan to make Robin's life better but you're going to have to trust me." She reached a hand in Dion's direction. "We need to visit Robin again, in the present time."

"Why? What's the plan?"

"I don't have time to explain. If we don't leave right now, we'll miss our chance."

Dion's eyebrows narrowed doubtfully, but she clasped Priela's hand. "Uh okay, I guess. Lady Raymere told us to listen to you." Then Dion began to recite a familiar sonnet, skipping ahead to the poem's last quatrain and finishing the final couplet before they were whisked away.

> *"Robin, to see you on a day unknown*
> *Where crazy tigers clad in stripes abound*
> *A fearful choice you may someday bemoan*
> *'Till poise and strength, your muse, in you has found*
>
> *To stay, to learn, a mind open to keep*
> *And then success, your dreams you now shall reap"*

The air was sharp this time, the light flashing in a fragmented rhythm. It carried the muses back to that Princeton University reception, landing them in the same striking house overlooking the city, with clusters of people sipping lemonade and chatting in vibrant orange and black attire. Uncle Richard was there again, welcoming students at the door, and Robin was still young and dressed in that same yellow outfit as before.

Although months had passed since their original visit and this moment wasn't the future anymore. It was the present day. The present time. Priela could tell because the shadows were aligned with the crowd's movements and everything was in focus, revealing the full grandeur of the view.

Priela moved closer to Robin until she could feel the girl's emotions fuse with her own, sensing her growing discomfort, her tense muscles, her quickly beating heart. And she could hear the words of Mrs. Tucker, that vile college counselor, already replaying through Robin's mind.

"Do you honestly believe that you'll measure up to those prep school kids, Robin? Do you really think they'll accept you? That you'll ever fit in at a place like Princeton?"

Robin's body began visibly cowering. She looked terrified.

"You need to stop her from running away, Dion," said Priela, firmly.

"No, I want Robin to run away. She shouldn't go to college at all."

"But this place is different from CSL."

"Why? She still can't afford it."

"I know, but Robin should strive for the best education possible. A school that will challenge her. A school that will value her. Like this one. It makes a difference."

Dion crossed her arms over her chest and frowned. "Even if I wanted to stop her, she's totally intimidated by these people. I can feel it."

"Yes, I feel it too." Priela pointed now at the man she called Uncle Richard. "Do you see that guy over there with the orange bowtie?"

"Yeah."

"Well, he went to college with my dad and he's the closest thing my father has to a brother. But it wasn't always like that. When they first met my dad was totally intimidated by Richard because he had everything… golf clubs, computer equipment. But my dad had no reason to feel inferior. And it's the same thing with Robin. She belongs here just as much as anyone else."

"Maybe, but…"

Robin's head tilted downward, her feet pivoted toward the exit, and she clutched her purse, about to flee.

"Dion, Lady Raymere told you to listen to me, right? I'm trying to fix things for Robin, but if we don't do this right now, we'll miss our chance."

"Alright, fine," she said. "I'll try." Then she closed her eyes, gritted her teeth, and time began to slow down. The guests' movements became more exaggerated and robotic before coming to a standstill, and Robin's escape was halted, her foot stalled mid-air.

Lady Raymere had talked about freezing time, but this was the first moment Priela had really seen it. When she had guided Noah with the letter, he was sitting all alone. Had time actually stopped then or had Noah merely paused long enough to hear her? The whole concept of freezing time had been an abstraction, an idea. But now there could be no doubt.

Someone in the crowd had flung a jacket over his shoulder and it was suspended in the air. Another guest was pouring lemonade and the liquid was now inert. The people looked eerie in their frozen state, like figures in a wax museum. It was disconcerting.

"Go ahead," said Priela, swiveling back to Dion and pulling on a curl. "Guide her."

"I want to, but I can't."

"What do you mean?"

"Dion's glimmers haven't become any stronger," said Edessa, shaking her head. "They're still really dim like before. They won't work."

"Maybe you could guide her, Priela?"

"Dion, you know it doesn't work that way. You're Robin's muse. You're the only one who can send her a glimmer." Priela glanced back at Robin. Her expression was so tortured. "Please, just try."

Dion sighed. "So what exactly am I supposed to tell her? Not to run away?"

"What should Robin hear right now? What does she *need* to hear?"

"Whatever it is," said Edessa, pointing. "You'd better hurry. I just saw that woman blink and there's one over there whose foot moved. They're all coming back to life. Time is about to start again."

Priela clasped Dion's hands in her own. "You can do this."

Dion nodded. Then she planted her feet firmly, looked over at Robin, and took a deep breath. "Robin, you are worthy," she said. Her tone was soft but deliberate, and her wings started glowing. "Stay at this party. Keep an open mind." She stepped closer and repeated her words, with more fervor this time. "You are worthy."

A glimmer arose from Dion's thoughts. The orb of light was faint. Its shape was round but lacking in firmness, and it was moving at a glacial pace. There was a chance it would dissolve into nothingness or simply fall apart before reaching Robin, but at least it was heading in the right direction and the distance was short.

A man in the crowd suddenly tilted his palm to one side. The lemonade started flowing.

"Come on. Come on," said Edessa.

Inch by inch the glimmer moved closer to Robin, its light becoming stronger as it traveled, its outline gaining definition. Then the orb touched Robin's forehead and it melted into her skin, like ice on hot pavement. There was a sizzling noise and the muses cheered. Not a moment later, the chatter of the party resumed and time began moving forward once more.

Robin spun back toward the party, straightened her spine, and expanded her chest, and Priela could hear her thoughts resonate.

"So what if I'm not dressed in those dumb tiger colors like everyone else?" she told herself. *"So what if I don't know anyone? I have just as much right to be at this party as anybody else. I'm just as worthy. Just as deserving. Just as capable."*

Robin's expression broadened into a smile and Priela could feel the girl's insecurities falling away, as if she were a butterfly shedding its chrysalis and emerging as a more magnificent being.

"Excuse me. Are you Robin? Robin Thompson?" said a woman, tapping her on the shoulder. The woman was wearing a tailored white suit that offset her dark complexion and her hair was woven into numerous tiny braids.

"Yes, that's me."

"Hi, I'm Evelyn Moore from Princeton's Admissions Office," she said, extending her hand. "I was hoping you'd be here. I just wanted to reassure you that the situation with Mrs. Tucker has been taken care of."

"What situation? What are you talking about?"

Evelyn bit her lip. "Oh… I thought you knew. Your college counselor contacted us."

"Why? What did she say? Please tell me."

Evelyn shook her head and her tone hardened. "Well, she claimed that you cheated on your standardized tests, but don't worry. There was an investigation and we didn't find any evidence of wrongdoing. So I visited East High to speak with Mrs. Tucker personally and I figured out what was really going on." Evelyn visibly tensed now, touching one hand to her temple and rubbing her dark skin with a thumb. "Let's just say that woman has no business being a college counselor and I can promise you that she won't be returning to East in the fall."

"She's leaving? Why?"

"I simply had a conversation with the school board and explained the situation."

"And they believed you? They believed you, instead of her?"

"What they believed was irrelevant. Princeton has relationships. So I informed them that if they wanted their students to gain admission to any selective institutions including ours in the future, they'd need credible college counselors in the district. Counselors who act in the best interests of their students. *All* of their students." Evelyn exhaled audibly and her tone took a gentle shift. "Now Robin, I'm really hoping you'll choose Princeton."

Robin twisted one foot behind the other. "I would love to, but I'm just not sure how I'm going to afford college. Any college."

"Listen, our financial aid packages are very generous. They include grants that don't need to be repaid. And even if you don't qualify, there are all kinds of ways we can help. There are campus jobs and outside scholarships. By any chance do you have an interest in engineering or computer science? Because I have a stack of scholarship information for young women pursing technical fields."

"Well," said Robin, her eyes sparkling. "I told myself to keep an open mind."

The wind began to swirl now, catapulting the muses deep into the future. Priela watched the air whirl by in giant chunks, catching glimpses of Robin between the pockets of brightness. But the sensation was more confused than usual, with Robin's image growing old, then young, then older again, as if the future were shifting in a new direction.

"Do you think my glimmer made a difference?" shouted Dion over the deafening whizz. "That it helped her?"

Priela narrowed her gaze. Robin would likely attend a more rigorous college institution now, one with a greater focus on academics than on churning through students. She might even choose a different field of study, one in greater demand. And Robin would likely accomplish it all with less debt. Much less. "I think so," she said, nodding.

A moment later, the muses found themselves in a large private office with striking mountain views. Robin was there behind a desk, her elbows resting lightly on its surface. She looked a bit older but her demeanor was calm, her skin glowing. Etched on a nameplate were the words, *"Robin Thompson, Executive Vice President."*

There was a knock and Priela's father entered the room briskly, taking a seat across the desk. Was Robin working for Priela's dad now at his software company?

"So Robin, you're starting maternity leave this Friday?" he said, the fine lines around his eyes more evident than normal.

"Uh, huh," said Robin, leaning backward in her chair and resting one hand on her belly. Her amber colored blouse did little to conceal that she was pregnant.

"Please tell me one more time that you'll be back because we really need you here. We've never had such a gifted software designer leading the division. My wife would say that you have an exceptional muse."

"Really?" whispered Dion and her wings began to flutter, turning from pink, to orange, to gold.

"You don't have to worry, Daniel," said Robin. "I'm coming back in August. My husband and I will figure out how to balance our family life with work. Honest. I'm not leaving. I love it here." Her smile was radiant. "Oh, and thanks again for the crib. That was a wonderful gift."

Edessa leaned in. "Priela, do you think we could fix Anton's future next? You have another discussion scheduled for next week, right? Just tell me what to do for homework. I'll do anything."

Priela didn't have a chance to respond. At that moment, the wind swept up and took her breath away.

Chapter Thirty-three
LEGACY

The world shifted the day Kalista's mother died. The change was almost imperceptible, like a drop of rain missing from a storm, but Priela could see it in her best friend's eyes where a light faded, leaving Kalista grounded in a stark reality from that day onward.

"When you were my age, who was your best friend?" Kalista had asked Priela's mother at the time.

"Her name was Ray," said Calliope, bringing over mugs of hot chocolate and wrapping a blanket around Kalista's shoulders.

"Is she still your best friend?"

"Well, I still care for her. But I'm afraid we chose different paths a long time ago."

Kalista turned sharply in Priela's direction and clutched her hand. "But that's not going to happen with us, right Priela? You'll never leave me."

"Never."

It wasn't until this week that Priela matched that memory from long ago with Lady Raymere. Her mother and her Muse Essentials instructor were once extremely close, but differing belief systems and an opposing set of choices drove them worlds apart. Still, the bond lingered. Lady Raymere continued to watch over Priela, like a strict fairy godmother. Priela was the one who'd broken her promise of friendship.

Now she ascended the stone front steps to Kalista's home, dressed in human clothing. But the clothes felt strange, the fabric itchy and stiff. She climbed the stairs one at a time, pausing, stalling, and then moving forward again, her thoughts overwhelmed with guilt.

Would Kalista still be able to see her? Priela had ignored her friend for months, not answering a single call or text. Did they still share an emotional connection, making Priela real in Kalista's world? Or would she remain in muse form, her body invisible, her knocking undetectable and silent?

Priela reached the top landing and raised up her hand, but the door swung open before she touched it.

"What do you want?" said Kalista, pushing her glasses across the bridge of her nose.

"I just wanted to see you."

"Uh, huh."

"I'm sorry I haven't returned your calls."

"That's it? Do you have any idea what you've put me through?"

"I know, I'm sure you were worried about me, but…"

"Worried? Priela, for months I've stood up for you against all of those rumors at school. I kept making excuses for why you weren't showing up, saying that you weren't feeling well, or that you'd had an emergency, and that you'd be back soon. Do you have any idea what it's like to apologize for someone all the time? And now everyone thinks I'm delusional."

"What rumors? What are they saying?"

Kalista pursed her lips and tapped one foot against the floor. "You can't be serious? Haven't you looked at anything that's been posted on your wall?"

Priela shook her head.

"They've been saying that you went crazy like your mother. That you were sent away to a mental institution or something. But I know that's not true. I know why you really left."

"You do?"

"Oh, don't pretend like you haven't figured it out," said Kalista, her irritation tangible. "I was the one who set you up with Noah under the bleachers. I thought you liked him and that he liked you. But I know it didn't go well. Noah said you yelled at him and ran away. And now you hate me."

"What? No, that's not it at all."

"It's okay. I know I messed up. But I would've thought you'd talk to me, or scream at me, or something. I never thought you'd just leave. I never thought you'd punish me like this for months."

"I didn't go away because of you."

"Sure."

"No, really. I left because… well, those rumors weren't wrong. In a way, I did turn in to my mother."

"So you're?"

"Different that's all. I'm just different now."

"And this whole time, you've been at an institution? With people who're… like you?"

"I guess you could say that."

"I don't believe you."

Priela twisted a long curl between her fingers and bit her lip. Then she pulled out her cell and swiped to a picture of her bedroom, taken before she'd ripped off the math equations from her walls. The place looked like the byproduct of a legitimately troubled mind.

"I know I should've talked to you Kalista, but I was afraid of what you'd think. I didn't want you to judge me."

"You know I'd never do that. You're my best friend."

"I'm so sorry."

Kalista lunged forward and hugged her, and Priela nestled into her warm embrace, "I've missed you so much."

"Me too."

Then they made their way inside, bee-lining to the kitchen, and Priela glanced around. The last time she'd been here, Noah was digging at the door with his screwdriver. It felt like a lifetime ago.

"Kalista, I know this is a strange question, but do you mind if I talk to your dad? I need his help with something."

"Why?" she asked, grabbing a plate of cookies and handing one over. "Are you sick? Because you know that he writes wills for people when they die."

"I know," said Priela, taking a bite and shaking her head. "It's not for me. It's for Mr. Stuart."

"Who?"

"Your dad knows him. Mr. Stuart is about to change his will, but it's a mistake."

Kalista gulped down the cookie and rolled her eyes. "I'm sure my dad knows what he's doing. Besides, why do you care? Is Mr. Stuart supposed to leave you money or something?"

"No, it's nothing like that. It's just… I've seen what happens to Mr. Stuart's sons in the future and that document is going to rip them apart."

"You saw the future?" she said with a laugh. "How? Did you discover a time machine or something? I guess you really did go crazy, huh?"

Priela stiffened and her hands turned cold. She had expected this reaction, fearing that her words wouldn't be believed, dreading the taunts that came with being different. But Kalista's mocking stung even more than she'd imagined. "Please don't say that, Kalista. Not you."

"You're being serious?"

Priela nodded.

"I'm sorry, I didn't mean it like that." Kalista moved closer and lowered her voice. "You know that you can talk to me about anything, right? Whenever you're ready. I swear, I won't judge. And it's fine if you want to talk to my dad. He should be home soon. But no guarantees that he'll listen. Just promise that you'll never disappear like that again."

Kalista reached out her hand and Priela took it, squeezing firmly.

"I promise."

***

The next day, Priela was back in her triangular classroom. Although this time Edessa and Dion arrived early, their wings fluttering excitedly, their arms overflowing with paintings and books.

Priela told them about Kalista's father, describing the man in affectionate terms, and holding out hope that her recommendations would be taken seriously.

"How do you know that he'll take your advice?" said Dion, her eyes wide.

"I don't."

"Okay, but if Kalista's father does say something then the brothers' lives will be better?" asked Edessa.

"I don't know that either. Anton and Garrett are pretty stubborn. So my talk with Kalista's dad might not have changed things at all."

"But it might have made a difference, right?"

Priela shook her head.

"Then let's go see them."

Edessa sprung up from her chair and grabbed her paintings. The first portrait was the same cubist image of Mr. Stuart that she'd used before, where the central figure was looking downward, and sideways, and a little over his shoulder at the same time. Although now, Priela could clearly identify Mr. Stuart and she recognized Kalista's abstracted father in the foreground too.

A moment later, the air was carrying the muses back to that same law office with its dark mahogany furnishings and its rows of books. But now, it was the present day, with shadows that tilted at precisely the right angle.

Kalista's father and Mr. Stuart were already engrossed in conversation, but something was different this time. Kalista's father had an intensity in his gaze that hadn't been there before and his jaw was now resting on his fist.

"That's right," said Mr. Stuart, clearing his throat and straightening his bowtie. "I want to leave the business to Anton in its entirety."

Kalista's father leaned in, "Can I offer some unsolicited advice?"

There was a pause and Mr. Stuart's eyes flickered to the ceiling. He seemed to be weighing the idea, afraid of what he might hear.

"Say, 'yes,'" whispered Priela. "Please just say, 'yes.'"

"Um, yeah. Okay."

"I really don't think it's wise to favor one son over the other. Not like this. Not in your will. Garrett deserves a level playing field, a chance to be successful."

"I understand what you're saying Hank, but you don't know my son. He's had some problems. He's been in rehab. He's been

271

in jail. He's emotionally…" Mr. Stuart strained his neck, searching for the right word. "Fragile. If I leave the business to both of them equally, I'm not sure if Garrett would even show up to work and Anton would have to deal with that. It's not right."

"Look, Anton's going to have to deal with Garrett no matter what you decide. This inheritance will only breed resentment. It sends Garrett the message that you don't trust him… that you think he's destined to fail."

"And what if he does fail? What if Garrett destroys the business for both of them? This way, at least Anton can financially support his brother and they'll both have a little money to live on."

"Is that really what you want? For Anton to become a caretaker and for Garrett to become a dependent? The boys will live up to the expectations you set." Kalista's father sighed deeply and tapped a pen against the desk. "Tell me, what was it that made Garrett so fragile? What caused his behavior to spiral out of control?"

Mr. Stuart cracked his knuckles in rapid succession and averted his eyes. His discomfort was palpable. "It's all my fault. When Sheila passed away I didn't handle it well. She was always so wonderful with the boys, so loving. I've never been very good with that kind of stuff and Garrett's never been the same."

"So there's your answer. If you want Garrett to turn his life around, you need to show him love. The hardware store is not your legacy. Those boys are."

"It's just too late, Hank. I've missed my chance. I'm dying."

"You're alive today. I wouldn't try to change your will right now. It's fine the way it was written originally, with both of your sons sharing in the business. Just go talk to them. Say whatever it is you need to say."

Mr. Stuart's hands stopped shaking and Priela could feel a shift in his energy. It was a reawakening of sorts, snapping him out of his desperate state and filling him with a sense of hope. He rose from his chair slowly and extended his hand. "Thank you. Thank you so much!"

Then the wind rose up and floated the muses into the future. Although the transition was swift this time, bringing them forward by only hours, and landing them at the small hardware store. Mr. Stuart was marching down an aisle, with his teenaged sons shuffling behind.

"See this?" he said, tapping one hand against a bin of screws. "We're almost out of the one inch size. It's time to reorder."

"Why are you telling us all this stuff, Dad?" said Garrett. "You hate it when we roam around here."

"Are you feeling okay?" asked Anton.

"No, but we'll get to that in a moment. Look, we're running low on drywall nails too."

Garrett growled. "Just tell us what's going on."

"I'm trying to teach you about the store."

"Yeah, I got that. But why?"

Mr. Stuart stopped moving and his muscles visibly tensed. "I know that I haven't been a very good father to you boys. When Sheila… when your mother… when…" He swallowed hard. "I know that I should have discussed it with you. Been there for you. Instead, I acted as if nothing happened. I didn't get us the help we all needed and I'm so sorry."

Garrett and Anton exchanged glances.

"Garrett, when we lost her you were just coming in to your own, and everything that's happened to you since then, the drinking, those nights in jail, it's all been my fault."

"I've made my own choices, Dad," said Garrett, gritting his teeth. "It has nothing to do with you or Mom."

"It has everything to do with me and the situation I've put you in. And I want you to know that I've never stopped loving you." He put a hand on his son's shoulder. His gaze was piercing. "You still have so much potential, Garrett. I believe in you."

Garrett pushed his father's hand away. "Uh, huh. Whatever."

"And I love you too, Anton," said Mr. Stuart, swiveling around. "You've always been so responsible, so conscientious, and those are wonderful traits. But I want you to remember that life is about balance. It's okay to live a little, to have some fun."

"Really?" said Garrett. "You're talking about balance? You've never missed a day of work, ever."

"Dad, be honest," said Anton. "What's this really about? You're scaring us."

Mr. Stuart's tone grew coarse, the words rolling off his tongue with an unnatural cadence, as if his mouth had suddenly gone dry and the muscles in his jaw had slackened.

"I'm dying," he said. "Soon, you will inherit my business, both of you equally. And I want you to know that it's just a store… if it survives… if it doesn't… it doesn't matter. The business isn't my legacy, you are. So whatever paths you take in life, I need you to know that I will always be proud."

Garrett and Anton exchanged glances again and their expressions changed, as if someone had removed meticulously crafted masks to reveal their true selves. Garrett's mask was arrogant and brash while Anton's was mature and steady, but beneath them they were both just frightened boys.

At that moment the air rose up, floating the muses forward to one last moment in time. Through the rings of brightness, Priela could make out the frame of the hardware store, melting, transforming, and then growing anew.

When the light stopped the muses were in the very same location, but years had passed and now the building was clad in walls of glass. The rows of screws, and paint, and tools were gone. In their place, were small cubicles filled with people. But these employees weren't wearing black aprons, like before. They were dressed eclectically and they were working as artists and designers, architects and engineers. The muses could just tell.

On the wall, a sign read, *"Stuart Brothers' Custom Design."* What was once a hardware store was now a full-fledged design firm.

Edessa's eyes darted around the space. "Anton can't even draw a stick figure no matter how many glimmers I send him. And now, he's giving all these artists a career? I can't believe it. He's bringing their gifts to the world!"

"And look," said Dion pointing, as Anton rushed by. "He's wearing a wedding ring. Wasn't he all alone before?"

"Yes," nodded Edessa. "He was so lonely. Maybe something his father said changed things? Maybe when he told him that life was about balance?"

The muses followed Anton into a corner conference room, where Garrett was already waiting. Anton had aged much the same as before, but Garrett looked significantly better this time around. His frame was more muscular, his teeth were whiter, and even his skin had a healthy glow. The brothers exchanged a smile, and employees started to shuffle in, filling the conference room to capacity.

"We have an important announcement," said Garrett, when the last employee squeezed into the space. Then he put an arm over his brother's shoulder and the room quieted down. "Years ago, when our father passed away and left this place to Anton and me, the first thing I wanted to do was burn it down, take the money, and run. But Anton was so stubborn, he wouldn't allow it." Garrett playfully pushed his brother away and the employees laughed.

"But over time, I came to love working here. It allowed me to make a difference, to take my father's store and build it into something new. Every day, I remembered what he said before he died, that he believed in me, and I just couldn't let him down. So today, Anton and I want to do something to show that we believe in all of you too. We're creating an educational scholarship fund for Stuart Brothers' employees and their families."

The employees clapped while Priela, Edessa, and Dion looked on, their eyes bright, their wings fluttering.

Chapter Thirty-four
CALLIOPE

Most sprites were green, but the one standing in Priela's garden had skin so paper-thin that its veins could be seen coursing beneath, giving him a purplish hue. Still, the creature was handsome and Priela guessed he was one of Dion's brothers because he shared her elongated proportions and enchanting eyes.

"Excuse me," said Priela, opening the sliding glass door and taking a step outside. But at that moment she transitioned between worlds, entering the human realm now, and the sprite promptly disappeared. She glanced around and saw her mother, standing behind an easel, her brush dancing effortlessly across the canvas. Had her mom caused her to switch worlds?

"Hi," said Priela, walking closer and looking at the art.

Calliope's painting was an accurate portrayal of the sprite, but from a human's perspective the image would have seemed eerie, the creature's smirk brazen, its frame alarmingly thin, like some demonic creature. And yet, the portrait was weirdly evocative.

"Who do you talk to when you're out here, Mom?"

"Sometimes I can still see them," she said, squinting at the spot where the sprite had been standing and exhaling loudly. "But they're so faint now. I'm not sure if there's actually something there, or if it's all just in my head."

Priela nodded. It was strange how much her perception of her mother had changed. She used to think Calliope was odd, but now as she watched her mother struggle to glimpse beyond her world, she seemed very human. Even her wings were different from other muses, still beautiful, but much more frail like appendages that had atrophied from little use.

"Mom, have you lost your powers?"

"It's like anything else, Priela. Imagine a person who learns a skill at an early age, like how to speak French, or how to play the piano, or how to dance ballet. Then years go by and she has no use for the skill. It's not that she's lost her power to speak French exactly. Although she may have forgotten how."

"So you can't fly anymore? You can't guide humans?"

"To be honest, I can't recall the last time I tried."

Priela traced one finger along the painting's frame. "At least you still have your art."

"Yes. I was never able to let that go."

"Why don't you sell your paintings, Mom? They're so amazing. They could inspire people."

Calliope shook her head. Then she lifted the canvas off the easel and set it aside. "I just don't think it would be fair for a muse to compete in the art world. It would be like a superhero racing in the Olympics. They would outrun everyone."

"But you're not really a muse anymore, Mom. You belong in this world. I can tell."

Calliope smiled weakly and her eyes shifted to the clouds. "I wish that were true, but I'm not sure I belong anywhere."

"Do you miss Gaia?"

"I don't regret my choices, if that's what you're asking. I have a wonderful life with Dad and you girls." She bit her lip and her eyes flickered across the sky. It was grey and dreary. "But yes, there are things that I miss."

"Like Lady Raymere? She misses you."

Calliope flinched, her head turning sharply in Priela's direction, her gaze snapping back into focus. "How do you know her?"

"She teaches Muse Essentials."

"Oh, that figures," she said with a laugh. "Ray was always pretty good at magic, but architecture was her true talent. Your Uncle Richard lives in one of her houses. It's this striking place on a hill. The very last structure she ever inspired."

"Her very last? What happened? Why did she stop?"

"Well you have to understand, Ray always saw the world through the lens of art, but that changed with Mr. Stuart. He was one of her charges."

"Lady Raymere was Mr. Stuart's muse?"

"Um, yes. And naturally she wanted to turn the guy into an architect. But it wasn't in him. Her glimmers only made Mr. Stuart more and more destitute. But then one day, he had the chance to buy this little hardware store. I pushed her and she guided him." Calliope folded up the easel now and leaned it against a wall. "That choice changed Mr. Stuart's future. His life was never particularly inspired, but after that it became much more stable. He could finally pay his rent. He married. Had two boys, I think. And Ray was never the same."

"So Lady Raymere abandoned architecture because her beliefs changed and she didn't want to break her oath? And you did the opposite, so you had to leave Gaia?"

"It's a little more complicated than that," said Calliope with a sigh. "I'm just glad that you've found your place there. The muse world is so unforgiving."

"Yeah," said Priela, yanking on a curl. "About that. There's something I haven't told you, Mom. And I know I should've said something sooner, but…"

At that moment, the glass door slid open and Priela's father stepped outside. "Hello," he said, walking closer and giving them each a kiss.

"Could you give us just a minute, Daniel?"

"No, it's okay. Dad should hear this too." Priela looked from her mother to her father and her stomach churned, the bile rising into her throat and tasting foul. "So I know you're going to be mad, but please just hear what I have to say. Please just give this idea a chance. You see, I was kicked out of class…"

"Why? What happened?" said her father, frowning.

"It's a long story, Dad. You wouldn't understand."

"Don't patronize me, Priela. What did you do?"

"Uh, okay," she said, shuffling her feet and swallowing hard. "This probably won't make sense, but about a month ago…"

"A month ago? You haven't been in class since then? Are you serious, Priela?"

"Yes, but it's alright because…"

"No, it's not alright." Priela's father shook his head furiously and the strength of his voice cranked up several notches. "You are not dropping out of high school, understand? If you're failing at the academy, then…"

"It's called the institute and I'm not flunking, Dad. I just kind of… broke the rules, but…"

"That's much worse, Priela. I realize things might be different at that place, but it doesn't mean you can just behave however you want. It doesn't mean you can disobey your teachers. You're going back to East High, starting tomorrow." Then he pivoted around and stomped back into the kitchen.

Priela chased after him. "But I can't go back there, Dad."

"This isn't negotiable."

"No, you don't get it…"

"No, you don't get it, Priela," he said, tensing his jaw. "I've given you a lot of leeway on this whole school choice thing. I even kept my mouth shut when I learned that you were only enrolled in a single course. I knew that you were going through a lot, and your mother said it would take time for you to adjust. But breaking the rules… getting kicked out of class… this crosses the line."

Calliope stepped between them. "Priela, if you haven't been going to school, then where have you been going every day? What have you been doing?"

"That's what I've been trying to tell you guys. It's not what you think. Technically, I'm still going to school. It's just that I'm not taking classes anymore. I'm teaching them now."

"You're doing what?" said Priela's father.

"I'm teaching some lessons."

"In what? Math?"

"No, my classes are about… It's hard to explain, Dad."

"Try me."

Priela rounded the kitchen counter and swallowed again, feeling the dry gulp push its way down her esophagus. Somehow, she had to make him understand. "So, I'm teaching muses about life-skills."

"What's that supposed to mean?"

"I got the idea from something Mom said once. She was talking about how giving humans financial freedom sets their talents free."

"And that's what your classes are about?"

"Yes. You see, everything makes sense to me now. I understand why Mom rejected Gaia. I understand…"

"Priela, your mother was an adult when she rejected that place. When you're an adult you can form your own belief-system too. You can even teach classes about it, if that's what you want. But for now, you need to stay in school."

"Daniel, I think there's a larger issue at stake here," said Calliope, nudging him aside. "Priela's lying. The institute would never allow the kinds of lessons she just described."

"I'm not lying, Mom. The headmistress agreed that there were things of value beyond art."

"That's not possible."

"It's the truth. Apparently, she really regretted what happened with you. She said you're deeply missed. So Lady Raymere convinced her not to make the same mistake twice."

Calliope gasped, her face turned ghostly pale, and she buckled over, as if she'd suddenly been punched in the gut.

"What's going on, Mom? Are you okay?"

Priela's father rubbed a hand along her back. "Take a deep breath, Calliope." Then he loosened his tie and glanced over one shoulder. "The headmistress is your grandmother, Priela."

"What? No. My grandmother's dead."

Priela's father shook his head.

"That's what Mom always told me. So she was lying this whole time?"

"I wasn't lying, Priela. I said that your grandmother wasn't a part of this world... that she was in a different dimension, a place of beauty."

"Uh, huh. And how was I supposed to interpret that information?"

"Enough with the sarcasm," said Priela's father. "It's the same thing. When you were born your mother reached out to her and she didn't want anything to do with you. Your mother hasn't spoken to her since."

"She didn't want to see me? Why?"

"Apparently, you broke the bloodline or something because you didn't have wings. Your mother was just trying to protect you."

A moment passed and Priela's wings darkened, fading from a pale pink, to a muted purple, to a deep blue. "Well, maybe now that I'm a muse…"

"Priela, what you are shouldn't matter," said Calliope, straightening her stance and gritting her teeth. "You're her granddaughter. She should love you no matter what. Support you no matter what. Believe in you no matter what."

"You're right, Mom. But please… you need to believe in me too. I'm not lying. I'm really teaching muses about life skills."

Calliope stepped closer and raised her chin as though her penetrating gaze could discern if Priela was telling the truth. "And these lessons are helping people?"

"Uh, huh."

"And my mother… she knows this? She's allowing it?"

"Yes. The whole reason I got kicked out of class was because I helped my charge to write a letter. But the letter helped him. It made his life better. And she saw that. It's like I've finally found my place. Like I'm still different from everyone else, but in a good way. And I think I was always meant to bring together Gaia and the human world. I think this was always my destiny."

A tear ran down Calliope's cheek and she wiped it away. "Daniel, we have to let Priela keep teaching. We must."

"This isn't about her lessons," he said, taking off his suit jacket and draping it across a chair. "Priela needs to stay in school. She can't just drop out. She's welcome to do whatever else she wants in her free time."

Priela glanced upward and ran her fingers through her hair. There had to be some way to do both, to attend classes and teach them too. But even if she auditioned at the institute again, her art hadn't improved, so she wasn't likely to be chosen for anything new. And just the thought of going back to East made her nauseated, the way a single incidence of food poisoning forever deterred people from eating a particular dish. Although Priela had endured the toxin of human-schooling for years, always hating how different she'd felt from everyone else. And now, her oddities would be greatly amplified.

"What if Priela enrolled in some classes at a local college in the fall?" said Calliope, tilting her head. "The math and science courses at East are too easy for her anyway. It's part of why she feels so out of place there. And a college schedule would give her the flexibility to keep teaching."

"Really? Calliope, you're the one who's always saying that she can't switch back and forth like that. You're the one who's always saying that she can live as a muse or as a human, but not both."

"I know," she said, placing a hand on Priela's shoulder now and squeezing it. "But we have to let her try."

"And you don't mind if she's around all those older college-kids? It doesn't worry you at all?"

"I can chaperone her, Daniel. I was thinking of applying for jobs as an art professor anyway. It's time I finally stopped being afraid to leave the house. It's time I finally stopped avoiding people and joined the human realm for real." Then she broadened her shoulders and her wings changed color, transforming from silver to a white that matched the kitchen, so that her wings seemed to fade into the background like a chameleon camouflaging its skin. "I'm ready."

He leaned in and embraced her. "You don't know how long I've been waiting to hear you say that, Calliope." Then he wiped his forehead and smiled at Priela. "What do you think, sweetheart? Do you want to enroll in some college classes?"

"Um, well. I'm definitely willing to give it a try."

"Alright, I can get behind this plan. But you're going to have to listen to your mother, Priela. No more breaking the rules, understand? And if there's anything I need to know about, you're going to tell me immediately."

"You're the best, Dad," she said, giving him a kiss on the cheek. "I love you."

"Uh huh, I love you too."

Chapter Thirty-five
WEALTH STUDIES

Priela tiptoed into the dark auditorium, her eyes blinking rapidly, her arms hugging the wall as she moved. Now that she'd fixed the future for Noah, and Robin, and Anton, and Garrett, she'd need another charge to help. So she was visiting the Pool of Polly to gaze into its murky depths. But when her eyes finally adjusted to the light, she realized she wasn't alone.

Clio was floating face down in the water. Her wings were perfectly still, but her hands were reaching for Violet's liquid incarnation which swirled before her with eyes as clear as glass. A last bubble of air broke the water's surface, and yet Clio remained limp. A moment passed. Then another. Then Clio's wings turned blue and her arms started to flail, until her body was thrashing violently.

Without giving it any thought, Priela dove into the water, swimming beneath Clio and then rising up behind her. She still didn't know how to swim with wings, but she'd grown much more adept at using them, understanding now how to synchronize her wings' movements with the rest of her body and knowing when she needed to bend or flex them. She linked one arm around Clio's waist, yanked her to the side of the pool, and dragged her out of the water.

Clio began coughing in abrupt, brutal gasps, spitting out mouthfuls of water. Her hair was flat against her scalp. Her clothing was clinging to her skin. And her body was shivering uncontrollably.

"Are you okay?" asked Priela.

Clio didn't answer. She just averted her eyes, wrapped her arms around her knees, and started rocking back and forth. Her expression was frightened and sad.

"Should I get some help?"

"Just leave me alone."

"Fine," said Priela, pivoting on one foot and heading toward the door. "You're welcome."

"And what am I supposed to be thanking you for, Priela?"

"Oh, I don't know, Clio. Maybe you could thank me for saving your life?"

"You think that deserves gratitude? I should have pulled you under and drowned us together. Or better yet, I should have let you drown all by yourself when I had the chance."

"You did this on purpose?"

Clio laughed, but her breaths were slow and pained. "Priela, you've destroyed everything I had to live for."

"What are you talking about?"

"Do you think I'm contented here, in this world? I'm a direct descendant of the original Clio. My mother, and my grandmother, and my great grandmother before her. I'm the only muse left in my line. The only one remaining. And the pressure on me is so great. If I'm not the best, the most talented, the most revered, then I'm nobody. Do you know what my mother said when you came to the institute, Priela? She said that if your talents ever surpassed mine she'd renounce me as her daughter."

Clio turned away, but her shoulders eased and her expression softened, as if she was too exhausted to remain angry, too overwhelmed with her own thoughts to direct any more hatred toward Priela.

"Sometimes I wish I could just leave this place forever and you have that freedom, Priela. You're a direct descendant too. Daughter of the most respected and reviled muse in recent history. Granddaughter of Headmistress Calliope. Another heir to another ancient line. But unlike me, you have the ability to make a choice. You exist in the human world, so you can leave this place whenever you want. While I'm… trapped."

Clio leaned forward now and gazed at her own reflection in the water's mirrored surface. "I wanted you to fail, Priela. I needed you to fail. I even had you thrown out of class, but you succeeded anyway. You're all anyone talks about anymore. How you're helping all of those humans and bringing art into their lives. I mean, before you came to Gaia nobody had even heard of computer science, and now Dion is writing a book about programming languages. How am I supposed to compete with that? It's like I was running a race on foot and you swept in on a racehorse."

"Clio, I was never trying to compete with you."

"And yet, you beat me anyway."

Priela took a step closer and crouched down by Clio's side. "Is that why you were trying to kill yourself? So that every literature muse would write a poem in your honor and every lyrical muse would sing a song? You thought that drowning was your path to immortality?"

"I don't care about that stuff. I just wanted it all to end."

Priela breathed in deeply and nodded, realizing that Clio's viciousness had never been about her. It was always about Clio's own self-loathing, her own inner doubts, her own jealousy. "You have so much to live for, Clio."

"Yeah, right," she said touching the water and Violet's face reappeared in broken threads. "I'm pathetic. I can't even get my stupid glimmers to work. Every time I visit Violet, I improve her singing voice more and more, but then I visit her future and nothing's different. She's still working in a horrible job at a warehouse. She's still coming home to this disgusting room with clothing everywhere and mice running around. She's still so miserable, putting her head in her hands and crying until she's practically numb. And I can feel her loneliness. I can feel her desperation."

"What if I helped you to help her?"

"Haven't you helped enough charges, Priela?" she sneered. "Now you want to add mine to your list?"

"No. I'm not trying to take the credit. You can say that you inspired Violet all by yourself, if that's what you want."

"And why would you do that?"

"Because I've never cared about being the best. All I ever wanted was to fit in somewhere."

Clio rolled her eyes.

"Look, before I came to Gaia, I tried to help Violet too. She was always so different. Special. And I think I tried to save her as a way of saving myself. But I failed." Priela reached a hand outward. "Come on, let's help her together. I promise, if it doesn't work out you can always kill yourself tomorrow."

Clio sat for a moment in silence, her glare piercing. "Fine," she said, rising to her feet and clasping Priela's hand. Then she started to sing.

> *"Violet a color, a flower, a name*
> *found in a dank place on a stormy Tuesday*
> *Will that devil of a man make you feel shame,*
> *or will you be saved from self-loathing?*

No longer to a place of glass and marble
a habit that will never be formed
Instead, the song on that stage still a mess, still a garble
allows your true talent to shine through, it will shine through

And because of a dress made from indigo blue
Oh Violet my human, my charge
One day in the future my heart, it will find you
inspiring others more than I ever could"

The music quickly swept them both away in a smooth, rapid motion bringing the muses once again to that dimly lit basement with its cinderblock walls and sour air. Although this time, it was clear from the way the light reflected, the way the humans were moving with a natural ease, that Clio and Priela were in the present watching events unfold in real time.

Violet was already there with that same worn backpack, but she was still very much her own person, still filled with passion and creativity. Priela could tell. Damien was there too, slinging a guitar over one shoulder, and behind him was that same disheveled band.

"You know," he said, with chilling indifference. "If you really wanna make it as a singer, you're gonna need to commit to the band full time. You get what that means, don't you Violet?"

"I know, Damien," she said, letting out a nervous laugh. "I can forget about high school, right?"

Priela gritted her teeth and looked away. It had been hard to watch Damien manipulate Violet the first time, sensing her vulnerability and her discomfort. But now that Priela knew what would happen in the future, now that she knew this moment would lead her down an awful path, it was even more painful to watch.

Violet dropped her backpack and pulled out an indigo gown. "But look, I have the perfect thing to wear on Thursday. I bought it at a thrift store but it's a Dior. Can you believe it? I got it for nothing."

"You need to look hot, not like a whale. That thing's enormous."

"I know, but don't you see? I could hem it. Take it in right here and clean it up. It would be beautiful."

She ran the couture cloth through her fingers and once again Priela could sense Violet's instinctive knowledge of design, her love of fashion. But the moment was short-lived. Damien grabbed a loose thread and started to unspool the fabric until a sleeve dropped to the floor. Then he ground the scrap into the filth with his heel.

"Don't…" said Violet, collapsing to the ground. "Please. The dress was so beautiful."

"It was crap. Now get up. We need to rehearse."

Priela tightened the muscles in her jaw. The conversation was excruciating. "Clio, you have to stop time, right now."

Clio nodded. Then she straightened her spine and focused her thoughts until the band's movements came to a halt and the instruments were silenced. Violet froze too, crouched amidst the fabric, her arms outstretched, her hands reaching.

"Okay," said Clio. "So if I'm not supposed to improve Violet's singing voice, then what should I tell her?"

Priela looked in Violet's eyes. Her pupils were unnaturally wide, her eyebrows were raised and drawn together, and her mouth was open slightly. It was a look of confusion, a look of panic. "Don't you see how frightened she is? Violet needs to stand up for herself. To believe in herself. It's the thing Damien is trying to steal. Her self-worth."

"Don't you think I know that?"

"So what's the problem?"

"Priela, confidence isn't an art form. We can't just guide Violet however we want. Muses have a very specific role, a very particular set of objectives…"

"Uh, huh. Clio, five minutes ago you were trying to kill yourself. Do you want to help Violet or not?"

Clio crossed her arms over her chest and groaned, "You'd better be right about this." Then she breathed in deeply, stretched her wings until they spanned virtually the width of the room, and began speaking to Violet with a slow, melodic intensity. "Believe in yourself, Violet. Stand up for yourself. You are talented. You are confident. You are strong."

A bright glimmer rose up from Clio's thoughts. It zoomed straight forward and landed squarely on Violet's forehead, releasing a discernible jolt and causing time to move again.

"Look," said Damien, adjusting his stance. "I just want you to wow Gloria, okay? She could really promote the band. I'll take you to buy something better. We'll go to that new Palomar Boutique place before the gig. Sound good?"

Violet remained still, but Priela could sense a change in her emotions. They were shifting from a quiet anxiety, to a fierce sense of conviction, as if a bomb had detonated inside of her and killed off any lingering fear. Then she swept the fabric into her backpack, rose to her feet, and placed her fists on her hips, striking a defiant pose. "No."

"You don't want a new dress?"

"No."

"You realize that you're acting like a spoiled brat, right?" said Damien, leaning in until his shadow darkened her face.

"This Thursday gig could change your pathetic life. How about showing some thanks?"

"No, you don't get it, Damien," she said, raising her head high and puffing out her chest. "I don't care about the stupid gig. I don't care about the music or the band. I never did. I just wanted your attention. I just wanted someone to think I was special for a change. But you know what? You think I'm special for all the wrong reasons. You've never taken the time to really know me or to understand how great I am."

"Yes, you're so phenomenal, Violet. Such an incredible talent. The only reason I picked you for the band was because those talent scouts are always looking for teenaged singers. Plus you were so desperate for attention that you'd do whatever I said. But if I'm being really honest, you've got no gift for singing, Violet. You're just a lonely, sad little girl, who's lucky I pulled you out of nowhere to give you this chance. So just stop your tantrum and get behind the microphone because we really need to rehearse."

"No, Damien," she said stomping her foot. "I'm not doing this anymore."

"So you're just going to ruin things for the entire band? Do you know how hard it was to book that gig on Thursday?"

"Fine, I'll come on Thursday. Not for you. But for Elsa, and Matt, and for our new drummer because I know how much they want this. But after that, you'll have to find another singer. After that, I'm done."

Then Violet turned around and raced up the basement stairwell, and suddenly Clio and Priela were in another location. Although the floating experience had been so fluid, so instantaneous, that Priela hadn't detected the motion at all.

They arrived in that same dark nightclub as before, and Violet was already singing onstage with Damien behind her. But this time, she wasn't wearing the revealing coral colored dress from the Palomar Boutique. Instead, she had never purchased the thing. She had never started a pattern of spending on items she couldn't afford. And her profound attachment to Damien was now shattered. Priela just knew.

In place of the coral dress, Violet was wearing a self-made outfit, sewn together from that couture indigo fabric. The dress had an angular neckline, an A-line skirt, and a missing sleeve where Damien had unspooled the thread. Although Violet had appropriated the rip into her design, and something about it was edgy and empowering.

The talent scout was sitting at the bar, just as before. Although she was leaning inward this time, and instead of bolting out the door in the middle of the set, she stayed. When the music ended, she approached Violet.

"Hey, great to see you, Gloria," said Damien, jumping between them and extending his hand.

"Nice to see you too," said the woman, clearing her throat. "Listen, I'm going to have to pass on the music. But I have a question for your lead singer."

"I'm Violet's manager. You can ask me."

"He's not my manager," said Violet, casting him an angry glance. "I'm perfectly capable of answering questions myself. Now, what did you want to know?"

"Um, okay. Listen, please don't take this the wrong way. I know you were hoping that I'd comment on the music. It just isn't for me. But I'm trying to develop a new look for one of my other clients and I think your outfit would be perfect. Where did you find that dress?"

"This one? I made it," said Violet, twirling around now and the skirt swooshed through the air.

"Really? You're quite gifted. Would you mind if I came by sometime to see your collection?"

"My collection? I'm still in high school."

The woman scowled at Damien and shook her head. "Well Violet, you should definitely cultivate that talent someday. But for now, I think it's time we just got you home." Then she linked an arm through Violet's and guided her toward the door, and Priela and Clio floated seamlessly to the next moment in time.

The muses landed in a classroom. It was Priela's classroom with its unmistakable triangular shape and its single window off to one side. But now, they were in the human version of the space, back at East High School where it all began. And here, the room still belonged to Mrs. Wilson, Priela's former algebra teacher.

Priela looked around. Something about the place was more welcoming than it had been, with colorful displays on the walls and desks arranged in a semi-circle.

"Now, who would like to read a quote from Hesiod's ancient Greek poem, *The Theogony?*" said Mrs. Wilson, with a smile. She looked the same as before. She was even dressed the same. But something was changed in her expression, so that it seemed less sinister, less intimidating.

A student raised her hand and Mrs. Wilson nodded in the girl's direction. "Happy is he whom the muses love, sweet flows speech from his mouth," read the girl.

"And what do you think that quote means?"

"I guess that muses can make a person's words nicer and more poetic?"

"Good job," said Mrs. Wilson, warmly.

A compliment? Really? Was this the same Mrs. Wilson? The same woman who had terrified her algebra students not so long ago? Clearly, she wasn't teaching math anymore. And her tone was different now. It was kinder and more encouraging. What had happened?

Priela thought back to that day when she had last seen Mrs. Wilson, the day she turned invisible. She'd yelled at her then. Although in retrospect, the woman wouldn't have been able to hear her insults. Still, what had she said? That Mrs. Wilson shouldn't be teaching math at all? That she shouldn't embarrass her students? Could Priela be her muse, having guided her somehow?

"Yes," said Mrs. Wilson. "Muses are special creatures. Hesiod believed that they knew the future and the past, and that they could pass on this knowledge and spread joy through art."

There was a quiet knock on the classroom door and Violet entered, her head held high, her face beaming. Mrs. Wilson rose from the edge of her desk and ushered her to the front of the room.

"Now, I'd like to introduce Violet, our special guest for today. She's an established fashion designer and I'm proud to say, one of my former students. Someone with the confidence to surpass my own mistaken expectations at the time and achieve brilliance." The students clapped excitedly and Mrs. Wilson and Violet embraced.

"Thank you," said Violet with enthusiasm. "I overheard your discussion about muses. And I have to confess that I've always believed I have a muse of my own. She inspired one of my very first dresses. A dress that turned my life around. I remember, I was in this dark basement and I could almost see her in the shadows with this bright purple gown." Violet shifted her eyes in Clio's direction and her jaw dropped. "She looked just like…"

Could Violet see Clio? Was that even possible? A human had to care about a muse for that to happen. Was a single moment of inspiration even enough?

It was clear from Clio's curious expression that she was having similar thoughts and her wings started to transition from purple, to yellow, to red, changing colors with rapid-fire succession as if something was being altered inside her, as if Clio had felt trapped for all of her life and now she'd found a door. She couldn't yet walk through that door. Priela could tell from her hesitant stance. But just finding a way out changed everything.

A light started to spin around, pulling Clio and Priela back to a different time and another dimension, although the pockets of air were warm now and strangely peaceful. They watched the classroom fade away and the students disappear into nothingness, until they were back in the dark auditorium.

"There's something I have to tell you, Priela," said Clio, pushing open the door and pointing at the money tree across the lawn. "Did you know that tree didn't exist in Gaia before you came here?"

"Really?"

"It was just this dead old stump, charred from a fire or something." She headed toward the tree now and Priela followed. "Maybe you did discover a new field of art after all? Maybe that money tree is your monument?"

"Doesn't someone have to build those monuments?"

"No, they're supposed to just rise up from the ground whenever a new art arrives at the institute, but I've never actually seen it happen before. What do you call your class anyway?"

"I don't know," said Priela, looking at the crisp green bills that were now waving in the breeze. "The lessons aren't really about money."

"No," said Clio, pulling her thaliation chalk from her gown. "They're about fulfillment. The true kind of wealth." Then she scrawled the words, *"Wealth Studies, founded by Priela,"* across the tree's trunk and the letters sank deep into the bark, changing from a chalky powder to a shimmering metallic silver that resembled an official emblem.

Priela touched the tree, feeling its leathery surface, and a light shined through the branches, illuminating her in a golden ray of sunshine.

Thank you for reading!

Dear Reader,

I hope that you've enjoyed Priela. Telling her story was definitely a labor of love.

So, what's next for Priela? Will her relationship with Noah deepen or will her invisibility keep them apart? Will she keep teaching? Is her sister Moriela a muse too or is she only human? I hope to explore these questions and more in the next book in the series.

But first, I need to ask you a favor. I'd genuinely appreciate an honest review. As you may know, reviews have the power to make or break a book, so please visit Priela on Amazon and provide your feedback.

Also, please visit my website at prielamuse.com where you'll find character photographs, a depiction of the muse realm, discussion questions, deleted chapters, and more. You can also find me on Facebook at Priela or you can email me directly at jocelyn@prielamuse.com.

I'd love to hear from you,

Jocelyn Bly Karney

Dedication & Acknowledgements

To my phenomenal editors: Cameron Fredman, Amber Tarshis, Benee Knauer, the Venture High creative writing class, and Brian Karney. A quick sample of their assistance...

Cameron
What if Priela didn't start the book as a muse? What if she started as a human and then grew wings?

Jocelyn
That's an interesting idea. I like it. Priela's mother would still have to start the book as a muse, but Priela could just think she's crazy.

Cameron
What if she is crazy? What if they're both crazy? What if this entire book is just Priela's decent into madness told from her point of view?

Jocelyn
Um, now you've taken it a little too far.

Amber
You can't say that Priela felt Noah's 'yearning.' This is for young adults. You need to keep it clean.

Jocelyn
Desire?

Amber
No.

Jocelyn
Excitement?

Amber
No.

Jocelyn
Energy?

Amber
Fine.

Dedication & Acknowledgements

Benee

You need to get into the characters' heads more. I'd like you to write a backstory for each major character. What happened to them before this book? What do they care about? What secrets are they hiding?

Jocelyn

Um, okay. Here are twenty five pages of backstory providing information about where the characters are from, their families, their interests, their hobbies.

Benee

You're not getting it. I want you to go deep.

Jocelyn

Uh, sure. Here's an additional twenty five pages. It discusses the characters' fears, their flaws, their strengths.

Benee

Go deeper.

Jocelyn

Fine. Here are 75 more pages. Now each character has a tragic event in their past – neglect, harassment, abuse, addiction, assault, incarceration, death.

Benee

Excellent work here, Jocelyn. Now don't use any of it.

Dedication & Acknowledgements

Venture High creative writing class where students read chapters and provided feedback:

> **Student**
>
> So Priela is invisible?
>
> **Jocelyn**
>
> Yes.
>
> **Student**
>
> Can animals see her?
>
> **Jocelyn**
>
> No, she's invisible.

Students appear distraught.

~ Two weeks later ~

> **Jocelyn**
>
> Okay, I've changed my mind. I've added a sequence where a cat sees Priela.
>
> **Student**
>
> Can dogs see her?
>
> **Jocelyn**
>
> No. I don't think so. I don't know. There aren't any dogs in the book. Do you think dogs should be able to see her?
>
> **Student**
>
> Well, cats are mystical creatures. Many ancient religions worshiped them and they're depicted in all kinds of literature, and mythology, and art. So, I think its fine if only cats can see Priela.
>
> **Jocelyn**
>
> Uh huh, good point.

Dedication & Acknowledgements

My husband, early in the process:

Brian

I don't get it.

Jocelyn

What don't you get?

Brian

The book. I don't like how it starts. You need to start with a bang. And I don't like the middle part. It's really slow and boring. And I don't like the ending. You shouldn't end it that way.

Jocelyn

Thanks. That was very helpful feedback. Just so you know, I'm hiring a professional editor. I'll share another draft when it's done.

~ Four years later ~

Jocelyn

Here's a finished draft. Don't say a word.

Additional thanks for the cover art to Elena Dudina (photoshop artist), Izabela Barisic (logo design), Stephanie Swift (vector artist), Mokhiber Family (cover model), Whitney Kofford (photographer), and Jennifer McGrew (costume designer).

CPSIA information can be obtained
at www.ICGtesting.com
Printed in the USA
LVHW01s0046091117
555586LV00001B/47/P